D1563538

D...... ......
... ....

# DISTANT COUSINS

## *and*

### OTHER STORIES OF COURAGE AND INSPIRATION

BY
EVA VOGIEL

THE JUDAICA PRESS, INC.

© Copyright 2004 by Eva Vogiel

ALL RIGHTS RESERVED.
NO PART OF THIS PUBLICATION MAY BE TRANSLATED, REPRODUCED,
STORED IN A RETRIEVAL SYSTEM OR TRANSMITTED, IN ANY FORM OR
BY ANY MEANS, ELECTRONIC, MECHANICAL, PHOTOCOPYING, RECORDING,
OR OTHERWISE, WITHOUT PERMISSION IN WRITING FROM THE PUBLISHER.

Cover design & typography by: Zisi Berkowitz
Editor: Bonnie Goldman


Library of Congress Cataloging-in-Publication Data

Vogiel, Eva.
  Distant cousins, and other stories of courage and inspiration / by Eva Vogiel.
    p. cm.
  ISBN 1-932443-17-7
  1.  Courage--Fiction. 2.  Jews--Fiction. 3.  Jewish fiction.  I. Title.
  PR6072.O28D57 2004
  823'.914--dc22
                          2004001687

Other books by Eva Vogiel

*Facing the Music*
*Friend or Foe?*
*Invisible Chains*

**THE JUDAICA PRESS, INC.**
718-972-6200    800-972-6201
info@judaicapress.com
www.judaicapress.com


Manufactured in the United States of America

# Acknowledgments

Writing a book is, in a way, like sailing a ship on the high seas. As you embark on the hazardous journey, you are not quite sure what obstacles you might be up against or, indeed, whether you will be able to steer your vessel safely to its destination. However, you put your trust in the Ribono Shel Olam to guide you and protect you and to help you reach your goal. I therefore give grateful thanks to Hashem Yisborach for the *siyata d'Shmaya*, without which I would have made no progress at all!

Thanks also to my wonderful crew, namely, my husband Nachman, my sisters Rebbitzen Ruth Padwa and Mrs. Esther Spitzer and my daughter-in-law Ruchi, who all helped me plan my course and who made sure I was pointing in the right direction as I went along. My sister, Mrs. Suri Kornbluh, was also there right at the start, giving my little ship an enthusiastic push into the water!

I am extremely grateful to Dayan Rabbi Osher Westheim, *shlita,* who was once again on the lookout, making sure I didn't hit any "icebergs," or become diverted from the course, regarding *hashkafa* and *halacha.*

Thanks to Mr. Nachum Shapiro, Bonnie Goldman and Zisi Berkowitz, as well as the rest of the Judaica Press staff, who were the best navigators ever, their guidance and expertise making the voyage smooth and pleasant right up to the moment of arrival!

A word of thanks to my computer teacher, Mrs. Naomi Rebenwurzel, who made a good maintenance officer, sorting out all my technical problems on board; also to my good friends Mrs. Chaya Gittleson and Rebbitzen Faigy Kupetz, who read the finished manuscript and formed my "reception committee" on shore, cheering my ship on as it sailed into harbor!

# Table of Contents

# The House Without Windows

here was a great deal of curiosity in our neighborhood about the people who had moved into No. 30 Milton Close. They were hardly ever seen and none of the Jewish inhabitants of the street had managed to exchange any words with them. Some of the neighbors had tried calling on them—especially Mrs. Mandelberg, who lived two doors away and had reported that she'd twice knocked on the door with a cake in her hands—but no one had ever answered.

We knew they were *yidden*—kosher milk was delivered to the door and was taken in, and a man could be seen emerging from the house early every morning with a tallis and tefillin bag under his arm. He would hurry to his car and drive off, obviously to go and daven in some shul in another area. On Shabbos he went to the local shul, but he managed to slip out before anyone had a chance to approach him.

The thing that intrigued us most was the fact that the curtains of the house were *always* drawn. My friends and I nicknamed it "the house without windows"! I could never walk past it without giving the place a curious glance. In style it was very much like the other houses on the street; a red bricked semi-detached house with bay windows to the left of the front door and three upstairs windows. There was a small garden, with a paved path running alongside the lawn towards the door. But, whereas most of the lawns on the street displayed flowery borders and some of the front doors were painted in bright, cheerful colors, the garden of this house was completely devoid of flora and the door was a dull, dark brown. Was it possible, I wondered, that someone was actually living in there? It looked so bleak and lifeless.

And then, one day, I thought I detected the slightest sign of life.

It was during the half-term holiday and the weather was fairly mild for the middle of February. Having no school, I was on my way to my friend Mashy's house and I had to walk through Milton Close to get there. As I passed the house at No. 30, my gaze was automatically drawn towards the house. Expecting it to look the same as it always did, I was aware, with a sudden sense of shock, of something happening!

I stared, not quite sure what I had seen. Had I imagined it, or had one of the upstairs curtains moved slightly? It certainly didn't look like it now, but something had definitely given me a jolt.

I stood gazing upwards for a few moments — then, shrugging my shoulders resignedly, I began to move on, but not before casting one last glance at the window. To my surprise, I saw it again!

This time I was sure it was not my imagination. What was

more, I was convinced I could see a person standing just behind the curtain. With a tingling feeling running down my spine, I stood rooted to the spot, not sure what to make of it. Who was up there, watching me? Perhaps it was someone who needed my help but could not call out! How could I just walk away without first trying to find out?

I don't know what made me do it. But on an impulse, I pushed open the wrought iron gate, walked up the path and rang the doorbell, jumping slightly at the shrill sharp sound it made. A moment later, I regretted my action, wondering nervously what I was going to say to whoever opened the door. But nobody *did* open the door. I stood waiting for a few moments and then, against my better judgement, I rang the bell again. Still nobody came.

There's no one in, I told myself. I must have imagined the whole thing.

With a mixture of disappointment and relief, I began to walk away. I went out through the gate into the street and involuntarily looked up at the house once more. To my utter amazement I saw that the curtain had been moved again! A hand was holding it slightly away from the window-frame and part of a face seemed to be peeping round it.

I just stood there for a moment, transfixed. Then, I don't know what got into me, but I stalked back up the path with a resolute air till I was standing right under the window.

"Open the door," I mouthed, pointing towards the front door. I could only see part of the person's head, but I could make out fair hair held back by a green hair-band, and I realized it was a girl. Shaking her head vigorously, she let the curtain drop back into place.

Having come this far, I wasn't going to leave things at that. Now I *had* to know what was going on! Spurred on by bafflement and intense curiosity, I rang the bell again and waited. Nothing happened. Not one to give up easily, I rang once more, keeping my finger on the bell for quite a while.

This time my efforts were rewarded. I could hear footsteps coming down the stairs, growing louder as they came across the hall, towards the front door. I held my breath, a quaking feeling inside me.

There was a metallic, rattling sound, which I recognized as a chain being pulled across the door and slotted in. Then the door was opened, very, very slightly and a timid, girlish voice came from behind it.

"What do *you* want?" she asked, somewhat nervously.

"C-can I come in?" I stammered, equally apprehensive.

"No!" the girl said, in a more positive tone. "I'm not allowed to let anyone in!"

"Why?" I asked, puzzled.

"I can't tell you," the girl replied and closed the door.

Having the door closed in my face irked me and I pressed the bell again. It was opened immediately, in the same way, with the chain still in place. The girl seemed to be standing right behind the door and I could not understand why she did not come round and face me.

"Why do you keep ringing the bell?" she asked, sounding upset.

"Because I don't like mysteries," I told her. "Who are you? What's your name?"

"Who are *you*?" the girl countered.

"My name is Tova Weinberg," I told her. "What's yours?"

There was quite a long pause before she answered. "Penina," she said eventually, her tone hesitant, "Penina Leifman..."

"Pleased to meet you, Penina," I said. "If one can call it

'meeting' when I haven't actually *seen* you. Even if you don't want to let me in, can't you just poke your head round the door so we can be introduced properly?"

"*No!*" she exclaimed vehemently. "That's just what I *can't* do!"

"Why not?" I asked, uneasily. There was something strange going on here and it was giving me goose pimples! I just *had* to know what it was all about! "I wish you'd tell me what you're talking about!"

"I can't!" There was a plaintive ring to her voice. "Please," she said imploringly, "don't ask me all those questions! Please go away — and leave me alone!"

I should have done as she asked and left her in peace. She sounded really upset. But, spurred on by my undying curiosity, I refused to give in.

"You must tell me!" I persisted. "You can't leave me hanging in mid-air, just like that! Please!" I begged, "I can't just walk away, all mystified. It wouldn't be fair!"

I thought it was the logic of my argument, plus my pleading tone, that did the trick, but later on I realized that that Penina was really just yearning to talk to someone.

In a low voice that trembled slightly, Penina began to tell me the whole horrific story.

It had all begun eight years ago, when she was a child of four. Her mother was making latkes and had just dropped the first few into the sizzling oil when the telephone rang in the living room. Turning the gas a little lower, she hurried to answer it, intending to be back a moment later. Penina had been sitting in the kitchen, playing busily with her doll. She could still remember that she had wanted to show her doll the latkes and had taken it up to the stove. The frying pan, of course, was far too high for her to see into it and she had stood on tiptoes and reached up for the handle, trying to tip it towards her. And then it had happened! The whole frying pan slid off the stove, pouring the boiling hot oil all over her face!

"Oh, no!" I gasped in horror. "How awful!"

"Yes, it was," Penina's voice was almost a whisper. "I can still remember how it felt. Sometimes I can still hear myself screaming!"

I wanted to say some words of sympathy but I was too shocked to speak. Besides, I was finding it unnerving to talk to a disembodied voice, though now I was finally beginning to understand why she didn't want to face me. She must be awfully scarred, I realized.

"What did your mother do?" I asked, eventually finding my voice.

"I can't remember all that clearly," Penina replied. "She came running in and I think she screamed as well, but everything began to happen at once. She pressed ice cubes or something onto my face and started doing all sorts of other things... I'm not sure what."

"And then, I suppose, she took you to hospital," I prompted.

"N-no, I don't think she did." Penina was obviously straining to remember.

"But she must have! How couldn't she?" I cried, incredulously.

"She was a qualified teacher and she'd studied first aid, so she knew what to do," Penina said, defensively. "She didn't need to take me to hospital! Anyway, she was afraid to."

"Afraid to? Why?"

"She says she might have been blamed for what happened. They could have prosecuted her for neglect and they would have taken me away from her and put me into foster care."

"Oh," I said, beginning to grasp the situation. "So that's why she keeps you locked up and doesn't let you go out."

"No!" Penina protested. "That's not the main reason. It's because of the way I look. She says people will stare at me and I'll get hurt. She says she wants to protect me from that."

"I'm sure it can't be that bad," I argued, in what my mother sometimes called my "bull-in-a-china-shop" manner. "After eight years, your scars must have faded quite a bit. I wish you'd come round the door and let me see you! I won't—"

"No!" Penina exclaimed, panic in her voice. "I can't! Please don't ask me to! I wish you'd go away! I shouldn't have told you all that. And my mother's just popped out shopping and she'll be back any minute! She'll be really cross with me for opening the door."

The urgency in her tone got through to me at last. Although there was so much I still wanted to ask her, I didn't want to cause her any trouble.

"Okay," I said, with a resigned sigh. "I'll go now. But I'd like to come and talk to you again. Can I?"

"N-no," she said, slightly hesitantly. "My mother doesn't go out very often. It's no use coming when she's in… she won't allow it at all. Please go now," she begged, "before it's too late!" She started pushing the door forward gently. It was obvious that she wanted to shut it firmly but didn't want to be rude.

"Okay," I said again. "Goodbye, Penina." I walked down the path. When I reached the gate, I turned to wave, but the front door was already closed.

I made my way to Mashy's, deep in thought. Poor Penina! It was bad enough to have suffered through such a horrifying experience. But then she had to deal with such devastating results— spending the rest of her life as a virtual prisoner, with no friends and nothing to enjoy. What a terrible existence! I couldn't possibly imagine spending all that time alone.

Mashy would surely ask me why I had taken so long to get there. What would I say? Would it be right to tell her the whole story, betraying Penina's confidence? Probably not. On the other hand, I felt so bad for Penina that I wanted to find a way to help her. Mashy might be able to suggest some way I could help.

By the time I reached my friend's house, I still hadn't decided what to do.

After my encounter with Penina, I could not get her out of my thoughts. I wished I could *do* something! Having resolved not to tell anyone her story, I realized I was probably the only one outside her family who knew of her plight, yet I couldn't begin to think of a way to help her!

She needed a friend, that was for sure! I would gladly have filled that need for her, but how could I get to her? I couldn't just knock on the door when her mother was at home. And I had no way of finding out when her mother would be out. Besides which, having been brought up to observe *kibud av va'em*, I was not sure if it was right to encourage Penina to go behind her mother's back.

If only I could speak to her mother and explain how important friendship was to a girl, whatever the circumstances! But that would mean revealing that Penina had told me everything.

It's no use, I told myself. You'll just have to keep out of it.

However, even though I was determined not to get involved, my thoughts kept returning to that poor girl, locked up in the "house without windows"! I found myself walking past frequently... my eyes automatically drawn towards the window where I had first seen her. It always looked the same—the curtains all drawn and the atmosphere bleak and somber.

Then, one afternoon, as I was walking down Milton Close, I saw a woman come out through the gate of No. 30, a large brown shoulder bag hanging from her right shoulder. She looked round a little furtively and then walked away from the house and went down the street. I knew instinctively that it was Penina's mother.

I quickened my pace and soon reached the house, stopping short just before I got to the gate. You're not going in! I told myself firmly. You'll only cause trouble if you do.

I stood for a moment, fighting a battle with myself—not wanting to break my resolve, but at the same time not wanting to go away. Involuntarily, I stole a quick look at the upstairs window. And then I saw it again! The curtain was moving—ever so slightly! That did it! I can't just walk away, I argued with myself. She's seen me. She'll be hurt if I walk past!

Without giving myself time to think, I marched up to the house and looked straight up at the window. I wanted to signal to her to come and open the door, but I couldn't actually see her and I felt rather stupid gesticulating to a practically closed curtain. I knew Penina was there, though, and the knowledge spurred me on. With a determined air, I went up to the front door and rang the bell insistently.

I waited a while but nothing happened. I rang once more and waited again. Still there was no response. Reluctant to give up so quickly, I pressed the bell again, promising myself that this would be my last attempt. This time, at last, I heard footsteps coming down the stairs. A moment later, the chain was once more hooked in place and the door was opened slightly, as before.

"What do you want?" she almost hissed. "Why have you come again?"

"Penina, I want to speak to you."

"Why?" she asked, her tone more puzzled than angry. "What for?"

"Because you need a friend," I replied, charging straight in, "and I would like to be your friend!"

"Oh," was all she said. I could tell she was taken completely by surprise.

"But I can't be friends with you if I haven't even seen you," I declared quickly, before she had a chance to collect herself. "So please, let me come in and talk to you, face to face!"

"No!" she cried, panic in her voice, "you can't!"

"Why not?" I persisted. "I don't mind *what* you look like! I won't stare at you."

"You will!" she declared. "You say you won't. But I know that you will! And you won't like what you'll see."

"I'm not afraid," I told her, "and you shouldn't be either. You can't go through life like that, hiding from everyone. You've got to be brave and face people! Where's your courage, Penina?"

"Courage?" she said, a bit listlessly.

"Yes, courage!" I forged on. "It takes courage to face the world with a problem like yours, but in the end, you'll see, people will get used to it and they won't even notice it any more. But they'll always admire you for your courage. Please, Penina," I cajoled, "be brave!"

There was a long silence and I waited with baited breath. Presently, I heard her give a deep sigh and she unhooked the chain and opened the door a little wider, still hiding behind it.

Suddenly taken aback, I had to brace myself to step inside. But step inside I did and at last I was treated to my first sight of Penina Leifman!

She was a little taller than me, though her posture seemed to droop slightly — obviously due to lack of exercise — and she wore her fair, shoulder-length hair held back with a blue hair-band. I took all this in at a glance, though my eyes were naturally immediately drawn to her face.

It took all my willpower not to flinch, even though I had actually expected it to be worse. Most of her face was covered in red patches, though I could see that they had obviously faded quite a bit. But the worst part was on her right cheek, where the hot oil must have made immediate contact. The skin was badly crinkled —rather like a garment that has been accidentally ironed with an iron that was too hot.

Penina was eyeing me anxiously, as if waiting for my verdict. Forcing myself to sound casual and unperturbed, I said, "it's not as bad as I expected."

"Really?" she said, sounding surprised.

"Yes, really. Don't you believe me?"

"I-I don't know what to believe," she stammered. "I don't really know what I look like."

"You don't?" this time it was my turn to sound surprised. "Have you never seen yourself in a mirror?"

"No. Mummy won't have any mirrors in the house."

"I see." I chewed over that piece of information for a moment. I suppose it really made sense. "But what about other people? Hasn't anyone else ever given you an opinion?"

"*What* other people?" Penina said, bitterness in her tone. "I never see *anyone* but my parents. And my father is out at work all day, so I hardly see him at all, except on Shabbos."

"Penina?" I said, beginning to get the picture, "didn't you ever go to school?"

"No, never," she told me. "My mother teaches me at home. She's a qualified teacher, you know, but she gave up her job to teach me instead."

"You probably know more than all of us, then," I commented, trying to bring a light-hearted note to the conversation. But then I couldn't help myself. "But wouldn't you like to go to school?" I probed.

"No!" she declared vehemently. "I'd hate everyone to stare at me and pull faces when they see me."

"They wouldn't do that!" I protested. "Not the girls in my school, in any case. If you'd only pluck up the courage to come and face them, you'd see it's not so bad! I think you should try to persuade your mother to let you."

"She wouldn't!" Penina interrupted emphatically. "She'd never allow it, even if *I* wanted to!"

"It might be worth a try," I said, a little lamely, already beginning to accept the fact that there was no point in pursuing that line.

It suddenly occurred to me that Penina did not seem on edge this time. She didn't seem to be worrying that her mother would come back. I made the observation to her, peering anxiously at the door myself.

"Oh, no," she said confidently. "She won't be back for a while. She's taken on a job giving private lessons every day to a child in another district. It's a half-an-hour's bus ride, so there's time."

"Oh, good!" I said spontaneously. "So we can still have a chat. And I could come again, sometimes, if you'd like me to. At least you'll have *one* friend then!"

This brought a smile to her face—the first one I had seen—and after a moment she said shyly, "Yes, I'd like that."

"Right! That's settled then. But I still feel you could do with more. Perhaps you'd like to meet my friend Mashy."

"Oh, no!" she seem to shrink away, "no more, please! I'd be happy with just you. You've seen me now, but I don't want anyone else to see me."

"But Mashy's not the sort that would stare or anything. She's a very matter-of-fact sort of person and she's terrific fun. You'll like her."

"All the same—" Penina began.

"Penina, be brave!" I cried persuasively. "Give it a chance! You'll be glad in the end."

I watched her face as she turned the matter over in her mind. I really liked Penina and I felt even more determined than ever to help her. I could see she was quite a strong person really and I had a feeling that I had awakened something in her that had hitherto been suppressed.

"Alright," she said, after a long deliberation, "if you're sure she won't shy away from me and that she definitely won't tell anyone."

"She won't! I'm sure of it!"

I stayed a little while longer and, before taking my leave, I made arrangements to come again—with Mashy, this time.

Was I imagining it, I wondered, or was Penina already a different person? She certainly seemed like it to me!

I became convinced, in the weeks that followed, that Penina really had undergone a change. Mashy and I visited her a few times a week and we all thoroughly enjoyed those visits, even though we could never stay long. We used to go straight after school and sometimes we had difficulty warding off the other girls, making sure they would not know where we were going. Then, of course, we had to be out well before it was time for Penina's mother to come home.

However, we managed to have a good time, doing all sorts of things while we were there. Penina took us into the living room, where we sat at the table, doing things like playing word games. Penina took to these quickly and, although she was a year younger than us, she often beat us hands down!

But the thing that gave us most pleasure was seeing her laugh! I don't think she had ever laughed in her life and, in fact, she seemed to find it hard to let go at first. But Mashy's jolly nature was infectious and Penina soon learnt from her how to enjoy a joke.

If only these afternoons at Penina's could have gone on indefinitely. But, one afternoon, they came to an abrupt end!

Mashy was reading some jokes to us from a book of school jokes and we were roaring with laughter, making such a noise that we didn't hear the key in the front door. We were not aware of Penina's mother entering the house, twenty minutes earlier than her usual time.

The living room door was suddenly flung open and Mrs. Leifman stood there, white-faced, her blue eyes almost popping out of her head. Mashy and I jumped up immediately and would have dashed out, had the doorway been clear. The silence in the room seemed loaded.

Presently, Mrs. Leifman found her voice. Turning from white to scarlet, she cried, "Who are you? And how dare you come barging in here like that!"

Not knowing what to say, we both began to mumble incoherently.

"Get out of here!" Mrs. Leifman shouted, moving away from the doorway. Feeling terribly guilty for leaving Penina to face the music alone, we nevertheless hurried out of the room. We were in the hall when we heard Penina say, "But Mummy, they're my friends!"

Expecting her mother to shout at her, I stood still for a moment, prepared to go back and help her out. But Mrs. Leifman didn't shout. I heard her say, in a sorrowful voice, "Oh, *Penina*! Penina darling, I can't let you get hurt!"

We didn't wait to hear more. Rushing out of the house, we ran all the way to my house, hardly pausing for breath.

It was only when I put the key into the lock that I realized my mother would notice that we were up to something. I stopped and took a few deep breaths before leading Mashy into the kitchen, determined to greet my mother in my usual easy manner. But Mummy was not in the kitchen when we entered. I could see her through the window, un-pegging washing from the line in the garden. I was glad that we had a few minutes, at least, to chew over what had happened.

"Whew!" I panted. "That was an amazing shock! I wonder why she came home early?"

"I suppose her pupil had an appointment, or something," Mashy commented. "But Tova, do you realize what this means? We won't be able to go to Penina any more."

"You're right!" I gasped. "We can't! But we must! Oh, no! Poor Penina!"

I don't know whether it was a delayed shock reaction, disappointment or concern for Penina that made me suddenly start crying. All I know is that I could not stop the tears pouring out. I sat at the table sobbing my heart out, with Mashy sitting next to me, her arm round my shoulders, also sniffing.

My mother came in from the garden carrying the washing.

"Tova! What's wrong?" she cried, her voice full of concern.

I didn't really want to tell her, but I just couldn't help myself. Before I knew what I was doing, I had poured the whole story out, with a bit of help from Mashy.

"I shouldn't really have told you," I said when I had finished. "It's sort of... you know... betraying a confidence."

"Yes, that's true," my mother agreed, "but don't worry. I'll keep it to myself. I can see you've got enough sense not to spread it around, too. All the same, you have both got to go and apologize to Penina's mother."

"Why? What for?" we both cried, aghast.

"For intruding on their privacy, for one thing. And for encouraging Penina to go behind her mother's back."

"But we *can't!*" I protested, with Mashy making agreeing noises in the background. "She'll slam the door in our faces! She was so *angry*, Mummy. You should've seen her!"

"I'm sure she was," my mother retorted. "That's *why* you've got to ask her *mechilah*. But don't go today. Give her a chance to calm down a bit. Leave it till tomorrow."

She was right, of course. We both knew it. But we couldn't help wishing there was some way we could get out of doing it!

We stood nervously at the door of the Leifmans' house, Mashy and I, and rang the bell. Nothing happened. We waited a while and rang again. Still no one came.

"Perhaps she's not in," Mashy said, a hopeful note in her voice. "Let's go."

I knew just how she felt. It would have been a good excuse to dodge an incredibly awkward situation. But what was the use? It would only have postponed the evil hour. Much better to get the ordeal over and done with.

I said as much to Mashy and rang the bell again. It took a few more rings before the door was pulled open by an irate-looking Mrs. Leifman.

"What?" she began, crossly. Then she saw us. "Oh, it's you!" she said, even more angrily. "What do you want? You can't see Penina… I won't allow it!"

"No," I said quickly. "It's you we've come to see. We want to apologize."

"Apologize?" she said, eyeing us suspiciously. "What for, may I ask?" There was an edge of sarcasm to her voice.

"For what we did," I replied, feeling rather foolish and wishing Mashy wasn't leaving me to do all the talking.

Looking round a little nervously, I guess to make sure none of the neighbors could see or hear us, Mrs. Leifman beckoned to us to come inside.

"And who, I'd like to know, told you to come and apologize?" she asked shrewdly, once we were on the other side of the front door. She was definitely not stupid! And one could tell by her tone of voice that she was a teacher. "I notice you weren't very apologetic when I caught you yesterday."

It would have been so easy to say "no one," but I couldn't lie to her and I told her it was my mother who had sent us.

"So you told her all about it, did you?"

"I didn't want to!" I protested, "but she could see I was upset, so I had to."

"So you *do* know the meaning of *kibud av va'em*," Mrs. Leifman said, her tone frigid. "Yet you encouraged *my* daughter to go against it. And who else have you told, may I know?"

"No one! I've told no one!" I declared emphatically.

"Well, it makes no difference. Your mother knows, so I suppose it'll be all round the neighborhood in no time," Mrs. Leifman commented, sounding defeated.

"*She* won't tell anyone, truly! She even forbade me to."

"I hope you're right, " she said. "Well, I accept your apology —as long as you know how wrong you were." She opened the front door and signaled to us to leave.

"Oh, please," I begged, "can we see Penina?"

"Certainly not!" she said sternly.

"But we're her friends!" I persisted.

"And she enjoys our company," Mashy added, finding her voice at last!

The expression on Mrs. Leifman's face suddenly softened. "Yes," she said quietly. "I know she does. Do you think I haven't noticed the change in her?" There was a long pause while she seemed to be turning the matter over in her mind. Presently she said, "Very well, yes, you can go on visiting her. Not just yet, though. Give her a few days to settle down... she's been quite upset. But you can start coming again next week... as long as you don't distract her too much from her studies. She's got quite a lot of learning to do."

We told her we'd comply and hurried away. We were utterly relieved that it had worked out so well. Much better, in fact, than we could ever imagine! We were excited that Penina would still be able to see us.

It was amazing being able to go on visiting Penina after all, especially as we didn't have to watch the clock any more, to make sure we were out before her mother came home. However, we usually left soon after Mrs. Leifman came in and I think she was grateful that we did.

I was still a bit worried, though. These sessions were doing Penina a lot of good, but they couldn't go on indefinitely, forever and ever. What about the future… Penina's future? She couldn't just stay locked in that "house without windows" for the rest of her life!

I voiced my concern to my mother one day. "I wish her mother would let her go to school, but she won't hear of it," I said, plaintively. "Penina's got to get out into the outside world at some time!"

"Yes," my mother agreed, "but I can understand Mrs. Leifman in a way, wanting to protect Penina from something as daunting as facing people with all her disfiguring scars." She was thoughtful for a few moments, then she said, "What she could use is some plastic surgery."

"Plastic surgery?" I asked. "What's that?"

My mother explained to me how operations are done to graft good skin in place of the damaged skin, hardly leaving a trace of scarring. "It's marvelous what they can do these days," she commented.

"Then that's what she ought to have!" I cried enthusiastically.

"Not so fast!" my mother laughed. "It's not that simple. For one thing it's extremely expensive."

"Oh," I said crestfallen. Then I perked up. "But couldn't she have it on the National Health—even if she does have to wait on a waiting list for months?"

"I don't know." Mummy sounded dubious. "Cosmetic surgery isn't usually covered by the National Health. Although, …" she lapse into thoughtfulness again, "there are some circumstances when it might be. I wonder…" She sat pondering for a little while. Then, abruptly, she changed the subject. "Go and wash for supper, Tova," she said briskly. "It's getting late and I've got to get on with my mending."

I found myself brooding a lot about that conversation, wondering what I could do about it. I toyed with the notion of broaching the subject to Penina's mother, but I soon rejected the idea. Mrs. Leifman might be more kindly disposed towards me these days, but she was still rather unapproachable. I couldn't mention it to Penina either, in case I raised her hopes for nothing. As usual, my hands were tied!

"Do you know your mother was here yesterday?" Penina said, a few days later. I had come on my own, as Mashy had a dentist's appointment.

"No, I didn't know!" I exclaimed, surprised. "How interesting! Did you see her?"

"No, I always have to go up to my room if someone comes — which doesn't happen too often! But I heard her introducing herself when Mummy opened the door."

"How come your mother opened the door?" I asked. "She doesn't usually — " I broke off, embarrassed.

To my relief, Penina laughed. "She rang the bell a minute after Mummy came in!" she said, "so she didn't have much of a choice."

"Did you hear what they talked about?" I asked, too puzzled to show amusement.

"No, of course not!" Penina sounded shocked. "I wouldn't eavesdrop! And, as I said, I went up to my room. Didn't your mother tell you she'd been?"

"No, she didn't," I replied. "But don't worry — I'm going to ask her!"

And ask her I did! "You didn't tell me you went to see Penina's mother," I said accusingly, as soon as I came home. "What did you talk to her about?"

I didn't think she would tell me but I was wrong. There were times lately when my mother treated me more like an adult, and this was one of those times.

"I suggested the possibility of plastic surgery," she began.

"And what did she say?" I interrupted eagerly.

"She said, as I knew she would, that she can't possibly afford it."

"But what about the National Health? Did you suggest she might try that?"

"Of course I did," my mother said, "but I'm afraid, Tova dear, that it's a little bit complicated. You see, Mrs. Leifman is still afraid of the authorities asking a lot of questions, and I must admit, she has a point. They could well do that."

Filled with disappointment, I realized there was nothing more to be said. But I could not stop thinking about it, wishing there was something I could do. The thought crossed my mind that we could approach some of the local charity organizations—or ask someone who was good at fundraising to collect the money. But that would have meant telling them who it was for and why.

After brooding about it for a while, the idea came to me in a flash! We could raise the money ourselves! I could enlist the help of many of my friends just by telling them that it was for someone who needed an operation. They would not need to know more than that.

Mashy thought it was a terrific idea. She helped me organize a sponsored swim. In no time at all, the girls in my class were circulating around in the neighborhood, asking people to sponsor them for a certain amount per length. That venture managed to raise fifty pounds.

"Not bad," I commented to Mashy, "but it's not nearly enough. What else can we do?"

"What about a bazaar?" Mashy suggested.

"Mmm," I murmured, a little doubtful at first. But the more I thought about it, the more I began to like the idea.

"It'll be loads of work collecting goods," I said, "but if everyone helps we should manage. Where can we have it, though?"

We pondered for a while, and then we decided we would ask Mrs. Solomons, our headmistress, if we could use the school Assembly Hall. We had to tell her more than we'd told the girls, but we didn't mention any names and she didn't ask. She readily agreed, telling us that she was glad we were involved with doing a mitzvah and that we were sensible to be discreet.

The bazaar was an amazing success and we raised the grand sum of two hundred pounds!

"Brilliant!" I exclaimed to Mashy, after we had counted the money. "That's two hundred and fifty altogether. It's surely enough! There might even be some left over for her to go for convalescence after the operation."

Dr. Feldman listened intently as I explained the reason for my visit to the doctor's office.

"Does your mother know about this?" was the first question he asked when I had finished.

A little taken aback, I assured him that she did. "I would have left it for her to come and speak to you," I told him, "but she's away for a few days and I was worried about leaving all that money in the house." I didn't add that I was eager to set the wheels in motion and had no patience to wait till Mummy came home.

"I see," the doctor said. "And how much money *have* you raised?"

"Two hundred and fifty pounds!" I said proudly, placing the envelope on his desk.

There was a strange expression on his face that I could not interpret, but he said nothing as he picked up the envelope and counted the money.

"You've done very well," he told me. "Leave this with me and I'll get in touch with a good plastic surgeon. I should have an answer for you within two weeks. Come and see me again then… or better still, ask your mother to come. Alright?"

With an encouraging smile, the doctor ushered me out of his office.

Things began to move quickly after that. My mother called Penina's parents and managed, albeit with a lot of difficulty, to persuade them to agree to the operation. Not having been present, I don't know exactly what was said, but I gathered from what Mummy told me afterwards that Mr. and Mrs. Leifman were still afraid the authorities would start probing. Mummy herself was not quite sure that they had nothing to worry about, but she did succeed in convincing them that they ought to give their daughter the chance for a better life. Mrs. Leifman, it seemed, had remained skeptical at first, but her husband declared that they owed it to Penina and that they would put their trust in Hashem that all would be well.

Very soon the wheels were set in motion and it was arranged for Penina to go into the hospital a month later.

"Professor Martin is an excellent surgeon," Dr. Feldman assured the anxious parents. "You can be sure he'll do a first class job."

Penina herself was terribly apprehensive.

"I'm scared," she told us, when I went with Mashy to see her the day before she went into the hospital. "I've never had an operation before. And what if they make me look even worse than I do now?"

"They know what they're doing," Mashy said, trying to sound grown up and knowledgeable. "They do hundreds of these operations—"

"And they wouldn't do them if they weren't sure they would be successful," I butted in, adding my comments to the discussion.

Penina, though, was ever so brave! She kept reassuring *us* that she would be alright!

When, after three weeks, her bandages were removed, we were excited, expecting Penina to look as if nothing had ever happened to her. To our disappointment, it wasn't quite like that. True, the ugly scars from the burns had gone, replaced by the smooth skin they had grafted on her, but there were red scars in the places where the joins had been made.

"The doctor says they will fade," Penina said, interpreting our expressions correctly.

"And guess what? I finally had a look in the mirror today," she told us. "It was awfully strange to see what I look like for the first time!"

The doctor was right. It took quite a long time, but the scars did fade eventually. They would always be there, of course, but they were hardly noticeable. Penina was taught how to cover them up with some cream she was given. Mashy and I marveled at the difference in her. She looked good and seemed more relaxed and confident—until we suggested the time was right for her to go out and meet people. Then the apprehension came back into her eyes.

"I can't!" she protested, a slight tremble in her voice. "Please don't make me!"

"Penina," I said persuasively, "what happened to your courage? Remember when you faced me for the first time? And, after that, when you met Mashy? You were brave enough then… and that was when you still had your scars! Now you look great, so you've got nothing to worry about!"

Mashy, too, began to cajole and coerce her and, eventually, we persuaded her to come to a school party. I don't think either of us quite knew what an ordeal it was for her, suddenly having to meet so many people, after being shut away from the world almost her entire life! It was only after the party, when she described her feelings to me, that I understood. It was like someone who can't swim being pushed into the deep end of the swimming pool. You feel as if you are going to drown, at first, but then you realize you must swim to save your life! And "swim" Penina certainly did! She made an enormous effort to overcome her self-consciousness and soon even began to enjoy herself. If any of the girls wondered what the slight scars on her face were, they gave no indication of it and they welcomed her warmly.

The next step, we decided, was to get Penina enrolled in our school. Penina herself like the idea, but she was afraid her parents would never agree.

"You'll have to find the right moment to suggest it to them," she told us. "I might hurt their feelings if I mention it. After all, they have done a good job teaching me and it would look as if I don't appreciate it."

The "right moment" I chose was Shabbos afternoon. I dropped in to visit Penina and found her learning Chumash and Rashi with her father, a refined looking man with a light brown beard. Whereas Mrs. Leifman taught her daughter *limudei chol*, it was Penina's father who took responsibility for her *limudei kodesh* education. In all the time I had known Penina, I had never met her father before. He traveled a lot for work and was otherwise very busy.

When I broached the subject of enrolling her in school, Mr. Leifman shook his head, saying, "It's Shabbos now. This is not the time to discuss it!"

He was right, of course, and I let the matter drop. But I came round again on Sunday and brought the subject up once more. This time, Mr. Leifman gave the suggestion proper consideration.

"I don't see why not," he finally said, after sitting quietly for a few minutes. "I think we've given her enough time to adapt now to being out in the world. It might be a good idea for Penina to have some school life. I will get in touch with your headmistress and put in an application. Let's hope she'll be accepted." A smile hovered round his lips and there was a twinkle in his eyes. "I don't mind letting someone else teach her for a bit. Perhaps then I'll have more time and can go to the *daf yomi shiur!*"

Of course, Penina was accepted into the school. Her first few days were rough. Starting school for the first time at her age took some getting used to. It was wonderful having Penina at school with us. Even though she was in a lower class and soon she made a lot of new friends, she still made sure to spend some time with Mashy and me.

Her mother, though still nervous and overprotective, seemed happy to let her go out and, indeed, Mrs. Leifman's attitude towards us had also changed. Even though she didn't actually express her gratitude, I could tell she really appreciated what we had done. Actually, I think she was kind of astonished at how it had all turned out. She had lived for so many years with such shame that seeing Penina accepted, with loads of friends, left her absolutely dumbfounded.

As a matter of fact, I couldn't help feeling a bit of pride myself, for being instrumental in bringing it all about. I wouldn't let myself get too smug, though, knowing that it was really *siyata d'Shmaya* that helped me raise the money for Penina's operation.

It was only years later that I became aware of the fact that the cost of the plastic surgery was actually a lot more than two hundred and fifty pounds!

Puzzled, I asked my mother about it. The secretive smile on her face reminded me of the expression I had seen on the doctor's face when I handed him the envelope. Then she told me what really happened.

"Dr. Feldman was most amused when you gave him the money, but he was also terribly moved. He decided not to disillusion you and, if necessary, collect the money himself. In the end he didn't even have to do that. Professor Martin was also extremely moved when he heard the story and he decided to do the operation for the sum you had raised.

"So, you see, the *siyata d'Shmaya* you had went even further than you realized!"

It's many years now since all this happened. We have all grown up and married. Mashy lives in Gateshead, where her husband learns in the *Kollel*. My husband is principal of a boys' *cheder* in another district of my old town, only a short bus ride away from my parents' house. Penina's husband, a much-respected *talmid chochom*, is a *maggid shiur* in a yeshiva in Eretz Yisroel. Although her parents miss her terribly, they go to see her whenever her mother, who now teaches in my old school, has holidays.

In fact, last week Mrs. Leifman telephoned me and told me that Penina was coming for a short stay with her four children.

"Great!" I exclaimed. "Can I come and visit her?"

"Of course, you must! She's longing to see you!"

So, there I was, pushing my youngest child, fifteen-month old Shmuli, in the buggy, as I walked down Milton Close once more.

I reached No. 30 and stopped short, wondering if I'd mistaken the house. How different it looked! A pram was standing in front of the door, with a blue blanket half hanging out of it. A doll's buggy with a doll inside was right near it and the front path was littered with toy bricks, a ball and a small tricycle.

I looked up at the windows, as I used to do in the past, and I saw that all the curtains were pulled right open. At one window, a teddy bear was perched on the sill and at the next window… yes, there was Penina, with a baby in her arms, waving to me!

I marveled at the scene in front of me. I remembered how dramatic Penina's change of appearance had been all those years ago. But nothing, I decided, was quite as amazing as the transformation of the house we had once called "the house without windows"!

# A Grandmother's Dilemma

"Ladies and gentlemen," a voice with a strong northern British accent came over the loudspeaker of the train, "I'm afraid we have run into some trouble. Due to the strong winds we've been having, a tree has fallen onto the track and we are unable to continue for the time being."

Oh, no! Rina Dorfberger could hardly believe what she was hearing. Of all times, this couldn't be happening now!

"… Needless to say," the guard's voice carried on, "work will begin shortly to move the tree and we hope to resume our journey soon. British Rail apologizes to passengers for the delay and for any inconvenience it may be causing."

Inconvenience! Rina thought indignantly—though she didn't

know whom she was blaming—it's *erev* Shabbos! If we don't move soon, I'll be in a pickle!

Rina hadn't been too worried at first, when the train had stopped in the middle of nowhere. Signals, probably, she told herself, confident that they would soon start moving again. But when, quarter of an hour later, they were still standing at the same spot, she began to feel the first flutterings of alarm. Then, that ominous announcement had come over the loudspeaker, causing a full-scale panic to rise inside her.

She shouldn't really have been on this train at all. All the other girls had traveled down last night in a hired bus and she would have preferred to go with them. She had been looking forward to this trip to London. The occasion was an annual event, when B'nos girls from London, Manchester and Gateshead came together for a weekend packed with *shiurim* and various activities. This year it was being held in London, and Rina was going as a *madrichah* for the first time.

"I really ought to be there right at the beginning," she had pointed out, but her mother had waved away her protests.

"You'll upset Aunty Rochel if you don't stay for the bar mitzvah," she had insisted. "You can take an early train on Friday morning. I'm sure you won't miss much."

Knowing she was right, Rina had agreed to stay, and as the 9:30 a.m. train had pulled out of Manchester, she had leaned back contentedly and admitted to herself that she had really enjoyed her cousin's bar mitzvah after all.

But now everything was suddenly going wrong! No way would her train be arriving in London at the scheduled time of 12:10, which meant she would have a mad rush to get to the house she was staying at in Stamford Hill and be ready and changed for Shabbos, which came in at 3:54.

Consulting her watch, Rina did some quick calculations. Don't panic, she told herself. It shouldn't take all that long to shift a tree. If we start moving within the next hour, I should be able to make it. In the worst case, I'll jump into a taxi at the station. But if it's any longer than that, *chas v'sholom*, I don't know what I'll do!

In spite of her determination to keep calm, the waiting soon began to prey on Rina's patience. If only the train would start moving already! She began to fidget, looking at her watch every few minutes and giving frustrated sighs as she drummed her fingers on the table in front of her.

"What's the matter with you?" the woman sitting opposite her complained. "You're getting on my nerves! You're not the only one stuck on this train, you know. We've all got to sit and wait!"

Yes, Rina thought to herself, but *you* haven't got to be somewhere in time for Shabbos! However, knowing that she could not explain that to this woman, she could only mumble a meek, "I'm sorry."

Gritting her teeth, Rina tried hard to keep the tension from building up inside her. She looked out of the window, knowing only too well that she would still see the same grassy slope, with the same wooden fence on top of it. The only difference was the sky above them, which had become black and menacing.

Then it began to snow. Watching the white flakes swirling through the air and bouncing off the train window, Rina could no longer suppress her anxiety. What was going to happen to her? Would she still be on this train when Shabbos came in? What was she supposed to do? There wasn't anyone there to ask! Desperately wiping away the tears that had welled up in her eyes, she groped in her bag and took out her little sefer Tehillim. Ignoring the strange looks she was getting from the woman facing her, she mouthed the words earnestly, praying for a way out of her predicament.

When she heard the click and crackle that usually preceded the guard's voice, she thought, for a blissful split second, that they were about to start moving. But the words that came across the loudspeaker dashed her hopes immediately.

"Ladies and gentlemen," the voice said, "due to the sudden bad weather, it is impossible to move the tree at the moment..." Exasperated sighs could be heard all around the carriage. "... and we cannot continue our journey for the present. We are just waiting for a clear signal and then we shall be pulling backwards to the nearest station — which is Tamworth."

The voice droned on, telling people what to do when they arrived at the station — how to get to their desired destination, or return to Manchester if they wished. But Rina was hardly listening. All she could think of, with immense disappointment, was that she would definitely *not* be in London for the weekend she had been looking forward to, after all. The time was now past two o'clock. Would she be able to get back to Manchester in time for Shabbos? The thought of being stranded in the middle of nowhere over Shabbos filled her with dread!

It took another twenty minutes to get into Tamworth station. Frantically, Rina grabbed her things and joined the throng of people pushing their way through the doors. Making a beeline for the telephones, she found them all occupied and had to wait for what seemed like an eternity till she could actually get through to her mother.

"Rina!" Mrs. Dorfberger shouted as soon as she heard her voice. "Why haven't you telephoned till now? I've been so worried! It must be hours since you got to London —"

"Mummy," Rina interrupted, her voice choked, "I'm not in London."

"What?! Where are you? What happened? Rina! Are you alright?"

The utter panic in her mother's voice released the tears Rina had been holding back. Amid sobs, she told her mother what had occurred. "What shall I do?" she wailed.

"Where did you say you are? Tamworth? That's quite near Birmingham, isn't it? Look, *shayfeleh*, there's no way you can get to London in time for Shabbos—and I don't think you could get back home either."

"But I can't stay here!" Rina cried, dissolving in another flood of tears.

"I know…" Mrs. Dorfberger said, sounded tearful too. "You'll have to go to Birmingham. But don't worry, Rina, there are quite a lot of *yidden* living there. Look, *sheyfeleh*, get a train or a bus to Birmingham and phone me as soon as you get there. You can give me the number of the phone and I'll phone you back. Meanwhile, I'll get in touch with Mrs. Weisner—she used to live in Birmingham—and ask her if there's somewhere you could stay. Okay? And Rina, darling, try not to—"

Whatever her mother was going to say was lost as a buzzing sound came over the line. Rina's money had run out. Fighting back more tears, she realized she had better follow her mother's instructions as quickly as possible.

The taxi drew up outside a pleasant looking house with a small front garden, which was covered with a thin white layer of snow. An attractive flower basket hung down over the front door, giving the place a welcoming look. It was the sort of house Rina would normally have enjoyed staying in, but just now it was definitely *not* where she really wanted to be! Still, she told herself, suppressing her disappointment as well as she could, she was lucky really. It could have been so much worse!

It hadn't been too difficult to get to Birmingham. A kind, elderly guard at Tamworth station, noting her distress, had checked the time of the next train for her and directed her to the right platform. Fortunately, a train came along soon and, after a twenty-minute journey, she was at Birmingham station, telephoning home. By then, her mother had already spoken to Mrs. Weisner, who had immediately contacted her friend in Birmingham, a Mrs. Kern. She had been told that, of course, Rina would be most welcome in the Kern home for Shabbos!

Aware that it must almost be Shabbos, Rina paid the taxi and pulled out her suitcase hastily, then gingerly made her way up the snow-covered drive and somewhat tentatively rang the doorbell.

The woman who opened the door was obviously already dressed for Shabbos. She was wearing a well-cut navy suit and her blonde sheitel was stylishly combed. She smiled warmly and Rina took to her immediately.

"I'm Rina Dorfberger—" she began to explain.

"—Yes, I know. Shoshana Weisner told me to expect you. *Sholom aleichem!* Come on in! I'm Leah Kern." Shaking Rina's hand, Mrs. Kern drew her inside. "You poor thing! What an ordeal you've been through!"

"Yes, it was rather frightening," Rina admitted.

"*Boruch Hashem*, at least you got here in time for Shabbos!" Mrs. Kern declared.

Rina looked up as a girl of about fifteen, clad in a lilac and green robe, her fair curly hair still wet, came walking down the stairs. "Ah, Dassy, you're out of the shower. Good. Take Rina quickly up to the guest room." Mrs. Kern turned to Rina. "You've just got time to have a quick shower. Shabbos is in twenty minutes and I want you to eat something before Shabbos. You must be starving!" Leaving Rina to follow Dassy up the stairs, Mrs. Kern hurried off towards the kitchen.

As long as Rina didn't allow her mind to dwell on what she would be doing now had she made it to London, she really enjoyed that Friday night. Earlier, realizing there was no time for conversation, Dassy had ushered her into the guest room, pointed out the bathroom and sped away to dry her hair. Rina had showered and gotten dressed in her Shabbos clothes in record time. Then she had gone down to the kitchen, from where the delicious and familiar smell of Shabbos food emanated. Mrs. Kern plied her with a welcome cup of tea and insisted she tasted some of her potato kugel. Then, with a quick glance at the clock, Mrs. Kern went into the dining room to light the Shabbos candles.

Dassy came in, looking quite different in a blue and cream dress, with her fair hair held back by a matching blue hair band. Now that Shabbos had come in and there was no longer any rush and panic, she was relaxed as she greeted Rina warmly, shaking her hand and leading her to the sofa, where she sat down beside her. Mrs. Kern came over to them and handed each girl a siddur, sitting down herself with her own siddur. There was a cozy atmosphere as they all davened kabbolas Shabbos and maariv together.

By the time Mr. Kern had come home from shul and made kiddush, Rina almost felt part of the family. As they all sat around the table, enjoying the meal, the conversation was lively. Even the two younger children, nine-year-old Mimi and six-year-old Danny, did their best to make Rina feel at home.

Answering all their many questions, Rina told them about life in Manchester.

"You're so lucky!" Dassy exclaimed when she heard about the B'nos group Rina belonged to. "There aren't enough of us here for that," she explained, a wistful note in her voice.

"What do you usually do on a Shabbos afternoon?" Rina asked her.

"In the summer, when Shabbos is longer, I get together with a few of my friends. But now, in the winter, there's just about time to go to the old age home where I go to visit an old woman named Mrs. Ginsberg. I usually go with my friend Esty, but she's away this week." She regarded Rina with an inquiring look. "Maybe you'd like to come with me."

"Yes, why not," Rina readily agreed. After all, what else was there for her to do? And, seeing that she was stuck here, she might as well spend some of the time doing a mitzvah.

By Shabbos afternoon, the weather had improved considerably. The blustery winds had abated and the thin layer of snow on the ground had been washed away by overnight rain. However, it was still bitterly cold as Rina and Dassy, wrapped up warmly in thick coats and scarves, made their way to the old age home, deep in conversation. Despite the two-years difference in their ages, the two girls had struck up a warm friendship. Rina told Dassy all about the gathering she had been traveling to and suggested that Dassy might accompany her after Shabbos and take part in the last lap of the weekend. It was a tempting proposition, and Dassy hoped her mother would agree to it.

As they approached the old age home, Dassy told Rina as much as she knew about the old woman they were going to visit.

"She's a Hungarian lady," she informed her companion.

"Oh, just like my grandmother!" Rina butted in. "She came to England from Hungary during the war."

"Well, Mrs. Ginsberg spent the war years in hiding in Hungary. It seems she was being taken away, together with her parents, to be killed, but she managed to escape and some good non-Jews took her in and hid her. After the war, when Communism took over, she couldn't get out—not until the Hungarian Revolution, in 1956—but she did manage to come to England then. I think she was about 35 at the time. Anyway, after a few months she married Mr. Ginsberg, who was also a Hungarian, and they settled here in Birmingham. I don't really remember her husband. She must have been alone for quite a long time now."

"Has she got any children?" Rina asked.

"Yes, she's got one son, but he lives in Devon—or somewhere—and I don't think he's very *frum*. He usually comes to see her once a week…"

"Is that *all*?" Rina exclaimed, aghast.

"Yes. I think she keeps on telling him off about his lack of *yiddishkeit*, so he steers clear as much as he can! Anyway, Mummy and some other ladies go a few times a week and they bring her things all the time. And I go every Shabbos afternoon. She's a nice old lady, even if she gets a bit cantankerous sometimes. I think you'll like her."

By now, they had arrived at the home and Dassy led Rina in through the large swing-doors. The entrance hall was a big, square area furnished with a few brown leather armchairs, two of which were occupied by elderly ladies, while some other old people were hobbling about with walking sticks. A nurse, serving tea and cake from a trolley, acknowledged Dassy with a nod and a smile.

"Come on," Dassy said, "she's on the second floor."

Rina followed her up the two flights of stairs and along a corridor, till Dassy stopped by a door with the number 25 on it, underneath which there was a small plaque bearing the name "Mrs. Ginsberg."

Dassy knocked and they went in. The old woman was sitting in a deep wicker chair, a large blanket wrapped round her. A cup of cold tea stood neglected on a small wooden table beside her.

"Where have you been?" she asked Dassy, her tone disgruntled. "I thought you were not coming already!"

"I'm not later than usual," Dassy told her gently. "And I've brought you another visitor. She's from Manchester and her name is Rina Dorfberger."

Mrs. Ginsberg turned and looked at Rina.

"From Manchester? *Sholom aleichem*," Mrs. Ginsberg gave her a somewhat grudging smile. "Take off your coat and sit down," she said, waving towards one of the chairs near her.

Rina was struck by a strange sensation. This woman reminded her so much of her grandmother! She studied her closely for a moment. Did she look like her? Not really, she decided. Was it the heavy Hungarian accent, then? Maybe. But she still had the feeling it was something else, too. Perhaps it was the way the woman tilted her head to one side when she spoke. Bubbe usually did that too. Whatever it was, the feeling was uncanny and she couldn't shake it off.

The nurse they had seen downstairs came in, a glass of water and a small container in her hand.

"Come on, Pearl," she said briskly, "time for your pills."

How strange, Rina thought. Fancy calling an old lady by her first name! But that's what nurses tended to do, she told herself, remembering a short stay she had had in hospital once. So Mrs. Ginsberg's name is Pearl, she reflected with some amusement.

Suddenly something struck a chord in her memory! Pearl… Perel… same name, really. All at once, without warning, her mind went back to an afternoon when she was sitting in her grandmother's flat in Manchester. Bubbe was telling her off because she'd had a big fight with her younger sister.

"Yoy, Rinaleh," her grandmother had said, shaking her head ruefully, "sisters shouldn't be *broigez* with each other! If only my sister had not been *broigez* with me… and now it's too late." There were tears in her eyes as she spoke.

"What do you mean, Bubbe?" Rina had asked, surprised. She knew her grandmother had had a sister who had been killed in the war, together with her parents. "What is it too late for?"

Her grandmother gave a deep sigh, two small tears rolling slowly down her cheeks.

"Once I did something that made Perel angry… yoy, how angry she was! She swore she would never ever forgive me! Even now I can understand how she felt and I was so sorry! I begged her, time and time again, but no… she just refused! Even when the people who took me out of Hungary with them arrived to fetch me, she wouldn't speak to me. And after that I never saw her again…" By now tears were pouring unchecked out of her eyes. She wiped them away with a tissue.

"But Bubbe," Rina wanted to know, "what could you have done that was so terrible?"

The old lady shook her head, giving Rina a wan smile. "No, *shayfeleh*," she said, "I'm not telling you that!"

Now, remembering that conversation, Rina scrutinized Mrs.

Ginsberg closely, then asked impulsively, "Mrs. Ginsberg, did you ever have a sister?"

The old lady seemed to turn pale for a split second. Then a pink flush replaced the pallor. Eyeing Rina searchingly for a moment, her lips suddenly set in a hard line and she turned her face away before answering with a curt "no!"

Her reply should have been enough to put an end to Rina's fanciful idea, but somehow she was unconvinced. She felt she had to probe further.

"Where about in Hungary did you live?" she asked, trying to sound as if she was merely being conversational.

The old lady turned to her, an angry look on her face. "Why do you want to know?" she snapped. "Do you *know* Hungary at all? Have you ever been there?"

"N-no..." Rina stammered uncomfortably.

"Your friend from Manchester asks too many questions!" Mrs. Ginsberg said sulkily, addressing Dassy. "Now tell me, Hadassah, what have you been doing with yourself all week?"

Feeling snubbed and embarrassed, Rina sat quietly and listened while Dassy chatted with Mrs. Ginsberg. She was quite glad when it was time to go.

"What was all that about?" Dassy asked, as soon as they were out of the building. "Why were you asking those strange questions?" There was an accusing note in her voice and she eyed her new friend as if there was something peculiar about her.

Feeling acutely embarrassed, Rina felt it was only fair to explain.

"Wow!" Dassy exclaimed when she had finished her narrative. "Do you really think she's your grandmother's sister? She said she never *had* a sister, and even though she's old, she wouldn't forget a thing like that!"

"I know…" Rina said, thoroughly confused. "But it was sort of… you know… funny, the way she said it. And I can't shake off that feeling that she reminds me of Bubbe. I wonder what her maiden name was…" she mused.

"Maybe Mummy would know," Dassy suggested. "She's known Mrs. Ginsberg a long time."

Mrs. Kern, however, was not much help. "Sorry," she said, shaking her head. "I wasn't even born when she came here! And I don't think anyone else will know because she only came to Birmingham *after* her marriage, so she's only been known here as Ginsberg." She smiled at Rina, aware of the disappointment on the girl's earnest face. The story the two girls told her had fascinated her, but she was inclined to think that Rina's imagination was running away with her a bit.

"What was your grandmother's maiden name?" she asked her.

"It was Kornzweig," Rina told her.

Hmm, not a common name, Mrs. Kern reflected. If she could only find out that Mrs. Ginsberg's name was something quite different, it would satisfy Rina and she would put the notion out of her head.

"I'll tell you what I *could* do," she suggested. "I could phone her son after Shabbos. When she moved into the old age home, he came and took everything out of her flat. He might well have a copy of his parents' marriage certificate."

"Oh, that would be terrific!" Rina cried, automatically glancing at the clock and hastily looking away again, ashamed of herself for wanting Shabbos to end!

Mrs. Kern noticed the gesture and laughed. "It won't help you, even if I phone tonight. You and Dassy will have to leave almost straight after *havdalah* — once Dassy's packed a few things, of course — or you'll miss the last train to London."

Mr. and Mrs. Kern had readily agreed to Rina's suggestion, glad for their daughter to have the chance to broaden her horizons and meet more Jewish girls of her age.

There was immense excitement when the two girls arrived, in time to join the girls for the tail end of the *melava malka*. Rina had contacted the weekend organizer before they left, asking her to inform the people who were putting her up, and Dassy's mother had promised to telephone her brother, who lived in Stamford Hill, telling him to expect his niece. The two girls had gone straight from the station to the school hall where the *melava malka* was being held.

Rina was given VIP treatment, with everybody crowding round her, clamoring to hear the details of her harrowing experience. After she had related the whole story, which she told with as much dramatic effect as she could lay on, they turned their attention to Dassy, welcoming her warmly.

"You know," one of the girls commented quietly to Rina, as they were walking home, "I think it was *bashert* that that would happen to you so that you would meet Dassy and bring her here to join us."

Yes, Rina reflected, but not only because of Dassy. Perhaps it was also because of two certain old ladies — one in Birmingham and one in Manchester!

Rina hurried up the path on Tuesday, eager to see her mother again. She had thoroughly enjoyed the two days in London, and the journey home by bus, together with the other girls, had been uneventful. But it was still nice to be home again.

Mrs. Dorfberger was already at the open front door, a welcoming smile on her face.

"*Sholom aleichem*, Rina! Did you have a good time in the end—after your awful experience?"

"Oh yes, it was terrific! And actually, Shabbos was nice too, after all. The Kern family made me feel at home."

"Yes, Mrs. Kern sounds extremely nice. I've just spoken to her, about an hour ago." Mrs. Dorfberger said.

"You spoke to her?" Rina sounded surprised. "Did you phone to thank her? I wish you'd waited till I was home so I could also thank her."

"Actually, no, I didn't phone her. She phoned me."

"Why? Isn't Dassy home yet?" There was alarm in Rina's voice. "Her uncle was taking her home by car and she said she'd be home before all of us."

"Rina, calm down!" her mother interrupted. "She was actually waiting for her daughter, who, she said, would be arriving soon. No, she phoned with a message for you."

"A message?" Rina sounded puzzled.

"Yes, a most peculiar message. I've no idea what it means! She said I should tell you that it seems you were right and that the name is the same. Do *you* know what it's all about?"

Rina's eyes lit up at her mother's words and a smile spread over her face. "Wow!" she exclaimed. "Mummy, I've got something so exciting to tell you!"

Following her mother into the kitchen, Rina threw her coat carelessly onto a chair and launched straight into her narrative. With a disapproving shake of her head, Mrs. Dorfberger picked up Rina's coat as she listened and was about to go and hang it up when the implications of Rina's story hit her. She stopped in her tracks and stared at her daughter in amazement! Was she hearing right? Could it be possible that an old lady Rina just happened to go and visit should turn out to be her own mother's sister? Unbelievable! With Rina's coat still over her arm, she sat down on a chair, a dazed expression on her face.

"B-but she was killed," she stammered after a few moments. "Someone told Bubbe that she saw her and her parents being led away."

"No, it seems *she* managed to escape," Rina told her. "She was in hiding in Hungary all through the war. She only came to England in 1956."

"I see," Mrs. Dorfberger was beginning to come to terms with the idea. "Bubbe will have to be told, of course. I hope it won't be too much of a shock for her."

To say it was a shock would be putting it mildly! Old Mrs. Brindler stared at her daughter and granddaughter with utter disbelief for a moment. Then her face, already deathly pale, crumpled up and she began to weep.

"I can't believe it!" she sobbed. "Perel... my own sister... still alive! Are you quite sure, Rinaleh? You haven't made a mistake, maybe?" Her tear-filled eyes peered at Rina searchingly.

"No!" Rina declared emphatically. "Her first name is the

same… *and* her maiden name! *And* she came from Hungary… just like you…"

"You should have *asked* her!" There was an accusing note in her grandmother's tone. "Why didn't you ask if she had a sister?"

"But I did!" Rina protested. She was eyeing her grandmother earnestly and was unaware that her mother was throwing her warning looks. "I asked her just that… but she said 'no'."

"She said 'no'?" Mrs. Brindler asked, suddenly sounding deflated.

By now Mrs. Dorfberger had managed to edge nearer to her daughter and give her a nudge. Rina immediately realized her mistake and tried to find a way out.

"She must have forgotten, after all these years," she said desperately. "Or maybe she thought it was none of my business."

But the old lady was not convinced. Shaking her head, she said sadly, "She still has not forgiven me. She *wants* to forget me!"

"Oh Bubbe!" Rina cried, "don't say that! When you see her, you can ask her yourself and I'm sure she will say she has!"

"No, no," Mrs. Brindler was adamant. "I *want* to see her… oh, I'd like to so much! But I just could not bear it if I would ask her *mechilah* and she would say 'no' again!"

For quite a long time, Rina and her mother tried to persuade her, but to no avail. They could not move her. Presently Mrs. Dorfberger stood up with a resigned air.

"Think it over, Mamme," she said with a sigh. "I've brought you some soup. It just needs warming up." She eyed her mother with concern. "Are you sure you'll be alright on your own? You've had a bit of a shock."

"Of course I will, Gittel." Mrs. Brindler gave her daughter a somewhat forced smile. "Don't worry about me. And thank you for the soup."

Mrs. Dorfberger was reluctant to leave her mother in the state she was in, but she knew she would hate it if she offered to stay with her. The old woman valued her independence above everything. Taking Rina by the arm she went to the door and, with one more wave, they left the flat.

Alone at last, the old lady sat quite still, staring at the wall. But it wasn't the wall of her kitchen that she saw. It was the floral wallpaper of the bedroom she shared with her sister Perel. No longer an old woman in her late seventies, she was pretty, twelve-year-old Minka—or Minku, as her family called her—admiring her new pink party dress in front of the mirror. Very soon her friend would be coming to fetch her and they would be going to another friend's bas mitzvah party. Her eye suddenly fell on a little red velvet box on the dressing table. She knew what it contained. It was Perel's engagement ring.

Perel had gone away for a few days, to help their aunt who had just had a baby. She had left the ring at home, knowing that she would be doing a lot of washing and cleaning and could either lose the ring or spoil it with too much water. On an impulse, Minku took the ring out of the box and slipped it onto her finger. How pretty it looked! If only she could wear it for the party. Why not? she thought suddenly. Perel would not be back till late that night, by which time she would be home and the ring would be safely back in its box. Perel would never even know.

Her conscience was just beginning to stab at her when her mother called her to say that her friend had come. With no time to think, she hurried out of the room to join her friend and together they set off for the party.

Quite a few girls noticed the ring and admired it, but nearly all of them could see that it was an engagement ring and they expressed surprise that her sister had allowed her to wear it. Feeling embarrassed, Minku took it off and slipped it into her pocket. It was only when she was back at home and had hastened to her room to replace the ring that she noticed it was missing!

Now, more than sixty years later, she could still remember the agony of the ensuing events… the frantic searching back at the house of the party and in the streets from there to her home. Then she recalled Perel's hysterical reaction and the terrible drama that followed when Perel's future mother-in-law found out. There had been such an angry scene when the *chosson*'s parents came round to their house. His mother had criticized Perel sharply for her carelessness and his father had demanded repayment for the ring. A bitter quarrel had taken place, harsh words were spoken and consequently the engagement was broken off.

She could still remember how she had found Perel weeping bitterly in their bedroom. She had tried to apologize, but Perel had turned to her with fury in her red-rimmed eyes and declared, "I will never forgive you for this! Never, never, ever!"

Those were the last words her sister ever spoke to her. Perel totally ignored her from then on. Perhaps, if she had become engaged again, Perel would have forgiven her. But it was not to be. The war broke out and, although Hungary was not immediately affected, things soon became difficult for the Jews. Many were drafted into the army and escape became almost impossible. When a neighboring couple called Lembiger managed to obtain papers to leave, they offered to take one of the Kornzweig girls with them as their own child, providing they could falsify a passport.

"Take Minku," Mrs. Kornzweig had said, her voice choked with tears. "She is only fifteen. Why should she live through these hard times?"

"No, Mamme, no!" she had protested pleadingly. But her mother had stood firm, trying nevertheless to appease her. "It won't be for long, *zeeseleh*," her mother had said, her voice shaking. "As soon as the war is over, you can come back to us."

And so, amid bitter tears, she had taken leave of her family. Only Perel had remained stony-faced, turning away from her. Little did Minku dream she would never see her family again!

The Lembigers took her to England and she was registered there as Minnie Lembiger. It was only after the war that she changed her surname back to Kornzweig. She had heard of the tragic fate that had befallen her parents, her sister and her two married brothers and she discovered that she was alone. Mr. and Mrs. Lembiger treated her like their own child, eventually marrying her off to a fine young man called Yakov Brindler. Then they were the typical contented grandparents to her six children. When they grew old, she looked after them in return. Now, many years later, Mrs. Brindler's three sons and one of her daughters had settled in Eretz Yisroel. Only Gittel and another daughter, Rochel, lived near her in Manchester.

And now, all of a sudden, her granddaughter had come and dropped a bombshell! Perel—her own sister Perel—was alive and was living in England!

How she longed to see Perel and speak to her! She was fully aware that her sister, seven years her senior and now an old woman in poor health, would not be the same as she remembered her, but then, wasn't she quite different too? Nevertheless, they were still Perel and Minku!

If only she could be sure Perel would be glad to see her. But, by the sound of what Rina had told her, it seemed unlikely. She didn't know if she could bear to be snubbed and rejected all over again!

No! She decided that there was no way she would be forced to go through that again! It was just too painful. And, after all the pain she had endured in her life, she didn't think she could endure any more. Gittel and Rina would just have to accept the fact and leave her in peace!

But she did not reckon with Rina's persistence. The girl refused to relinquish the picture in her mind of the sisters' grand reunion. She came round constantly, trying everything she could think of to convince her grandmother to make the trip to Birmingham. And each time Rina went away disappointed.

Oddly, it was her son-in-law who finally persuaded her. He dropped in one afternoon to deliver some fish her daughter had cooked for her. It was not long before he steered the conversation round to the subject of her sister.

"Oh, no!" Mrs. Brindler complained, looking pained. "Not you as well! I've had enough of it! Why can't you all understand that I *can't* go! If this goes on much longer, I'll end up quarrelling with my own daughter and granddaughter!"

"But, Shvigger," Mr. Dorfberger protested calmly, "it's the Ribono Shel Olom you're quarrelling with, not them!"

The old woman stared at her son-in-law open-mouthed. "What do you mean, I'm quarrelling with the *Eibeshter*? How can you ever say such a thing?"

"Don't you see?" Chaim Dorfberger explained gently, aware that he had upset his mother-in-law, but convinced that he must nevertheless press on with his argument, "Don't you think there was a reason Rina's train journey was delayed and she ended up in Birmingham? It was bashert that she would meet this woman who would turn out to be your sister. It is bashert that the two of you should be reunited after more than half a century. The Ribono Shel Olom has done His share but now you are refusing to do yours!"

Mrs. Brindler continued to gape, her face a delicate shade of pink. "Oh Chaim," she said presently, in an awed voice, "I hadn't thought of it like that!"

"So you'll go?"

"I-I don't know," she said, hesitantly, her voice soft and thoughtful. "It's not that I don't want to. You don't know how I long to see Perel again… and to ask her *mechilah*. But, to be honest, I am afraid. What if she refuses?"

"I'm sure she won't. And, anyway, whatever happens, it would be tragic if you missed this opportunity to see her again," Mr. Dorfberger said, standing up. "Well, think it over. I have to go now. I'm late for my *shiur*." He went to the door and turned round to smile encouragingly at his mother-in-law. "Enjoy the fish. And don't look so worried. I'm sure it will turn out alright."

After he went, Mrs. Brindler sat still, turning her dilemma over in her mind. What should she do? Chaim was right, of course, but she still felt she could not bear it if things turned out the way *she* imagined they would.

It took at least half-an-hour of soul-searching and deliberating before she finally made up her mind.

On the Sunday afternoon after his visit, Mr. Dorfberger drove his car into the car park of the old age home in Birmingham and stopped, allowing his three passengers to alight. He could not help noticing how tense and nervous his mother-in-law looked as her daughter and granddaughter helped her out of the car.

"Take your time," he said, taking a small *gemara* out of the glove compartment. "I'll be waiting right here. And Shvigger, don't worry. Remember what I told you. If you keep your side of the bargain, the Ribono Shel Olom will do the rest!" He gave her a wink, aware that Rina and her mother were staring at him. They both had been astonished when Mrs. Brindler had told them of her intentions. Though they praised her courage, they had no idea what had prompted her decision. Realizing now that Mr. Dorfberger had had something to do with it, neither commented, both intending to question him later. The object now, though, was to get Mrs. Brindler over the hurdle she was dreading as quickly as possible.

As she walked between them, her arms linked with theirs, they could feel her body tense up, which seemed to intensify as they entered the building. A nurse, not the one Rina had seen when she had been before, met them in the entrance and asked them whom they had come to see.

"Ah yes," she said, when they told her, "Mrs. Ginsberg is in quite good spirits today. She will enjoy having visitors."

They took the lift to the second floor and Rina led them to room 25. Rina put her hand out, ready to knock at the door, when her grandmother suddenly pulled her back.

"No, no!" Mrs. Brindler whispered, her face white. "I can't go in!"

"Oh, Bubbe…" There was exasperation in Rina's tone. "You can't back out now. You've already come so far! Please, Bubbe."

They watched anxiously as Mrs. Brindler struggled with herself once again. After a few moments, a resigned expression came into her tired grey eyes. "No, you are right," she said, somewhat hesitantly, "I can't back out now." She sighed. "Come on then, let's go in. What will be will be!"

"That's the idea!" Mrs. Dorfberger said approvingly, while Rina's comment was, "Oh Bubbe, you're so brave!"

Rina knocked, and as soon as they heard the meek "come in," she pushed open the door and ushered her grandmother into the room.

The frail old lady in the rose-patterned armchair stared at her visitors, looking puzzled. "Who are you?" she asked.

"Hullo, Mrs. Ginsberg," Rina said, immediately. "Do you remember me? I came here on Shabbos, with Dassy Kern."

"Oh, yes!" Recognition sprang into the old lady's eyes. "The girl from Manchester who asked a lot of questions!"

"That's right!" Rina laughed. "But this time I've come to bring you a special visitor. Someone you know very well but haven't seen for quite a while."

Mrs. Ginsberg's gaze went straight to the other occupants of the room, a hopeful gleam in her eyes. But the expression was immediately replaced by a blank stare.

"Who are you?" she asked again, looking puzzled.

"Perel, don't you know me?" Mrs. Brindler said, an almost pleading note in her voice.

Mrs. Ginsberg turned pale on hearing the name she had not been called for a long time. "Wh-who are you?" she said once more, her voice shaking.

"Perel, it's me! Minku!"

"*Minku*?" The old woman drew in her breath sharply as she slowly scrutinized the speaker. Then, without warning, she turned her face away. The hearts of her three visitors plummeted.

"I told you!" Mrs. Brindler spoke accusingly to Rina, her eyes filled with tears. "Why did you make me come? Take me home at once!" She began to walk towards the door and neither Rina or her mother attempted to stop her. She had just reached it when there was a cry from the armchair.

"No! Minku, don't go!"

Turning towards the sound of the cry, they saw old Mrs. Ginsberg trying to rise from her chair, tears rolling down her cheeks. Quickly, Mrs. Brindler rushed to her side, grabbing the wrinkled thin hands that were outstretched towards her. Still holding them, she sat down on a wooden chair beside Mrs. Ginsberg.

"Minku, Minku! " the old lady sobbed. "Can it really be you?"

"Yes, yes!" her sister cried in a choked voice. The two old women began to carry on a tearful conversation in Hungarian. Neither Rina nor her mother understood much, and, though they could imagine the gist of it, Rina could not help wishing she knew what they were saying. Perhaps it would give some indication of the issue they had quarreled about. She was so curious to know what it was, but she realized she would have to resign herself to the fact that it was something she would never find out. And, in any case, it didn't matter now that they had been reunited.

They heard Mrs. Brindler say the word *moichel* and Mrs. Ginsberg saying an emphatic, *"igen, igen!"* which they knew meant, "yes, yes!" in Hungarian.

The two sisters began to weep profusely, handkerchiefs suddenly appeared in their hands and soon their arms were round each other. Mrs. Dorfberger signaled to Rina and the two of them crept noiselessly out of the room, their own eyes wet with tears.

"Well, Rina," Mrs. Dorfberger said, dabbing her eyes with a tissue and smiling at her daughter, "are you still disappointed that you missed that Shabbos in London?"

"Oh, I got over the disappointment quickly," Rina told her. "Although I must admit it *was* a bit scary when I didn't know where I was going to end up for Shabbos! But now I understand that it was meant to happen that way, so I could be instrumental in reuniting two sisters." Her eyes strayed towards the closed door, picturing what was going on behind it. "Now I'm positively grateful that Hashem made that tree fall onto the tracks!"

# The Wheel of Fortune

The telephone rang out shrilly in Menashe Baronsky's study, interrupting his concentration. With an exasperated sigh, he placed a piece of paper onto his *gemara* to mark his place and walked across to a small table by the window, where the telephone rested. Picking up the receiver, he stared at it for a moment, not quite sure which way to hold it, then listened with rising irritation to his manager telling him about an appointment he had arranged for Menashe for the next day, giving him lengthy, detailed explanations. Muttering his agreement somewhat impatiently, he replaced the receiver and went back to his *gemara*, but found, to his annoyance, that he had lost his train of thought due to the interruption.

If not for that "thing" — he eyed the telephone crossly — he would not have been disturbed from learning. He hadn't really wanted to have the telephones installed — neither in the office nor in his home. His father, a Polish immigrant, had come to England at the end of the nineteenth century and, after trying various jobs and losing them when he refused to work on Shabbos, he had started his own business, making wheels for carts and carriages. Menashe had eventually taken over and the business had flourished, making him a rich man. And all this, he had declared, had been achieved without the use of a telephone!

"Maybe," his manager had argued, "but that was then. Things are different now. It's 1925! No business can function nowadays without a telephone. One has to move with the times!"

And so Menashe had allowed himself to be persuaded. Yet there were many times when he had cause to regret his decision. Like now, for instance.

Menashe's main ambition was to be able to spend as much time as he could learning Torah. Now that his business was thriving and he had the ability to employ a manager, he had decided to stay in the office only in the mornings, spending the afternoons at home, poring over his beloved *seforim*. He had told his manager not to disturb him at home. Why couldn't the man understand and obey his instructions?

Casting another baleful glance at the object of his momentary displeasure, he was aware of a figure walking past the window. He recognized him immediately. It was Herschel Berkowitz, the local butcher, delivering their weekly meat order. At least, Menashe told himself, Dinah has to buy *meat* from a *heimishe Yid*. Since they had acquired the telephone, his wife had taken to buying fruit and vegetables from a large shop in town because she could make her order over the telephone. Menashe had not been happy about it, preferring to patronize the local Jewish shops.

"Why can't you send the housekeeper down to Melsky's shop to make the order?" he had asked her. "They'll deliver it just as promptly."

"Mrs. Katzfeld has enough to do here without spending time going to the shops," Dinah had retorted. "And what's the use of having a telephone in the house if we can't use it to save time and energy?"

Reflecting on the situation, Menashe sighed. It had been difficult to argue against that piece of logic.

On an impulse, he left the study and went out through the front door, just in time to catch Herschel on his way back to his horse and cart.

"A *gutten tug*, Reb Herschel!" he called out. "How are things with you?"

"*Boruch Hashem*! *Boruch Hashem*!" Herschel replied heartily. "Couldn't be better!"

"You're looking extremely pleased about something," Menashe commented. "Business doing well?"

"Not bad, *Boruch Hashem*," Herschel replied. "The reason why I'm looking pleased is because my wife has just given birth to a baby girl! Our tenth child, *b'li ayin hora*!"

"*Mazel tov*! That *is* good news! You should have a lot of *nachas*!" Menashe exclaimed, giving Herschel an affable slap on the back. "Well, you'll certainly need a successful *parnossoh* with a family that size! How do you manage?"

"*Boruch Hashem*," Herschel repeated, "we're managing quite well. We've got what we need. Who wants more?" With a smile and a cheerful wave, he climbed up onto his cart and, whipping his horse into action, he rode off.

Menashe watched him drive off, a thoughtful expression on his face. How did Herschel manage to keep so cheerful when it was obviously not easy for him to support his large family? His manner was positively carefree! A strange feeling of envy swept over Menashe. There *he* was, a successful, wealthy businessman with every comfort and luxury one could wish for, yet he never felt calm and relaxed. Furthermore, he couldn't say his family was bringing him a lot of *nachas*. His wife, Dinah, never seemed satisfied, always making changes in the house or looking for some new way to improve her lifestyle. His seventeen-year-old son Tuvya was a constant source of worry to him. Never one to take his learning seriously, he had recently failed a *farher*, effectively ruining his chance to go to the Brisk Yeshiva in Poland. His young daughters, Sheindel and Shifra, seemed to think of nothing but clothes and wasted their time doing nothing in particular all day.

Was this what wealth was doing to them all?

He sat brooding about it, a distant look on his face, hardly glancing at the open *gemara* in front of him. Did he ever imagine, he asked himself, that a time would come when he would almost wish his business had not been so successful? He had been so enthusiastic when he had taken it over, putting time and energy into it, yet making sure his *yiddishkeit* did not suffer. He kept rigidly to his learning time and did his best to see that his son learnt diligently too. Was it his fault that the boy did not stick to his guidelines?

An astonishing idea suddenly came into his head, almost making him fall off his chair! Is that what he should do? Would that solve the problem?

No, no! His mind rejected the notion immediately. How could he bring himself to make such a sacrifice? Forget it, he told himself emphatically. And yet, an inner voice nagged at him... you're not satisfied with the present situation. Go on, it urged, take the plunge. Eventually, you'll be glad you did.

Conflict raged inside him until, unable to cope with it, he forced it out of his mind and returned his attention to his *gemara*, giving it all he was worth.

The next day he went on with his usual routine, hardly giving a thought to the previous day's idea. If it did cross his mind, he quickly pushed it away. He did not feel like arguing with that inner voice again.

It was an incident that happened in the afternoon that brought it to the forefront once more.

Relieved that the telephone seemed to be staying silent, Menashe was once again immersed in his precious *Torah* learning when he was disturbed suddenly by a commotion outside in the hall. The hysterical voice of his daughter Sheindel could clearly be heard. He hardly had time to wonder what was going on before there was a frantic, impatient knocking on his study door. Fortunately, his children *did* obey his orders never to come in without knocking.

"Come in!" he barked, somewhat gruffly.

The door was flung open immediately and Sheindel burst in, a wild look in her eyes.

"Tatty, I'm so *angry!*" she cried vehemently. "I could *scream!*"

"Please don't!" he begged. "Calm down, Sheindel! Why are you so angry? And with whom are you angry?"

"With Mrs. Steinman!" Sheindel cried, as if that explained everything.

"Mrs. Steinman?" Menashe repeated, looking blank. "Who's that?"

"Oh Tatty, you know! She's the dressmaker!"

"I see," Menashe said, comprehension dawning at last. "And what has she done to make you so cross? You always seem so happy with the dresses she makes you."

"I *am*!" his daughter declared. "That's just it! She made me a beautiful dress for Rachel Goldfeld's *chasunah*. I chose a stunning material from the samples she brought me and it came out gorgeous..."

"Well? ..." Menashe prompted, baffled.

"Well, I've just found out that she's made her daughter a dress in the *same* material!"

"So? It shows that you've got good taste if someone else has the same."

"Oh, Tatty, you don't understand! I can't go to the *chasunah* wearing a dress that looks the same as the one the *dressmaker's* daughter is wearing! She had no right to do it! I don't think you should pay her, Tatty! She ought to make me another dress!"

"Nonsense!" This time Menashe raised his voice. His daughter's snobbish attitude annoyed him immensely. "Of course I will pay her for her work. And you will have to wear that dress, whether you like it or not. I am certainly not paying for another one! It's utter *bal tashchis*! I cannot stand waste!"

Sheindel stared at him in disbelief for a moment. Then her face crumpled up and she burst into tears. "I'm not going to the *chasunah* then!" she cried and rushed out of the room, sobbing loudly.

Menashe sighed deeply and sat staring in front of him for a while, wondering why the incident had unnerved him so. It was not the first time he was faced with this type of situation. He had experienced similar outbursts many times with his daughters—and even occasionally with his wife—but he had always taken them with a pinch of salt. Why did he feel so upset now?

The "inner voice" of yesterday suddenly spoke up again. It's because it only confirms what you have been worrying about, it told him. Your family's *midos* are straying from the right path! You have got to do something, before it's too late!

It's true, he realized. He would never forgive himself if his children turned out wrong. He must act quickly!

He knew that his plan would not be an easy one to carry out and he prayed quietly to Hashem that his courage would not fail him in the last minute.

Rav Telzow finished his *shiur* and bade the attending members of his congregation a good evening. The men all stood up and, chatting amicably with one another, slowly filed out of the shul. Only two people remained. One was the Rav, who was busy putting away the *seforim* he had used, and the other was Menashe Baronsky.

"Rav Telzow, could I have a word with you?" Menashe approached the Rav somewhat tentatively.

"Of course, Reb Menashe. Come and sit down here," the Rav replied in a friendly tone, indicating a chair near him. But one look at the man's worried expression made him change his mind. This was obviously a serious matter that should be discussed in less public surroundings. "No, wait a minute. Why don't you come next door to my house and we can talk there?"

"Yes, I would prefer that. Thank you," Menashe said, relieved. Perhaps the homier atmosphere of the Rav's home would make his ordeal a little easier.

Rav Telzow finished replacing the *seforim* on the bookshelves, then led the way across the hall to the door that was the entrance to his own house. Unlocking it, he ushered his visitor in and took him to his study, where bookshelves with *seforim* covered every wall.

"Nu, Reb Menashe," the Rav said, once they were both seated at the table, "what is it you want to speak to me about?"

Menashe began to explain the reason for his visit, a little reticently at first, but sounding more positive as his narrative progressed. Rav Telzow listened intently, utterly amazed by what he was hearing. However, being a man of immense self-control, he was able to conceal his surprise.

"Are you sure you want to do this?" he asked, a note of caution in his voice, when Menashe finished speaking. "Have you really considered what it would mean to you?"

"Yes, I have," Menashe replied soberly, "and believe me, it was no easy decision. But don't you agree that it is the only way?" His tone was almost imploring—as if he was begging the Rav not to talk him out of it.

"Yes, I do see your point of view and I must say I admire your courage. All I can say is I wish you a lot of *hatzlochoh*. Now tell me, in which way can I help you?"

"By advising me how to dispose of my fortune—helping me decide which *tzedokos* would have the most benefit. I know you have your own charity fund for needy families and, of course, I would like to give a tidy sum to that, but, as you know, yeshivos are close to my heart and if I can give one or two yeshivos a substantial amount, then maybe in that *zechus* my own son might still become a *masmid*. Perhaps you would know which yeshivos require the most help."

"Well, I would say they all do," the Rav commented, "but I understand what you mean. Give me a bit of time to make inquiries and I will let you know."

"Thank you," Menashe stood up and extended his hand. The Rav grasped it in a firm grip.

"This is indeed an extraordinary thing that you are doing," he said, his voice full of admiration, "and I'm sure you will have *siyata d'Shmaya* and will never regret your decision."

The Baronskys sat round the highly polished mahogany dining room table, gazing at the head of their family, who was standing at the top end. They were all wondering why Menashe had summoned them and were eagerly awaiting his explanation.

Menashe stood surveying them for a moment. His wife Dinah, impeccable as ever in her well-set blonde wig and a navy and gold brocade robe, looked slightly impatient. She was used to her husband's generous gestures, and if this was another one then she had better things to do than listen to a long rigmarole about something she took for granted in any case. Tuvya and the two girls all wore expectant looks, waiting for their father's announcement, which could only be something good and exciting. For a moment, Menashe could not help feeling sorry for them. How would they take the bombshell he was about to drop on them? But his sympathy soon evaporated. After all, it was their fault that he was forced to make this great sacrifice.

"You are all wondering why I have called this meeting," he said, his tone indicating that this was merely a statement. "Well, I have something to tell you which will come as quite a shock. It is not good news, I am afraid." Anxious looks began to replace his audience's former smug expressions. "As you might have realized," he went on, "my business has been lately suffering a slightly downward trend. The truth is, carriage wheels are not as much in demand as they used to be. Many people are changing over to the motor car."

"Yes," Tuvya butted in sulkily, "but you won't buy *me* one!"

"I'm afraid, Tuvya, my boy, you will have to learn to do without a lot of things that you *do* already have!"

"What do you mean?" Dinah asked sharply, suddenly alert.

"Exactly what I said," her husband replied. "We are all going to have to adjust to a much, *much* more modest lifestyle..."

Everyone suddenly sat bolt upright, staring at him but saying nothing.

Menashe continued. "I have done a deal which years ago might have been profitable, but now has resulted in me losing everything... plunging me into debt, in fact!" There were horrified gasps round the table. Ignoring them, Menashe went on. "We will have to live quite differently from now on. No luxuries... no fancy clothes... no servants..."

"*What!*" Dinah shrieked, "not even Mrs. Katzfeld?"

"Definitely not Mrs. Katzfeld!" Menashe replied emphatically.

"But you can't mean that!" his wife protested. "How can I run a big house like this without her?"

"You won't have to run a big house like this without her," Menashe told her, "because you won't have a big house like this to run." Dinah stared at him, aghast, as he hastened to explain. "I will have to sell this house to pay off my debts. There might just be enough left over to buy a small house, but that is all we will have."

"You... you mean I will have to do the housework? To cook and everything? I can't! I haven't cooked for ages! I wouldn't know where to begin!" She began to weep bitterly. Her children just stared at her in stunned silence. The sight of his family looking so utterly broken quite unnerved Menashe, leaving him unable to carry on.

Mumbling a barely coherent, "We'll talk more about this later," he hurried out of the room, feeling terribly cruel. What was he doing to them? Was he not being a bit too harsh? Maybe he should back down. No! he told himself, his determination returning, it's too late for that now! He would have to keep going and not allow *anything* to break his resolve. It will be good in the end, he reflected, in a valiant attempt to convince himself. There was nothing he could do now but pray for strength and for *siyata d'Shmaya*!

The wagon carrying the Baronsky family's possessions stopped outside a house in London's East End and even Menashe's heart sank when he saw it! Small and shabby-looking, with the paint peeling off the front door and the window frames, it was almost impossible to imagine that they would be living in it from now on!

Having sold his house and his business, Menashe had taking the enormous amount of money to Rav Telzow, instructing him to divide it into three; a third each to be given to the two yeshivos the Rav had chosen and the remaining third to be kept for the Rav's own charity fund. All he had kept was some money to send Tuvya to a yeshiva in Poland and enough to buy a small house in the provincial town where he had lived all his life.

The decision to move to London had been brought on by Dinah. She became quite hysterical, protesting that she could not stay and face all the people she knew.

"What will they all think?" she had sobbed. "I'm so ashamed! I simply *cannot* stay in this town anymore!"

Fully understanding how she felt, Menashe had agreed to move, choosing London because it was a place where other *yidden* lived, yet it was large enough to be anonymous. He was fairly certain that no one in London had heard of the wealthy Menashe Baronsky.

The money he had set aside for buying a house might have bought a small but pleasant house with a little garden in the provinces, but in the capital, where prices of homes were much higher, it would only suffice to purchase a terraced house leading straight onto the street, in the poorer part of the East End. Adamantly refusing to use some of the money for Tuvya's yeshiva fees, Menashe had little choice. Leaving the matter in the hands of an agent, he had agreed to whatever the agent chose.

Now, seeing the house for the first time, he fought back a pang of regret. His dismay, however, was minimal compared to that expressed in no uncertain terms by his family. Dinah let out a wail that was surely heard by the neighbors and the girls shrieked in unison, declaring that it was too awful to live in! Tuvya announced that he was *glad* he was going to yeshiva. Surely he would be more comfortable there, whatever the conditions! Hoping he had not made a dreadful mistake, Menashe prayed inwardly again that things would yet turn out for the good.

To say things were difficult in the weeks that followed would be putting it mildly. Menashe himself was quite happy. He had secured a job as *shamash* in the local shul, an occupation he really quite enjoyed. Once he had tidied up and arranged everything that was necessary in the shul, he could sit down and learn out of the many *seforim* that were at his disposal. (He had not been able to take many of his own *seforim* with him and had asked Rav Telzow to keep them for him for the time being.) Rabbi Greenfein, the shul's rabbi, realizing that Menashe had once been well off but had fallen on hard times, was extremely kind to him, paying him little extras from time to time and occasionally bringing him some tasty dish for his family that the Rebbitzen had cooked. Menashe was grateful for that, as these dishes were more or less the only cooked food they had. Dinah refused to cook on what she called "that primitive stove," relying mostly on canned food and raw fruit and vegetables. His younger daughter, Shifra, had been enrolled in the local school and informed her parents that she hated every minute of it. The non-Jewish girls, she said, were horrid and the Jewish girls were "not her type"! A job had been found for Sheindel as apprentice to a dressmaker, but she never stopped grumbling about that too, complaining that Mrs. Jacobs made her pick up pins all day long. Tuvya's letters from yeshiva were also full of grumbles and the reports from his *mashgiach* were not complimentary.

Life went on in this unsatisfactory way for a while, but Menashe, a man of tremendous *bitachon*, remained convinced that things would soon improve.

The turning point came eventually, brought about—surprisingly—by a fish.

Menashe, who did most of the shopping, brought it home from the market one day, deciding that it was time Dinah learnt to do some proper cooking. He placed it on the kitchen table and went back to the shul to work, the sound of his wife's loud protestations ringing in his ears.

Left alone with the fish, Dinah stared at it, overcome with revulsion. There it lay, on a piece of old newspaper, its mouth open and its eyes seeming to return her stare. For one split second she imagined it was winking at her. No way, she resolved, was she going to touch the thing! Utterly frustrated, she sat down on a chair, as far away from the kitchen table as possible, and wept. She was sobbing so loudly that she did not hear the soft knocking on the front door and was startled suddenly by a gentle female voice.

"Is anything the matter?" the voice said, sounding worried. Dinah gaped in surprise at the sight of its owner, a middle-aged woman who was wearing a floral housedress, a similarly patterned turban on her head. Her long, narrow face looked kind and there was concern in her bright blue eyes.

"Wh-who are you?" Dinah asked, bewildered, as she desperately wiped her eyes and tried to look as if nothing was amiss.

"My name is Blumberg—Sarah Blumberg. I live two doors away…"

"Oh," Dina said, surprise in her voice. She couldn't remember ever seeing her.

"I was away when you moved in," Mrs. Blumberg explained, interpreting Dinah's expression correctly. "In fact, I've only been back a few days and haven't had time to come in and say *sholom aleichem* till now. I hope you don't mind me walking in like this. I did knock but you must not have heard me. I found the door open, so I just came in."

"My husband can't have closed it properly," Dinah said. Suddenly remembering how Menashe had gone out, leaving her with that dreadful fish, she heaved a deep sigh.

"I can see you're upset about something," Mrs. Blumberg said solicitously. "I don't want to pry, but is it something I can help with?"

Dinah opened her mouth to protest, but the kindness in the woman's voice suddenly released another flood of tears. Unable to stop herself, she began to pour out her tale of woe. "It's this fish!" she cried, looking at it and shuddering. "I'm suppose to clean it and cook it," she went on, amid sobs, "but I can't bear to touch it... and I don't even know how to cook it! I don't know how to cook *anything*!" She burst out, her voice choked.

Mrs. Blumberg's reaction to this outburst was to stare at her in surprise. "I-I don't understand..." she stammered. "Pardon me for asking, but how come you can't cook? I hope you don't mind me saying so, but you don't look like a newly married young woman..." She broke off anxiously, afraid she may have offended this poor, distressed person.

"I've never *had* to cook," Dinah explained, her tone rueful. "I used to have servants and a cook... and a beautiful large house..." She stopped, too overcome to say any more.

"I see," her visitor said softly, her voice full of understanding and sympathy. "What happened?"

"My husband lost all his money... every penny! We had to sell the house and now we are here and I'm suppose to do things that I'm not used to doing! How am I ever going to learn?"

"I can teach you, if you'd like me to," Mrs, Blumberg offered. Dinah nodded, somewhat diffidently, and Mrs. Blumberg walked over to the table and lifted up the fish's head, holding it by the gills. "If you'll give me a knife," she said authoritatively, "we'll clean this fish and then I'll show you how to cook it."

Menashe thought he was dreaming when he came home that night. A delicious smell greeted him as soon as he entered the house! He went into the kitchen and noticed a large pot bubbling on the stove. He also saw that the fish no longer lay on the kitchen table where he had left it.

"You cooked the fish!" he said, his voice full of wonder.

"I did not!" his wife hastily informed him, and told him about Sarah Blumberg's visit and how she had cleaned and cooked the fish for her.

Menashe could not help feeling disappointed. Still, he and his family enjoyed the meal and, to his surprise, he found he was deriving some pleasure from the sight of Dinah serving it up— just like any housewife, he thought to himself. Little did he know it then, but that day was the beginning of better things to come!

Sarah Blumberg become a constant visitor to the Baronsky household. She came every day and, in her forthright way, set about teaching Dinah how to cook. Dinah could not help being impressed, and bit by bit her resistance began to wane. She watched intently, determined to learn the ropes. It became challenging and she began to enjoy learning this new skill. She longed to prove herself just as good as her neighbor. Sometimes she would get up early, hurriedly putting some dish on the stove herself, before Mrs. Blumberg had a chance to come in and take over. These attempts often resulted in disasters—too much salt or too little flavoring altogether—and sometimes they bore a closer resemblance to burnt offerings than food!

Eager to encourage his wife, Menashe would eat these calamities without a word of complaint. However, it did not take long for Dinah to master the art, becoming quite an accomplished cook. Sarah Blumberg also taught her to bake and that was where Dinah really excelled. She made *challos* and a variety of cakes, but nothing gave her as much pleasure as baking fancy little tarts and elaborate pastries. The kitchen was now her domain and Menashe knew better than to get in her way when she was busy.

Indeed, he was only too happy to retreat to the dining room, where he could sit and learn with complete peace of mind.

He was doing just that one evening when Sheindel knocked and came in. As she opened the door, the delicious aroma of baking drifted in. He sniffed appreciatively.

"Lovely smell, isn't it?" Sheindel commented.

"Yes, it is," Menashe agreed. "Your mother's in her element, I'm pleased to say."

As she approached the table, Sheindel's eye fell on a letter lying next to her father.

"A letter from Tuvya," she said, recognizing the writing. "What does he write?"

"Oh, it's full of *divrei Torah*," Menashe said. "I must say, he seems to be doing well in yeshiva at last."

"You know something, Tatty," Sheindel said, philosophically, "when you told us you'd lost all your money, it seemed like the end of the world to us. But now I sometimes think it's *gam zu l'tovah*."

"I couldn't agree more!" Menashe said, enjoying the earnest expression on his daughter's young face. "Your mother is finding talents she didn't know she had... and Tuvya is at last getting pleasure out of learning. What about you, Sheindel? How are you getting on with your dressmaking?"

"Very well!" Sheindel replied enthusiastically. "Mrs. Jacob says I have real aptitude. She allows me to help with the sewing now and I actually made a dress almost on my own. You don't know what a thrill it is to make a garment, Tatty!"

Menashe could not help but smile when he remembered how condescendingly Sheindel had spoken about another dressmaker, not so long ago.

"I'm glad to hear it," he said encouragingly. "You're doing something extremely useful."

"That's what I really came to talk to you about. If I had my own sewing machine, I could do work at home and even make clothes for us. Oh, I know you can't afford to buy me one," she said quickly, as Menashe opened his mouth to speak, "but Mrs. Jacobs is buying a new machine and she wants to sell me hers. She really wants to pay me a bigger wage now that I am doing more work, but she said she would give me the machine and leave my wages as they are until I have paid it off. Would you agree to that, Tatty?" She eyed her father pleadingly.

"Why not?" Menashe said, smiling. "It sounds like a good arrangement to me."

"Oh Tatty, thank you!" Sheindel cried, jumping up. "You're so wonderful! I'll make good use of it, you'll see!" And with that she bounced out of the room with the air of an excited child with a new toy!

As time went by, the transformation of the Baronsky family became more and more apparent. Even Menashe himself was different. In his affluent days he had always appeared stressed, continually under pressure to keep his success going. Now he was calm and relaxed.

Dinah was a different person altogether. Gone was that bored "every-day's-the-same" look she had in the old days, and so was the bitterness she had displayed when their circumstances had changed. She now had a sense of purpose and satisfaction as she went about her work in the house, determined to perform each chore to perfection. It was this quest for perfectionism that drove her on. Her main pleasure now came from creating artistic fancy cakes and biscuits. She was restricted, however, due to the fact that the ingredients were more expensive than she could afford. It was Sarah Blumberg who came up with an idea that solved her problem. The two women, who had become firm friends, formed a partnership, baking for people's simchas. This would not have been too profitable in their immediate community, where people could not afford many luxuries, but their fame soon spread to other districts of London where Jews lived and Dinah was able to indulge in her favorite pastime and contribute to the family's financial situation at the same time.

Sheindel had, by now, become an accomplished dressmaker, spending a lot of time at her beloved sewing machine and deriving great satisfaction from her creations.

Shifra, too, was settling down. Having taken on a few holiday jobs minding people's children, she had discovered that she had a way with children and, now that she was about to leave school, she had found a job as a nursery teacher in a Jewish kindergarten.

The one who brought Menashe most pleasure, however, was Tuvya. He had obviously turned into a *masmid* at last, and the reports Menashe received from the *mashgiach* and the *Rosh Yeshiva* were excellent. Just recently, when Tuvya had been home for Pesach, Menashe had asked him how this had come about.

"It was when I realized what an immense sacrifice you were making to send me to Yeshiva," Tuvya told him, a serious expression on his face. "It suddenly struck me that I can't let you do this for nothing and I started learning more seriously. And then, once I did that, I saw what I'd been missing all those years. Learning Torah gives me so much satisfaction, Tatte!" His words gave Menashe a warm glow.

If he had ever had any doubts or regrets about the drastic step he had taken, he certainly did not have them any more!

The London-bound train jostled along the track, shaking its passengers about relentlessly. Rav Telzow's bones were beginning to ache and he found it difficult to learn out of the small *sefer* he had taken with him. He didn't travel by train often and, when he did, he could not say he enjoyed it. However, he could not forego a chance to see Reb Menashe again. He had not seen him since he left five years ago, but he thought of Menashe often, wondering how he was faring and whether things were turning out as he had hoped.

And last week he had received a letter from Menashe, inviting him to his daughter's engagement. He hoped it did not mean that Menashe was having regrets and wanted his advice on how to retrace his steps. After all, marrying off a daughter… No! He must not think like that! he told himself guiltily. But he could not help feeling worried, all the same.

The train arrived in London at last. Rav Telzow stood up, rubbed his aching limbs and put his *sefer* into his small, black leather overnight case. He stepped off the train and joined the throng of people making their way off the platform. What a busy place London is! he thought, as he looked, a little helplessly, around the station for the right way to go. Eventually he found himself outside and he pulled out Menashe's letter, scanning the instructions he had been given on how to get to the Baronskys' address. He found the right tram and asked the driver to call out the required stop, as Menashe had advised him.

Once off the tram it was not hard to find the street he wanted. Eventually he found himself outside number 23. Already surprised by the area he was walking in, he could not help staring at the house. A vision of Menashe's beautiful house, back in his own town, sprang up in his mind... elegant and imposing with its spacious front lawn, featuring colorful flower beds and a water fountain in the center. What a contrast to the house he was now facing! Small and plain, the front door came straight out onto the street and the door and window frames looked badly in need of a coat of paint. Perhaps it's the wrong house — maybe even the wrong street — he thought hopefully.

Noticing a *mezuzah* on the door, he examined at it and recognized it immediately. It was the *mezuzah* he himself had given Menashe as a parting gift!

Tentatively, he rang the bell, dreading the moment he would face his old congregant, who he feared would be looking strained and sad. But the man who opened the door — Menashe himself — looked quite well and robust, greeting him with a beaming smile.

"*Sholom aleichem!*" Menashe cried heartily. "Come in, come in! It's so good of you to come, Rav Telzow!"

"I was happy to," the Rav assured him as he followed his host into the tiny hall. Watching Menashe hang his coat up on the hall stand, he could not help noticing how shiny and spick-and-span the house looked. So Mrs. Baronsky does seem to have some help, he reflected. Perhaps things aren't so bad, then.

"*Mazel Tov*, Reb Menashe!" he said, shaking his hand. "Who is the *chosson*?"

"His name is Eliezer Gluckstein. He's from New York and he's Tuvya's *chavrusoh* in Mir Yeshiva. Tuvya speaks highly of him. He says he's a *talmid chochom*, if ever there was one! They have been learning together for a long time."

"Is that so? And how is your son doing, Reb Menashe?"

"Very well, *boruch Hashem*! In fact, I would like to show you the last report I received from his *mashgiach*."

He led his guest into the dining room, where the tables were already prepared for the engagement. Rav Telzow gazed in surprise at the fabulous trays of fancy cakes that were laid out. Things can't be too bad, he thought, if they can afford to buy this variety of cakes.

"I'm glad you've come early," Menashe said. "I'm sorry I couldn't come and pick you up, but the *oilom* will be arriving in about half-an-hour, complete with *chosson* and *mechutonim*. Now, please drink a *l'chayim* before coming into the kitchen. I'd like to offer you some warm food. You must be hungry after your long journey." Menashe poured out a small glass of brandy and handed it to the Rav. Then he picked up a tray of cakes. "And please taste some of these cakes. My wife baked them all herself!" he said proudly.

"*Did* she?" Rav Telzow could not conceal his surprise. "I didn't know she could do that!"

"No, neither did she!" Menashe declared. He proceed to tell the Rav all that had transpired in the last few years; how difficult life had been for everyone at first and how gradually they had adjusted, with each member of the family discovering their capabilities and deriving pleasure and satisfaction from their achievements.

"And you, Menashe? Are you satisfied with your lifestyle?" the Rav asked him searchingly.

"*Boruch Hashem*, more than satisfied!" Menashe replied vehemently. "I would not go back to my former life for anything! My wife is happy, my daughters are happy and my son has developed a zest for learning at last! I have all I need—more than I need, in fact. *And* I am about to acquire a son-in-law who is a *talmid chochom*. What more could I want?"

As Rav Telzow listened to him, some words from *Pirkei Avos* flashed through his mind. *Eizehu oshir? Hasomeyach b'chelko.* Who is rich? He who is happy with his lot.

Regarding his host now and noting how contented he looked, the Rav reflected how well it applied here. Whatever it was Menashe Baronsky had been previously, he thought, it can only *now* be truly said that he had become a rich man!

# Go for the Truth

Sitting by the little wooden desk in her bedroom, with the light from a small black bedside lamp shining onto her history textbook, Naomi Rothman, a serious-looking bespectacled girl with straight, flaxen hair, could feel her eyes begin to droop. Giving her head a vigorous shake, she made a desperate attempt to keep herself awake. She just *had* to absorb all the facts tonight and memorize them for tomorrow's exam! If only she could be sure she would remember them!

Why did it have to be so difficult? It wasn't that her intelligence was below average. She was good at math—a subject that didn't require memorizing anything—and her essays and reading comprehension were not bad at all. But when it came to learning poems by heart or remembering names and dates — not to mention French vocabulary — her memory just let her down.

Come on, she told herself, looking at her book with a determined air, you're going to learn it this time, and you're going to remember it!

She plodded diligently through the facts of the Civil War. Then she closed the textbook and tried to memorize them. One or two names and dates did come up in her mind but they just seemed to stick there, blocking out everything else. What was she going to do? Perhaps if she wrote them down it would be easier to remember them.

Taking a notepad, she scanned the textbook again and began to copy down as many facts and dates as she could: *Roundheads (Parliamentarians); Cavaliers (Royalists); no Parliament for eleven years (1629-40); Long Parliament (1642-49); Civil War (1648); Charles I executed (1649); Oliver Cromwell ruled as Protector (1649-58); Charles II returned from exile and acclaimed king (1660);* and so on, until she had filled up a whole page. She skimmed over the notes she had written, but she found that she was too tired to take them in properly. Better go to sleep now, she told herself. She would glance through her notes once more in the morning.

If only these exams were over and she could start relaxing again! It wasn't even as if she felt ambitious to get good results. *She* didn't really care. It was her parents who did. They never stopped reminding her how lucky she was to go to a Jewish school and to have a good education, something that neither of them was privileged to have had, due to the war.

Her father, originally from Vienna, Austria, had endured unspeakable horrors in a Nazi concentration camp, missing out on his chance to follow in his father's footsteps and become a qualified engineer, as well as study in a yeshiva for a few years. Her mother, who came from Poland, had been sent with her family to Siberia, where they had been forced to work hard, with little food. Many people, including members of her own family, had died of disease and malnutrition.

Having undergone so much suffering themselves, Mr. and Mrs. Rothman felt that Naomi ought to know the truth about what happened to the Jews during the war.

"If the next generation isn't told about it," they reasoned, "the truth will be forgotten and eventually people will claim that it never really happened."

Apart from that, they thought their daughter ought to appreciate her good fortune and make the most of her opportunities.

Naomi disliked hearing all the gruesome details and — afraid they would give her nightmares — she forced herself to shut them out of her mind. She hated the thought of her parents undergoing so much suffering. She wished they could forget about it, too.

After all, it was 1970 now, long enough for their wounds to have healed. All the same, she felt she owed it to her parents to do well at school, knowing how much it meant to them. She worked with diligence and achieved reasonably good results. It was just this dreadful memory of hers. ...

Naomi slept restlessly that night and woke up with a heavy feeling, thinking of the history exam ahead of her. Before going down to daven and eat breakfast, she glanced quickly over the notes she had written down. Collecting all her books and her pencil case, she pushed them hastily into her briefcase, including the page from her notepad. Then, on a sudden impulse, she took the notebook out of her briefcase, tore out the page of notes and stuffed it up the sleeve of her sweater. If she could have opened her head and pushed it in there, she would have done so! As it was, having it so close to her gave her a certain amount of reassurance. Perhaps, knowing it was there would help her remember what was written on it.

There was almost complete silence in the classroom as the pupils sat hunched over their exam papers. The only sounds that could be heard were the scratching of pens and the occasional creaking of benches, as the more fidgety girls amongst them shuffled about a bit.

Naomi scanned the printed paper in front of her with some trepidation. Would she be able to answer all the questions? She looked at the first questions and felt reassured. *In which year was Charles I executed?* Ah yes, she knew that! Picking up her pen she wrote *1649* with confidence. She also remembered that Oliver Cromwell was known as the Protector. It was the question after that that stumped her. *What were the words spoken by the Speaker when the King entered Parliament to arrest five men?* They had been told to memorize the quotation when the teacher had taught them about it and Naomi had tried to learn it but, as usual, it had refused to stick in her memory. Last night, she had jotted it down and tried to memorize it again. Automatically, she patted her sleeve and could feel the paper folded up against her arm. It was all there, written down! If only her arm could transmit the infor-mation to her brain!

Tugging gently at her sleeve and peering in, she could see the note lying snugly inside. *"Come on,"* she urged it mentally, *"tell me what it is!"*

It's not fair! she thought bitterly. The other girls are lucky enough to write things in their heads and refer to them when they need to. If my head won't retain the knowledge, why can't I do the same with a piece of paper? At the back of her mind, she knew she was wrong, but temptation, egged on by her frustration, seemed to take hold of her. She gave a quick pull and suddenly the note was lying in her lap.

I only want to see the first few words, she told herself, then I'll remember the rest. And there it was — the whole quotation! "*I have neither eyes to see, nor mouth to speak, save that which I am instructed by this House.*" Oh yes, now she remembered!

Pushing the paper back up her sleeve, she wrote down the first few words, convinced that the rest would automatically follow. *I have neither eyes to see…* she wrote confidently. How did it carry on? She could not remember! After struggling for a few moments to recall the rest of the sentence, she pulled the paper out again and took a quick peek. It was a good thing, she told herself, that Esty Jacobs, who normally shared the desk with her, was away for her brother's *chasunah*. She would never have been able to do this if someone had been sitting beside her.

By the time she got to the end of the exam paper, she found she had had to pull the paper out many times for a quick peek. Breathing a sigh of relief, she handed in her paper, wishing it had not been necessary to keep looking up the answers, but she was thankful that her ordeal was over. It was only when she saw the teacher walking out of the room with the papers of the whole class in her arms, that she was suddenly struck by the impact of what she had done. She had *cheated*! What a horrible thought! She had never ever done such a thing before! What should she do? She couldn't very well run after the teacher and ask for her paper back, telling her the reason. The mortification would be too much to bear! No, it was too late! She would just have to keep the knowledge to herself, however bad it made her feel.

Guilt weighed heavily on her heart for the rest of the day. At night, after trying unsuccessfully to study the French vocabulary for the next day's exam, she lay in bed, unable to sleep. One thought went round and round in her head. *I cheated! I cheated!* If only she could undo what she had done! It wasn't even as if she cared whether she got a good mark or not. She was not really an ambitious girl. But her parents *did* care. Their desire for her to do well was so strong that she felt she could not let them down. Nevertheless, they too would be horrified to discover that she had cheated!

She remembered once learning in a *mussar* lesson that if one is truly sorry for doing an *aveirah*, the proof of proper *teshuvah* is being in the same situation again but refraining from doing it. She promised herself faithfully that she would never ever do it again, and her conscience began to ease a little.

True to her resolutions, Naomi plodded through the rest of the exams as well as she could, not even thinking of cheating, and her guilt feeling gradually abated. She did have a feeling of discomfort when they were given the results and she saw she had a mark of 98% for history. But there was nothing she could do about it now and, relieved that she had at least managed to rid herself of that bad *midah*, she tried to push it out of her mind.

The feeling of remorse came over her again with a vengeance a few days later, when Mrs. Glass, the headmistress, made an announcement about the forthcoming prize-giving afternoon.

"There is no time for me to read out the names of all the prize-winners now, but I have pinned up a list on the notice-board in the hall."

There was immense excitement as all the girls gathered at the notice-board, eager to see who the lucky girls were. Naomi hovered around, too, but did not push herself forward to get a look.

She did not expect to be one of the prize-winners. She had done well in the math exam but Miriam Stansky had obtained two marks higher than hers and would therefore be the winner of the math prize.

"Hey, Naomi!" Her friend Shanny Fisher came towards her, a beaming smile on her face. "You're getting the history prize! *Mazel tov!*"

Naomi's heart sank. Oh, no, not that! she cried inwardly. How could she possibly accept a prize she didn't deserve? On the other hand, how could she refuse the prize without confessing to what she had done?

Of one thing she was certain. She would not tell her parents about it. How could she bear to see the pride on their faces, when she knew how misplaced it was? It would be better if they knew nothing about the prize-giving afternoon altogether. Maybe she should dodge the occasion herself. She could pretend to have a sore throat or something. No, that would not help either. Someone would probably bring her prize round to her house and the cat would truly be out of the bag!

Naomi's heart grew heavier and heavier as prize-giving day approached. Then, just a week before the big day, she tripped in the school playground and sank to the ground, and a fiery pain shot through her ankle. Mrs. Glass was summoned and immediately telephoned Naomi's mother. An anxious-looking Mrs. Rothman arrived on the scene and bore her daughter quickly off in a taxi to the nearest hospital. It occurred to Naomi on the way there that if, as she suspected, her ankle was broken, she would not be able to attend the prize-giving after all. She wondered if that would be a good thing or not.

However, when the doctor at the hospital examined her X-rays, he told them that Naomi had luckily not broken anything. "It's just a bad sprain," he explained to her mother. "Keep her at home for two or three days and make sure she keeps off her foot. After that she can go back to school, but make sure that she rests her foot as much as she can. And keep it bandaged up for at least two weeks."

So that was that, Naomi thought. A bandaged ankle was no excuse for missing school, let alone the prize-giving.

Shanny Fisher came round to visit that evening. Mrs. Rothman ushered her into the living room, where Naomi was sitting on the sofa, with her bandaged foot resting on a stool in front of her.

"Hi, Naomi!" Shanny greeted her. "How's the ankle? What have you done to it?"

"It's not as bad as we thought, *boruch Hashem*," Mrs. Rothman answered before Naomi had a chance to speak. "It's only a sprain. She'll be back in school in two or three days, hopefully."

"Oh, that's good!" Shanny said. "I'm glad you haven't broken it. And it's a good thing it happened now and not next week!"

"Why? What's special about next week?" Mrs. Rothman asked, smiling expectantly at Shanny.

Naomi's heart sank. Please, Shanny, she prayed silently, please don't say anything! She tried to throw her friend a warning look but Shanny wasn't looking in her direction. She was staring at Mrs. Rothman with a quizzical look.

"It's prize-giving day," she said, surprised. "Didn't Naomi tell you?"

"No, I don't think she did," Mrs. Rothman sounded equally puzzled. "Did you tell me, Naomi?"

"I must have forgotten," Naomi replied lamely, aware that she was blushing.

"Forgotten?" Shanny exclaimed, incredulously. "Fancy forgetting, when you're going to get a prize!"

Quaking inwardly, Naomi could feel her color heightening. How was she going to get out of this?

"A prize?" Mrs. Rothman eyed her daughter, a beaming smile on her face. "Naomi! Why didn't you tell us?"

"She must have been too modest," Shanny commented, "though, if you ask me, it's carrying modesty a bit too far! She got a brilliant mark for history," she told Naomi's mother, "so she's getting the history prize!"

"That's wonderful!" Mrs. Rothman cried, immense pride in her voice. "This I really must see! When did you say this prize-giving is?"

"Next Tuesday at two o'clock," Shanny told her, "in the school ha—"

"—But Mummy," Naomi interrupted, clutching at straws, "you only get home from work at one o'clock. It will be such a rush for you."

"So what?" her mother countered. "It's worth it to see you getting a prize! I'll ask my boss if I can leave a bit earlier for once. And I'm sure Papa will take the afternoon off too. He wouldn't miss this for anything! Oh, I can't wait to tell him!"

Shanny could not understand why Naomi was so quiet and withdrawn for the rest of her visit, hardly talking to her. So, as soon as Shanny could, she took her leave and went home, trying to remember exactly what had happened when her friend had tripped. Was it possible that, even though Shanny could not remember such a thing happening, Naomi had somehow bumped her head when she fell?

The week that followed was extremely difficult for Naomi. For the first two days, as she sat in the armchair with her foot resting on the stool, she was forced to listen to her parents endlessly proclaiming their pride in her and how much they were looking forward to seeing her receive a prize. Every word they spoke was like a knife in her heart, stabbing at her conscience.

When at last the pain in her ankle had eased off enough for her to go to school, Naomi was relieved. But she found it was no better there. There was an atmosphere of excitement about the place as the school prepared itself for the event, which only helped to accentuate Naomi's guilt pangs.

The Big Day arrived — all too quickly for Naomi — and the girls were given the morning off, with instructions to be at school by one o'clock, looking clean and tidy in their school uniform. The apprehensive feeling with which Naomi awoke that morning increased when, a little later, her mother poked her head into the dining room, where Naomi was davening.

"I'm off to work now, Naomi," she said, "but I might be back before you go to school. Mr. Witman has given me permission to leave an hour early. Papa has also got the afternoon off, so we'll both be there to clap and cheer for you!" With a cheerful wave and instructions to "eat your breakfast," she went out.

Naomi's low spirits sank even further and she found it difficult to concentrate on her davening. She felt as if she had a big hole in her stomach. All she could think of was what a fraud she felt like and how she hated the sensation! With an effort, she applied her mind to the *tefillos*, but before long her thoughts began to wander again. She pictured herself walking up onto the stage with the eyes of the entire audience on her as she accepted her prize — a prize that she didn't deserve! There would be clapping and cheering, of course — they applauded everyone who won a prize—but the others were entitled to theirs and she wasn't! How could she do it? On the other hand, how could she get out of it? It was too late for that now.

Tormented by the conflict raging within her, Naomi carried on davening, inwardly praying for some sort of guidance. All of a sudden it came to her, with absolute clarity. She knew what she must do! A moment later, however, her mind rejected the notion. No, no! She couldn't do that! The shame and humiliation would be too much to bear!

Thus she debated with herself for most of the morning, only picking at the food her mother had prepared for her and trying to quell the quaking feeling inside her. Eventually, she came to the conclusion that she would have no peace until she did what she had decided to do, however difficult it would be. Desperate to be out of the house before her mother returned, she hurriedly dressed in her freshly laundered school uniform, combed her hair and went out.

The walk to school took a little longer than usual, due to her still painful ankle, which gave her more time to think and argue with herself. Did she really want to take this drastic step, announcing what she had done and being disgraced? In her heart of hearts she knew there was no other way, if she wanted to be able to live with her conscience.

By the time she reached the school, she was feeling more resolute and she braced herself to get over her ordeal as quickly as possible.

It was only once she was inside the school building that her courage began to fail her again. There was not one other pupil in sight; only members of the teaching staff, moving busily about, and the place seemed somehow austere and forbidding. A fit of panic seized Naomi. Her only thought was to slip unobtrusively into the classroom and hide there till all the other girls arrived.

She began to creep surreptitiously along the corridor when, to her shock and horror, she came face to face with Mrs. Glass!

The headmistress, on her way to her office with a pile of books in her arms, seemed surprised to see her. She knew Naomi Rothman was a diligent pupil but she wouldn't have expected her to go as far as coming an hour early for the prize-giving.

"Hullo, Naomi," she greeted her with a welcoming smile. "You're early!"

Feeling like a cornered rat, Naomi realized there was no escape. She had no alternative but to face the music!

Taking her courage in her hands she blurted out, "Mrs. Glass, could I talk with you about something?"

The headmistress's first reaction was one of irritation. The pile of books she was holding was beginning to feel heavy and she still had to write all the inscriptions in them. What a time to choose to come and speak to her!

But one look at the girl's pale face and worried expression told her intuitively that it was a matter that could not wait.

"Of course, Naomi," she said. "Come into the office with me."

With Naomi following, Mrs. Glass led the way to her office and pushed the door open gently with her foot. Naomi followed and closed the door.

"I've just got to write this last lot of inscriptions," she said chattily, placing the books on the desk, where another pile of books already rested. "Your prize is in the first pile. I must say I was really pleased —"

Her sentence was cut short as Naomi, her face flushed and tears forming in her eyes, burst out, "Mrs. Glass, please don't give me that prize!"

Mrs. Glass stared at her, aghast. "Naomi," she said, concern in her voice, "what is all this?"

By now Naomi had taken off her glasses and was weeping bitterly, her hands covering her face. Extremely alarmed, Mrs. Glass nevertheless sat waiting patiently for Naomi's outburst to finish. Presently Naomi's sobbing subsided and she answered in a jerky voice, "I can't accept the prize. I don't deserve it!"

"Nonsense!" the headmistress protested, "you did excellently! You had the highest mark in the exam."

"But I shouldn't have had!" Naomi cried desperately. "I *cheated*!"

"You *what*?" Mrs. Glass stared at the girl in front of her, her tone shocked. A moment later, however, her glance softened and she suppressed a smile. Typical of a fourteen-year-old girl, she thought, with some amusement, and an essentially honest girl like Naomi in particular. Probably her eye had inadvertently caught sight of someone else's answer and she had written it down, then classed it as cheating in her mind, making her feel guilty.

"How did you cheat?" she asked, expecting to be able to reassure her. But as she listened to Naomi's account, she began to feel uneasy. It was not as she had imagined after all. The girl really *had* cheated! And in an underhanded way she would never have expected of Naomi. There's more to this than meets the eye, she told herself, resolving to get to the bottom of it.

"Why did you do it, Naomi?" she asked quietly. "I'm always pleased to see a girl take her work seriously and strive to get a good mark, but does it mean so much to you that you had to resort to deception to get it?"

Naomi eyed the headmistress nervously. She had expected Mrs. Glass to be furious with her but she sounded more upset than angry.

"You don't understand! It wasn't for me!" she cried, bursting into another flood of tears. "It was for my parents! You see, it means so much to *them*... and after all they've suffered, I couldn't let them down..."

"Tell me more," Mrs. Glass prompted softly, and suddenly Naomi could not help herself. Amid sobs she poured everything out, telling the headmistress how her parents would recount the nightmarish details of what they had been through; how she had striven to shut them out of her mind, determined never to remember them; but how she knew she had an obligation to make it up to them somehow by making the most of her chances and doing well at school.

The poor girl, Mrs. Glass thought as she listened. What pressure she is under! The story Naomi had just told her explained a lot. Yet there was one thing that still puzzled her.

"What I can't understand," she said, eyeing Naomi searchingly, "is why you found it necessary to look up the answers at all. You're not lacking in intelligence and if, as you say, you studied it all the night before, you should have remembered it all the same."

"I know..." Naomi agreed ruefully, the flush returning to her face. "But that's my trouble, you see. I've got a terrible memory! I learn things like names and dates and vocabulary and I'm sure I'll remember them, but a little while later they've just gone out of my head!"

It sounded like the typical excuse girls make for their failures, but Mrs. Glass sensed that this was not the case here. It was obviously a genuine problem that was causing Naomi a great deal of aggravation.

She felt an overwhelming pity for this girl, who was sitting in front of her looking so forlorn and frustrated. Her sympathy, however, left her in a dilemma. She would dearly have loved to give Naomi her prize all the same, but how could she? She could not appear to condone cheating under *any* circumstances!

"Naomi, you showed a lot of courage, coming here to confess to me and I admire you for it," she said, "but you must understand that I can't give you the prize."

"Yes, that's what I thought," Naomi replied quietly, looking down. Then, lifting her head, she eyed the headmistress anxiously. "Are you extremely angry with me?" she asked.

"No, Naomi, I am not angry with you at all and I am not going to punish you. You shouldn't have done it, as you well know, but it is not really like you and I know you have done *teshuvah* for it. I'm sure it is something you will never do again!"

Naomi's reply was to nod emphatically.

"Go and join the others now," the headmistress said, glancing at the wall-clock. "It's almost one o'clock so most of them should be here now. And, Naomi," she said, as her pupil stood up, "I'm sure your friends will ask you why you weren't given the prize, but I must ask you not to tell them the reason."

"But surely..." Naomi began, looking uneasy.

"Believe me, it's better if they are not told—even your best friend. They can't possibly understand and it will be hard for them not to think badly of you. I'd prefer to avoid that."

"But what *should* I tell them?"

"Just say that this is between the two of us and that I have ordered you not to tell. They might be curious but they wouldn't try to make you disobey me."

"But what about my parents?" Naomi asked, bewildered. All the implications of the situation were beginning to hit her. "I'll have to tell *them* something." An expression of distress came into her eyes. "They've made a special effort to be here today! They've gotten permission to leave work early and everything!"

"Yes, you are right," the headmistress said. "Of course they are entitled to an explanation."

"But what shall I tell them?" Naomi cried, near to tears again. "They will be so hurt and disappointed! How can I do it to them?" There was desperation in her tone.

Mrs. Glass stood up and went up to Naomi, putting a hand on her shoulder. There was deep concern in her eyes. The task of explaining to the Rothmans would be an unbearable one for their daughter, she knew. How could the poor girl be expected to shoulder yet another burden?

"They do have to be told the truth," she said gently, "but I don't think you should be the one to do it. Leave it to me, Naomi. I will see to it."

For the second time that afternoon, Mrs. Glass experienced a powerful feeling of sympathy.

A few hours earlier, it had been with Naomi Rothman. Now it was directed at her parents. She studied them as they sat opposite her in her office—Mr. Rothman, tall and gaunt, with a small greying moustache and slightly drooping shoulders, while his wife, a navy felt hat covering most of her mid-brown sheitel, was plumper and looked more robust, yet had deep lines on her forehead and her blue eyes bore signs of suffering.

They looked so dejected as they tried to absorb what she had just told them. She hated having to do it, but there was no way she could cushion the truth. And now they were staring at her in disbelief, looking as if the bottom had dropped out of their world.

"Why?" Mrs. Rothman asked, when she found her voice. "Why did she do it?"

"We've always taught her to be *emmesdig*," her husband commented, his tone almost pleading. "I can't believe she would..." he broke off, throwing up his hands as if to indicate that he would rather not say the ugly word.

As reluctant as she was to deal them another blow, Mrs. Glass realized that some hard truths were required here. They would never understand their daughter if the truth of what they were doing to her was not pointed out to them. With tact and kindness and without a hint of reproach, she explained to them how much Naomi suffered from the pressure they were putting on her.

In spite of the hurt way they regarded her, the headmistress was gratified to note that they *were* taking in what she was saying and that they seemed to acknowledge the sense in her explanation.

"W-we didn't realize..." Mrs. Rothman stammered, wiping away a tear from her eye.

"We wanted her to have the best chances," Mr. Rothman explained. "Not like us..."

"Yes, I understand," Mrs. Glass reassured him. "And Naomi does too. She is a very good girl and you can both be *immensely* proud of her. It took tremendous courage for her to come and tell me what she had done, yet her natural truthfulness wouldn't let her do otherwise. Her one concern was how much all this would hurt you both."

"Poor thing!" Mrs. Rothman whispered tearfully.

"Let me tell you," Mrs. Glass went on, "that she is bright and intelligent and one of the most diligent girls in the school. She works hard and always tries her best. You really should be proud of her!" she repeated, making sure to emphasize the point.

"Yes, we are!" Mrs. Rothman said. "But there is something I

still don't understand. She's been studying hard for her exams, sitting up quite late most nights. Surely she should have known enough of the answers without having to… er… cheat."

"Yes, I would have thought so, too," the headmistress agreed. "But Naomi explained it to me. It seems her one big problem is that she has a bad memory. She has trouble remembering facts even when she has recently learnt them."

"But why should a bright, intelligent girl have a bad memory?" Mr. Rothman asked, perplexed. "She's still young. It's not as if she's an old lady…"

"Yes, I agree. It is a bit of a puzzle," Mrs. Glass said. "Actually I have a theory about that, but I'm no psychologist and I might be wrong." Aware that they were looking at her eagerly, awaiting an explanation, she went on. "Naomi tells me that you sometimes told her things about what happened to you during the war…" She hesitated for a moment, wondering if she was going too far.

"We felt she ought to know…" Mr. Rothman began to justify himself once more.

"Yes, I know, and believe me I am not criticizing you, but for Naomi these tales of her own parents' suffering were pure torture and she did her best to shut them out of her memory. It could be that's the reason her memory stopped functioning so well. It's almost as if her memory was saying 'I know when I'm not wanted!'… if you see what I mean."

The Rothmans took in this notion in silence, guilt reflected on both their faces. Feeling that she must say something to alleviate their pain, Mrs. Glass carried on speaking. "Please don't blame yourselves…" she began.

"We have been bad parents," Mrs. Rothman declared, her tone sorrowful.

"No!" the headmistress protested vehemently. "On the contrary! You are good, caring parents and Naomi appreciates you both. I know you want to do what's best for her and my advice to you is to encourage her to do just what she is capable of — and believe me, that is no small amount — but don't expect more from her than that. That way she will thrive, you'll see! I wish you a lot of *nachas* from her, which I am sure you will have!"

Thanking her profusely, Mr. and Mrs. Rothman stood up and took their leave. Watching them go out, their expressions thoughtful, Mrs. Glass could not help feeling that they looked as if a weight had been lifted from their shoulders.

It had been one of the hardest interviews she had ever had and she had felt terribly cruel through most of it. In fact, she had wondered at times whether she was doing the right thing. But, she told herself, remembering the principle she always instilled in her pupils, you never go wrong if you go for the truth!

Naomi hurried home from school, extremely worried about her parents. She had seen Mrs. Levy, the school secretary, approach them and direct them to the headmistress's office and she wondered what they had been told. Knowing Mrs. Glass's passion for *emmes*, she was sure they had been put completely in the picture. How had they taken it? They must have been so hurt and disappointed! And it was all her fault!

As soon as all the parents had left, the girls had been given orders to go to the gym, where refreshments had been prepared for them. Naomi had had no choice but to go. The atmosphere there had been jolly and festive, but for Naomi it had been torture. Besides worrying about how her parents had reacted, she found herself in the uncomfortable position of being bombarded with questions by her friends.

"Naomi, what happened to your prize?" Gitty Holtz, a tall girl with a loud voice called out.

"That's right! You didn't get it, did you?" another girl commented, puzzlement in her tone.

"I know," Naomi replied, making a valiant attempt to brazen it out.

"What happened? Why didn't you get it?" her friend Shanny asked softly, her voice full of concern. She couldn't help remembering Naomi's strange behavior when she had visited her and she began to wonder again whether her friend had suffered more than a sprained ankle when she had fallen.

"I can't really talk about it," Naomi answered, trying to sound calm. "Mrs. Glass has forbidden me to talk about it!"

Although the girls persevered, they soon realized they could not question Naomi further after that, but it did not stop them from giving Naomi strange and curious looks. Feeling acutely embarrassed, Naomi found it impossible to join in the festivities. As soon as it was time to go, she rushed out, anxious to get home quickly.

Running up the steps to the front door, in spite of her troublesome ankle, she turned her key in the lock, then stopped, suddenly reluctant to go inside.

How could she go in and face them? The sight of her mother and father looking so upset — and maybe angry with her — would cut into her like a knife! All at once, she wanted to run off and be miles away!

"Is that you, Naomi?" her mother called out, sounding perfectly normal.

A little surprised, Naomi braced herself to go in. Sitting at the table in the living room, drinking tea, her parents smiled warmly at her as she entered.

There was not a sign of distress or reproach on their faces as they greeted her. All Naomi could see in their eyes was love and protectiveness… and pride!

# A Taste of Shabbos

Yechiel Wollinger's family knew better than to ask him any questions when he returned home from work on Friday afternoon. Naturally they were all anxious to know whether, for a change, he had managed to hang on to a job in spite of his refusal to work on Shabbos. But they knew Reb Yechiel would not tell them anything.

If the news was bad—as it usually was—he would never let it disturb their Shabbos. If it was good news, there was a danger that they would not be able to stop talking about it, thereby profaning to the holiest day of the week!

As soon as he came home, Reb Yechiel's whole being became immersed in preparations for Shabbos. By the time Shabbos came in, he had shrugged off all his worries, bringing a serenity to the house that rubbed off onto the whole family.

Even after he had made *havdoloh*, this air of tranquility remained. Still dressed in their Shabbos clothes, the family would eat *melava malka* and sing *zemiros* in a relaxed manner, taking their leave of the *Shabbos Hamalka* in the appropriate way. This week was no different from any other.

It was only on Sunday morning that the worried lines reappeared on Reb Yechiel's face. He caught sight of his oldest son, seventeen-year-old Doniel, making his way to the door with a *gemara* tucked under his arm, on his way to the *beis medrash*, and Reb Yechiel sighed deeply. If only it had not become necessary to do what had to be done. He knew how Doniel longed to go to yeshiva and he yearned to be able to send him. But it was becoming impossible now — there was barely enough money to feed his family, and his aged father, who was confined to a wheelchair, lived with them now as well.

He beckoned to his son to come and sit beside him at the kitchen table. Doniel complied immediately.

"Doniel, my son," he said in a sorrowful voice, "you know it has happened again. I was told not to come back to work if I didn't come in on Shabbos."

"I know, Tatte," Doniel said. "I can see how worried you look this morning. But what can you do? You can't possibly work on Shabbos!"

"Quite right!" his father agreed. "That is something I will never do! But I don't think my father realized what the situation was when he decided to emigrate from Poland all those years ago." A faraway look came into his eyes as he reminisced... "I was twelve years old when we sailed to England in 1882. My father, not a young man then, had grown weary of the difficult conditions back home and decided to try his luck here in England. He hadn't been here long when he began to regret his decision. *Parnossoh* wasn't much better here than it was in *der heim*, but the worst part of all was the lack of *yiddishkeit* around him. It just wasn't the same here! But what could he do? There was no going back!"

"Yes, I know, Tatte," Doniel said. "Zeide still talks about it, even now."

"We were lucky, really," Reb Yechiel went on. "We managed to settle in an area where there was still a crowd of *yidden* who stuck strictly to their *yiddishkeit*. But I'm sorry to say, the next generation are not all so steadfast," he shook his head sadly. "Your Zeide, he should have *arichas yomim*, instilled in me a love of Torah and taught me to treat Shabbos like a precious gift."

"And *you* have taught that to *your* children!" Doniel remarked.

"Yes, *boruch Hashem*," his father said. "And now the time has come for your *yiras Shomayim* to be put to the test."

"What do you mean, Tatte?" Doniel asked, looking puzzled.

Reb Yechiel gave another sigh and eyed his son searchingly for a moment, before replying. "I didn't want this to happen just yet, but I'm afraid you will have to go and find a job," he said quietly. "I think I have tried every job out there already. There is nothing left for me. Now it is your turn."

Doniel said nothing, but just looked at his father with consternation on his face and a hint of tears in his brown eyes.

"I know you want to spend your time learning… that is what I wanted for you, too… but you will have to confine it mostly to evenings now. I'm sorry, Doniel." Reb Yechiel sounded near to tears himself.

"But Tatte," Doniel said, when he found his voice at last. "What makes you think I will keep down a job if you couldn't? After all, I won't work on Shabbos either!"

"I should hope not!" his father declared vehemently. "But I am already in my forties, whereas you are still young. If you work well, some employer might be so eager to employ you that he will let you have Shabbos off all the same."

Doniel laughed. "That sounds ideal," he said. "But how do I go about finding such an unlikely job?"

"I've been thinking about that," Reb Yechiel said. "I did hear of someone who is looking for workers. I would have applied for it myself, but I know he's after a much younger work force. Have you heard of Harry Colman?"

"The raincoat manufacturer? Yes, I have heard of him. Someone told me he's Jewish."

"Yes, he is, though you would hardly know it!" Reb Yechiel shook his head from side to side in a disapproving manner. "I'm not sure if he really knows it himself! His grandfather, Shia Kalmowitch, was such an *ehrliche yid*. He came here from Russia many years before we came and he was a *chazzan* in a shul not far from here. What a voice he had! They used to say that his davening on the *Yomim Nora'im* inspired many people to do *teshuvah*. Unfortunately, he didn't have much influence on his own children. He wasn't aware of the dangers and the pitfalls until it was too late and his children quickly strayed from the path. Harry's father started the raincoat factory and kept it open on Shabbos right from the start. He was bad enough, but Harry, who changed his name from Kalmowitch to Colman, is completely assimilated."

"Then he's hardly likely to agree to me not working on Shabbos," Doniel observed.

"Although I fear that you're right," his father said sadly, "it's worth a try. What have you got to lose?"

This time it was Doniel's turn to sigh. "Yes, Tatte," he said solemnly. "I know you wouldn't ask me to do this if it wasn't necessary. I'll go tomorrow."

"Good boy," Reb Yechiel said approvingly. "Now hurry along to the *beis medrash* and *chapp arein* while you can!"

Monday morning found Doniel boarding a tram for the short ride to where Colman's factory was situated. It took a bit of searching, but eventually he came to a building with a large board outside displaying the words: "COLRAYNE RAINCOATS. (prop. H. Colman). Established 1887." Underneath this notice, a small wooden board had been nailed on with the words: "Machine operators required. Apply within."

Still trying to pluck up the courage to go inside, Doniel stood and surveyed the grey brick building for a few moments. It did not look especially inviting, with its two long rows of barred windows giving it an austere appearance.

Bracing himself, Doniel went up to the door and found it unlocked. He went inside, somewhat tentatively, and looked about him. The place seemed to be buzzing with the whirring sound of machinery. One of the doors downstairs was open and he caught a glimpse of people and machines, constantly on the move. He tried to see exactly what they were doing but he was startled suddenly by a man's voice.

"Are you looking for someone?" it asked, and Doniel spun round to face a rather nondescript-looking middle-aged man with bleary eyes and greasy greying hair.

"Oh… er… are you Mr. Colman?" he asked nervously.

The man's mouth twisted into what could perhaps be called

a smile and he gave a short, mirthless laugh. "Oh, no!" he said, "I'm just the caretaker. Are you looking for a job?"

Doniel nodded.

"Well, wait here while I tell the boss you're here." The man shuffled off down the corridor and knocked on a door. Doniel tried to have another peek into the room where all the activity was going on, but before he had a chance to see very much, he could hear the shuffling footsteps returning. The caretaker beckoned to Doniel to follow him. He led him to a heavy oak door marked "OFFICE," with the word "PRIVATE" underneath.

The office, though expensively furnished, with a wall-to-wall thick grey carpet, brown leather armchairs and a large oak desk, gave the impression of untidiness. The books on the shelves seemed to have been tossed there in a haphazard manner and the desk was littered with an assortment of papers. Harry Colman sat behind the desk, smoking a cigar. In his mid-fifties, he wore a starched white shirt and a well-cut suit. His already greying brown hair was plastered down with hair oil. A pair of brown eyes peered at Doniel through gold-rimmed spectacles that rested on a hooked nose. It occurred to Doniel that it would be useless for Mr. Colman to deny the fact that he was Jewish with his unmistakably Jewish features.

Harry Colman took a puff of his cigar and put it down on a glass ashtray, regarding Doniel with a cynical smile.

"Not another one of those!" he said, throwing his glance up at the ceiling in an exaggerated expression of long-sufferance.

He was probably referring to Doniel's yarmulke and *peyos*. He had recognized him as observant.

Then his gaze returned to Doniel. "You want a job, do you?" he said. "What's your name?"

"Doniel Wollinger, Sir."

"Wollinger... Wollinger..." Colman repeated the name as if trying to jog his memory. "I think someone of that name applied for a job once. Must have been your father. Well, he was a bit too old, for one thing, and then he informed me that he would not work on Saturday," he shrugged dismissively.

Doniel had intended not to mention Shabbos immediately. There would have been time for that on Friday afternoon, after he had done a good week's work. But now he felt it could not be left unsaid.

"I won't work on Saturday either, Sir."

The smirk returned to Mr. Colman's face. "Most of them say that at first," he said, "but they soon get enough sense not to throw away a good wage. If you work well — *and* come in on Saturday — you will have a well-paid job. However, if you fail to appear on Saturday, you needn't bother to return on Monday!"

Doniel said nothing, though his resolve did not falter for a moment. Perhaps he'll change his mind, he thought, if I do a really excellent job. And if not... well, at least I'll get paid for the work I do until Friday.

Mr. Colman picked up a bell on his desk and rang it. A moment later, the caretaker reappeared.

"Jack, take this young man to the pressing-room," Mr. Colman said, "and give him an overall and cap." He went up to Doniel and flicked one of his *peyos*. "I ought to tell you to cut these off," he said. "But I don't suppose you will. All the same," he pointed to the yarmulke on the boy's head, "I insist you take this off and keep it in your pocket!"

Filled with dismay, Doniel decided to ignore the order. Mr. Colman might not find out, he thought, and if he does and I get sacked, so be it!

The caretaker took Doniel upstairs to the pressing-room,

which seemed to be filled with steam. He handed him a grey cotton overall and a strange looking cap made of the same material. Doniel was relieved. At least he could keep his head covered without disobeying orders.

Taking him over to a large steam press, Jack told a man who was working there to explain to Doniel what to do. Jack smiled at Doniel and walked away.

Doniel couldn't see the other man clearly through the cloud of steam. He nearly jumped out of his skin in surprise when he heard the man say, "Aren't you Yechiel Wollinger's boy?"

Shocked, Doniel waved away some of the steam and peered though the mist. Soon he recognized the man as someone from his neighborhood. It was Berel Scheinman, whom he knew vaguely. Had he also just started working here? It didn't seem like it. He obviously seemed to have some experience. Perhaps Mr. Colman did sometimes give in about Shabbos after all. He decided to ask Mr. Scheinman about it.

Berel Scheinman sighed and shook his head in a resigned manner. "No such luck!" he exclaimed. "I wouldn't have this job if I took a day off! I can't afford to risk that, with a family to support. You realize that there are practically no jobs in this entire area that give off for Shabbos?"

"You mean you work on Shabbos?" There was incredulity in Doniel's voice.

Berel Scheinman visibly blanched at Doniel's tone. "Well, I try to avoid doing things that are actually *mechalel Shabbos*," Mr. Scheinman said defensively. "Don't think I don't keep Shabbos at all. Haven't you heard of the early morning workers' minyan? We daven all the Shabbos davening, *shacharis* and *mussaf* and all. And we *lein* the weekly *parshah*! If you're really desperate for the work, I'm afraid you'll soon be joining us."

"No! Never!" Doniel declared emphatically.

Mr. Scheinman shrugged. "I envy you for your *emunah*," he said, "but you're still young. Wait till you have a family who need to eat!"

Doniel opened his mouth to protest further but Mr. Scheinman carried on speaking. "Did you know that about seventy percent of the workforce here is Jewish? Most of them are *frum*. You'll meet them all in the canteen during the lunch break."

"The *canteen*?" Doniel cried out, aghast. "You mean—"

"Oh, no! We don't eat the *treif* food, *chas v'sholom*! Only the *goyishe* workers do. But we're not allowed to eat anywhere else in the building, so we take our sandwiches there. Have you brought sandwiches? If not, you can share mine. My wife always prepares a lot to eat."

Doniel thanked him and assured him that he had brought some food, though he privately thought he would not be able to eat. He suddenly felt a little nauseated. Mr. Scheinman's revelations had quite taken away his appetite!

The factory canteen was full of workers when Mr. Scheinman and Doniel entered carrying their packets of sandwiches. The non-Jewish employees brought their trays of hot food to a table near the counter, where they sat down to eat. By the far wall, a bunch of men were squashed together at another table, eating sandwiches.

Doniel stared when he saw them. He recognized so many of them! There were quite a few older men, married with families, as well as younger ones and boys, some of whom had even gone to the *cheder* that he had attended.

His first inclination was to get out of there as quickly as possible and never come back. How could this have happened? How could so many of the men he knew have become *mechalelei Shabbos*? But he began to think about his parents and their constant struggle to make ends meet. Then there was also his grandfather, confined to a wheelchair and requiring medicines they could ill afford. No, he was determined to at least give it a try. So many people were counting on him! He wouldn't disappoint them! But he firmly resolved not to let this weak crowd of men influence him.

He was noticeably quiet as he sat amongst them, resisting all attempts to be drawn into the conversation. It was Mr. Scheinman who finally explained the reason for Doniel's reticence. At once some of the men turned on him and began to bombard him with their excuses.

"This is your first job, isn't it?" a young man called Gavriel Viederman asked patronizingly. "Wait till you've lost a few and see how you feel then!"

"It doesn't mean that we're not *shomer Shabbos*," middle-aged Hershel Blau protested plaintively. "We just can't afford to lose our jobs, but we try not to do things that are actually *mechalel Shabbos*... if we can," he added lamely.

"You're only a *bochur* still," Zev Kransky, a recently married young man, pointed out. "I've got a wife to support now. And quite a demanding one too!"

The rest of the men just shook their heads sadly. Although each of the men had some reason to give and tried to convince Doniel that they were really justified, just listening to them made Doniel want to scream.

It was a relief to him when the bell rang for the end of the lunch hour and his table companions began to bentch hurriedly and rush back to their work.

When Doniel unburdened himself to his father that night, Reb Yechiel shook his head sadly. "*Nebech*!" he sighed. "Because Harry Colman's Jewish, they all hoped they would be able to persuade him when they started, but it didn't work. Harry couldn't care less about Shabbos."

"But why do they stay?"

"I'm sure they all didn't really want to, but the *nisayon* was too great for them." Reb Yechiel put an arm round his son's shoulder. "*Boruch Hashem*, you're strong enough to resist it, even if it does mean you'll be out of work by the end of the week!"

His father's faith in him was immensely gratifying, but Doniel could not help but brood about the situation his fellow workers had gotten themselves into. How could he just stand by and watch them desecrate the Torah? Was it right for him to keep quiet? His dilemma nagged at him for the next few days. By Thursday he had decided that he must do something about it. This was the last chance he would get as tomorrow was *erev* Shabbos, and after that he would surely not be coming back any more. As they all sat together at their table eating in the canteen, Doniel quietly put forward the suggestion that they should all stay away, en masse, on Shabbos.

"Are you mad?" Zev Kransky hissed at him, making sure to keep his voice down, so as not to attract the attention of the non-Jewish workers at the other table. "That would definitely be asking for trouble!"

Some of the others murmured their agreement.

"But don't you see!" Doniel persisted. "He can't get rid of three-quarters of his workforce! His factory would grind to a halt! We have power even if we're unaware of it!"

"You know, Doniel has a point!" Gavriel Viederman declared eagerly. "I vote we give it a try!"

A lively argument broke out, mostly in Yiddish, which was just as well, as the men didn't all manage to keep their voices low. However, most of them were eventually won over, with the reluctant minority finally also agreeing, simply because they felt ashamed not to.

Doniel went home that night feeling triumphant, yet with a slight feeling of trepidation. What had he done? Would it work out as he predicted? It was a long shot, he knew, but it was meant *l'shem Shomayim* and because of that, he told himself, it would surely pay off!

Harry Colman woke up wondering what day it was. While his wife had been alive, the household had revolved round her social routine, but now, five years after Eunice had died, he was living in this big house all alone. Alone, that was, except for his manservant, Angus. Without Eunice, though, every day seemed the same.

As he dressed in the suit and freshly laundered shirt Angus had laid out for him, he remembered that it was Saturday. He had better get to the factory early and make sure the orders would be made up, ready for collection on Monday.

Calling to Angus not to bother making porridge today, he ate two slices of toast with a cup of coffee, promising himself that he would have a good meal later on, at one of the restaurants he frequented often.

Slipping into the seat of his car, he cheered up a little, in spite of the bleak, cloudy weather. Not many people owned a car and sitting behind the wheel of his shiny Ford made him feel important.

When he arrived at the factory, he went straight into the office and picked up the mail, already lying on his desk waiting for his arrival. Ah! There was a letter from Garments Limited. No doubt it was a renewal of their contract. Garments Limited was one of the largest wholesalers in the country and he had been lucky to secure a contract with them. He opened the letter eagerly and began to read. A moment later, he turned pale and the letter fell out of his hand. What was this? They had found another manufacturer whose terms they preferred and they would not renew their contract with him!

This was a calamity! What was he going to do?

A knock at the door interrupted his thoughts. "Yes!" he snapped. "Come in!"

His caretaker Jack entered, looking extremely worried. "S-sir," he stammered. "I'm afraid there is a bit of trouble."

"Trouble? What trouble?" Mr. Colman barked. He could not be bothered with anything just now.

"Only a handful of men have turned up for work," Jack said meekly.

"*What*? What do you mean? Who are they?" Mr. Colman asked, somewhat foolishly. It didn't really matter who had come. It was more important to know who hadn't.

"I don't know offhand," Jack replied, a little flustered. "But I've noticed one thing. The ones who are not here are all the Jewish workers."

"Is that so?" Colman's eyes narrowed. "Well, we'll see about that! What I want you to do, Jack, is draw up a list of the men who are here and I'll compare it to my general list to see if you are right."

"Yes, sir," Jack sped off quickly and Harry sat drumming his fingers on the desk, wondering why this had to happen just now!

A short while later, there was a knock at the door.

"That was quick!" Harry thought. But it was not Jack who responded to his "come in." There stood Joe Bates, one of his oldest workers, his ample frame filling the doorway.

"Sir," Joe said immediately. "Can we go home?"

"Certainly you can not! You're needed more than ever at the moment!"

"But sir..." Joe persisted. "We can't get on with the work with most of the men missing! It's a waste of time getting the machines going."

Mr. Colman stared at Joe for a minute. There was nothing Mr. Colman could do but agree. Joe hurried off to impart the news to the others, making sure they all got out before, as he put it, "the old man changes his mind!"

Harry Colman remained sitting at his desk for a while, seething. It did not take long for him to work out who was behind this. It had to be that new boy... young Wollinger. Well, he would have it out with him! In fact, he would go right now!

Looking up the Wollingers' address in one of his ledgers, he jotted it down and went out, getting into his car and driving it out of the garage.

He found the house easily enough and stopped his car outside it, turning off the motor and preparing to get out. To his surprise, the front door suddenly opened and a handful of men, dressed in their best clothes, began to pour out of the house. What was going on? Had something serious occurred? Watching for a few moments, he soon realized it was nothing of the sort. They all seemed cheerful, waving to one another as they went off in various directions.

As soon as he was convinced no one else was coming out, he got out of his car and marched up to the front door, the angry speech he had rehearsed already on his lips. He reached for the knocker and, to his surprise, the door opened slightly. Obviously someone had not closed it properly.

So much the better, he told himself. I'll just go in and surprise them. That way young Doniel won't have a chance to hide from me!

Pushing the door open gently, he edged his way round it and crept into the house. It seemed extremely quiet. Was there anyone about? he wondered, looking around. His gaze fell upon the open door of the dining room facing him, and he could see a number of people inside, though no one seemed to be speaking or moving about. He inched closer to the door, not sure what his course of action should be. Should he burst in and surprise them all, giving vent to his wrath in no uncertain terms?

He was about to do that when, for some reason, he stopped short, staring transfixed at the man who stood at the head of the table, a silver goblet of wine in his hand. The eyes of all the people in the room were upon him and there was a look of serenity about him as he began to recite some foreign words in a beautiful, lilting tune.

A strange sensation came over Harry. He felt as though he were being transported somewhere, but he didn't know where. There was something familiar about that tune—and those words—but the feeling was too vague for him to place them. He stood listening, trying to bring it to the forefront of his mind, but it continued to elude him. It was only when the man, whom he recognized as Doniel's father, had finished his chanting, that the sensation began to wear off, replaced instead by a feeling of panic. It was as if he was being pulled in a direction he did not want to go. He felt he must get out of this house to escape from it!

Turning quickly, he made a dive for the front door, hoping to get out before he was seen. He was never quite sure what really happened then. He either tripped or lost his balance and he fell forward heavily, knocking his head on the front door with a loud thump!

Pandemonium suddenly broke loose! Children began to scream hysterically in shock and fear and Reb Yechiel and Doniel rushed forward to see who the intruder was. When they saw him, they both gasped in surprise.

Mr. Colman was holding his head and swaying precariously. He felt extremely dizzy and looked as if he was about to faint. Instinctively, Doniel and his father grabbed hold of him and, leading him into the dining room, they sat him down in an arm-chair by the fire.

Wondering why Harry Colman had suddenly appeared in his house, Reb Yechiel threw a puzzled glance in his son's direction. One look at Doniel's face told him that the boy knew what all this was about. Later, after they had attended to the man's needs, he would ask his son for an explanation.

Doniel, visibly shaken, was beginning to wonder whether he had been right after all, making that suggestion in the canteen. This was the last thing he had expected to happen!

He had found it almost impossible to concentrate on the dav-ening that Shabbos morning, wondering whether his fellow workers had stuck to their pledge and stayed away from work. He hoped they had, but hoping was about all he could do. He had no control over their actions. He knew one thing, though. He was glad he was at home, enjoying Shabbos as it was meant to be enjoyed.

The minyan, which took place in their house every Shabbos because Reb Aaron Wollinger, Reb Yechiel's elderly father, was confined to a wheelchair and could not go to shul, had just come to an end. The men who had taken part in it bade everyone "*gut* Shabbos" and went home, leaving the Wollinger family to get on with their Shabbos meal.

And now, suddenly, the tranquil atmosphere had been shattered and he, Doniel, was responsible!

Harry Colman was feeling completely disoriented. Here he was, in alien surroundings, with a shaky feeling and an aching head, not quite sure what he was supposed to be doing. Gingerly, he touched the painful spot on his forehead and winced.

"Does it still hurt?" a woman, who was obviously Mrs. Wollinger, asked solicitously, coming towards him with a glass of lemon tea and a piece of cake on a plate.

Mr. Colman took the tea and began to sip it, feeling slightly better. Then, realizing he was hungry, having had only a small breakfast that morning, he bit into the cake, grudgingly admitting to himself that it was delicious.

"Perhaps you will join us for the Shabbos meal," Mr. Wollinger began.

Suddenly Mr. Colman's head cleared. Shabbos! Yes, that's what it had all been about! Anger overtook him again as he remembered that he had come here to rant and rave at Doniel. He wanted to do so now, but as soon as he prepared to start shouting his head began to throb again. He certainly didn't have the energy to exert himself just now.

He shook his head, a sullen expression on his face, and leaned back resignedly, wishing he felt steady enough to get up and go home.

Soon, the family all left the dining room and filed into the kitchen. Then, one by one, they returned silently to the table, looking expectantly toward Reb Yechiel. In spite of himself, Mr. Colman could not help being fascinated. He had never seen anything like it... or had he? There it was again... that vague sensation!

Reb Yechiel lifted up the blue velvet cover that was covering a large plate in front of him and revealed two beautifully plaited loaves. At the sight of them, Mr. Colman was conscious, yet again, of a vague memory passing over him, as elusive as the previous ones. He watched Reb Yechiel hold the loaves, say some foreign words and then tear pieces of bread off and dip them in salt.

When a slice of the bread was offered to him, he was tempted to accept it but he stopped himself, determined not to take part in this meal that seemed full of antiquated rituals. He refused all the dishes that were offered, with a vehement shake of his head.

Presently a steaming plate of hot food was held in front of him, containing, as far as he could see, meat, beans and potatoes. He was about to turn his face away when the aroma suddenly reached his nostrils. Again that strange aura of familiarity swept over him, this time even stronger than before. What was it that dish reminded him of? If only he could remember. And yet... at the same time... he didn't *want* to remember!

Panic gripped him again and he began to feel trapped. He must get away at once, no matter how unsteady he felt! With an effort, he pulled himself out of the armchair and stood up straight.

"I'm going home now!" he announced as firmly as he could.

"Are you sure you're feeling up to it?" Mrs. Wollinger asked anxiously. "You still look so pale. Please stay and rest."

"I'm perfectly alright, thank you!" Mr. Colman said stiffly, walking towards the door.

Reb Yechiel had secretly nursed a hope that a Shabbos spent with them might arouse some feeling of *yiddishkeit* in this man's heart. He decided to make one last attempt to keep Mr. Colman with them a little longer.

"I'm not sure if you're ready to go home just yet," he said. "Please, Mr. Colman, stay a little while here." His tone was persuasive. But Mr. Colman, informing Reb Yechiel curtly that he wouldn't dream of staying longer than necessary, pulled open the front door and left.

The family stood watching him go down the steps, somewhat unsteadily, and walk towards his car.

"I should have realized he came by car," Reb Yechiel thought regretfully. "Why didn't I try harder to stop him going? I could have prevented him from driving for one Shabbos at least!" However, he was aware that it would have been futile to try. Mr. Colman was determined to leave and it was completely inappropriate to try to detain him forcibly.

Harry Colman knew he must drive carefully in the state that he was in, but it wasn't easy. He was still rather shaken up from his experience. For some odd reason, his mind was in a turmoil. To make matters worse, the entire visit had all been for nothing. He hadn't achieved what he had set out to do.

Anger overtook him again and he felt determined to show all those rebels that they couldn't mess him about. He would get rid of them all when they turned up on Monday morning!

Then he shook his head. Although he'd love to do that, he knew he couldn't. What would happen to his factory then? That belligerent Joe Bates would probably incite the non-Jewish workers to walk out too and then he would have no one! Very well, he decided, he would let them stay this time, with a warning. But that Wollinger boy would have to go! After all, he was the one who had caused all the trouble!

He arrived home and let himself into the house. It suddenly looked bleaker than ever, filling Harry with a feeling of desolation. Although he could feel hunger pangs, he had no appetite to eat anything and he didn't feel up to going to the restaurant, as he had intended. Apart from the fact that he still felt a bit weak, he had a bump on his forehead, which undoubtedly everyone would stare at.

He was met in the hall by Angus, who eyed him with concern. Not wishing to explain what had happened, he was forced to make up some cock-and-bull story by way of explanation.

Ordering Angus to bring him a glass of whiskey, he went into the sitting room and sat down in one of his soft, comfortable armchairs and presently he fell into a deep sleep.

He awoke to the sound of the doorbell chiming. A glance at the grandfather clock in the corner told him that it was eight o'clock. He had slept for six hours! And now, he wondered, who could be calling on him at this time of the evening?

Angus opened the sitting room door and ushered in two boys. One of them was Doniel Wollinger and the other boy he recognized as one of the boys he had seen at their house, obviously Doniel's younger brother.

"What do you want?" he snapped at them.

"My mother asked us to come and see how you are," Doniel said, "and she sent you this." He held out a wicker basket covered with brown paper.

"What is it?" Mr. Colman asked, somewhat gruffly.

"It's just a bit of food that she thought you might enjoy for your supper," Doniel explained.

Mr. Colman would have liked to refuse it but, realizing it would be utterly churlish of him, he refrained.

"Tell your mother I thank her for her kindness," he said politely, if somewhat grudgingly, "and tell her that I'm feeling much better, thank you."

"*Boruch Hashem*," the two boys muttered under their breath. Mr. Colman was about to ask them what they had said, but thought better of it. He didn't really want to know. They stood there for a few minutes awkwardly and then the boys said good-bye and left.

After they were gone, Mr. Colman peeked into the basket they had placed on the table. There was a piece of fish on a plate, with slices of cucumber round it and two tasty looking rolls next to it. In a cardboard box were some slices of cake and an apple lay beside the box.

Harry Colman suddenly found himself moved beyond words! Since Eunice had died, no one had taken care of him… not even Marilyn, his only daughter, who lived far away in South Africa and hardly ever contacted him.

And these people, who should have been furious with him for the way he had barged in on them and the way he had behaved while he was there, had shown him nothing but kindness and concern. To his utter amazement and chagrin, he felt tears pricking his eyes, threatening to spill out!

One thing he suddenly knew. After this there was no way he could fire Doniel Wollinger. Not this time, at any rate!

The week that followed was the most unusual one that Mr. Colman had ever experienced. Being essentially a creature of habit, he generally conducted his business on regular lines, plodding along, week after week, in the same manner. But this week everything seemed to be turning upside down!

On Monday morning, all the Jewish workers showed up looking wary, but nothing was said and they realized they had not been dismissed. Relieved, they all threw themselves into their work enthusiastically, some of them even staying on a little later than their usual time.

All the same, Mr. Colman told himself, he could not allow this situation to continue. If they all stayed away next Saturday, the non-Jewish workers would not come in either. There was no choice; they either came in on Saturday or he would have to find new men.

He said nothing for a few days. On Wednesday, he summoned Doniel to his office. As young as he was, the boy seemed to have become the spokesman for the others and Mr. Colman therefore decided to tell him of his decision, giving him the task of imparting the information to the rest.

Doniel listened silently, then he turned his earnest brown eyes on his employer and said quietly, "Mr. Colman, you're also Jewish, aren't you?" It was more of a statement than a question.

Mr. Colman looked ready to explode. "And what has *that* to do with it?" he shouted.

"Everything! Your factory shouldn't really be open on Shabbos!"

"Oh, is that so?" Mr. Colman's tone was icy. He knew he ought to throw Doniel out, there and then, but he was somehow fascinated by the boy's courage. He certainly had guts!

"Yes," Doniel said. "Shabbos is a holy day! You must know

that. You've had a taste of Shabbos now. Surely you must have felt something!"

Mr. Colman's fury suddenly gave way to that strange feeling again... the sensation of being pulled. He remembered that he had meant to try and fathom what that vague memory was, but, once home, he had forgotten about it. Now it came back to nag him again.

"But," he said, wondering why he was trying to justify himself to this youngster, "Saturday is my busiest day. How can I be closed?"

"Nobody has ever lost out through keeping Shabbos," Doniel argued. "On the contrary. You'll have more success if you close on Shabbos."

"Is that so?" Mr. Colman said again, his tone less cold and angry this time but sarcastic, nevertheless. Then, suddenly, the lost contract from Garments Limited sprang to mind.

Harry Colman was in a quandary. He really didn't want to take notice of what this boy was saying, but he had a strange feeling now that it would be unlucky for him to fire his Jewish workers. He would have to let them have Saturday off and that would mean giving the non-Jewish men the day off too. He might just as well be closed. In any case, he told himself, since he had lost his biggest customer, there was considerably less work for them all at the moment.

Desperate not to appear to be giving in, he sighed deeply and said, "It seems I don't have any choice. There is no point in opening the factory and switching on the machines for a handful of workers. I can't say this will be a permanent arrangement, but for the time being we will be closed on Saturday."

Harry Colman was at his wit's end, not quite sure what to do with himself. There was no point in going to the factory on Saturday as it was closed for the day. He had plenty of time on his hands to do... absolutely nothing! Always completely wrapped up in his business, he had never developed any other interests or hobbies.

He was alone in the house, except for Angus who, never very talkative, was carrying on his duties silently. Mrs. Grimley, the housekeeper had left a few weeks ago, deciding it was time for her to give up work. She had gone to live with her daughter in Devon. Harry had no choice but to take most of his main meals in a nearby restaurant, having been too busy to look for another housekeeper.

He eased himself into an armchair and lay back, staring aimlessly up to the ceiling. Soon his mind began to wander and memories of the previous week, when he had had that mishap at the Wollingers, came back to him. It might have been distressing, but at least the place had been full of people—not lonely and empty, like this house. A picture rose up in front of him of Mr. Wollinger, wine cup in hand, saying the blessing in that pleasant, lilting melody.

And then, suddenly, the image changed! It was not Mr. Wollinger whom he saw, but a much older man, with a flowing white beard. He, too, was holding a silver goblet in his hand and he was singing a similar melodious tune.

Clinging to the memory, Harry Colman forced his mind back and soon he remembered who it was. It was his own grandfather! Strange that he should have forgotten all about him and the visits he used to make, as a very young boy, to his grandfather's house.

Now the memories came flooding back, unchecked. He used

to love going there. His grandfather had a beautiful voice and would sometimes sing specially for him. He remembered the plaited loaves his grandmother had on the table and how eagerly he had eaten the slice she had given him. He had enjoyed the rest of the meal too. It was so different from the food his mother usually served.

And then, one day, his father had found out about those visits and had put a stop to them.

"You're not to go there any more!" he had shouted. "I'm not having my father turning you into one of those *frummies*! I had enough trouble myself, breaking away. Do you hear me, Harry? Keep away from there! If I catch you going there, you'll be sorry!"

Harry had reluctantly obeyed and eventually the pull of his grandfather's house had worn off. He never went there again and gradually the memory of his grandparents faded out of his mind.

Now, though disturbed by these reminiscences, he was relieved that the strange sensation he had felt last week was no longer a mystery to him.

All the same, he told himself, it's no good dwelling on it now. It's a thing of the past and best forgotten.

The letter from Garments Limited arrived the following Friday morning. Mr. Colman stared at it, surprised, before picking it up and opening the envelope. What could they possibly want now? he wondered. They had already severed their connection with him. His astonishment grew as he read the letter. In it, the large wholesale firm stated that they wished to reconsider their original intention and renew the contract after all, as they had found the goods of the other firm to be far inferior to his. If he was in agreement, they wrote, they were ready to place a large order with him immediately.

Mr. Colman could not believe his luck! Of course he agreed! Who wouldn't? He would answer them right away and set about increasing his production output at once!

But how could he do that if his factory was closed for one whole day in the week? Too bad if he'd promised, he decided. He would have to reopen on Saturdays. It was too late for this week, of course. He would risk a complete walkout if he sprung it on them without even a day's notice, but next Thursday he would tell them all to come in on Saturday!

The next morning, he woke up late. As he sat down to his breakfast of toast and scrambled eggs, he thought about the long, tedious day that stretched ahead of him. Never mind, he told himself, it's only for one more Saturday. Next week it's back to normal again!

He was quite unprepared for a little voice inside him that suddenly spoke up—the voice of his conscience.

"*Harry, wait a minute!*" it said. "*Have you thought about what you're doing? Maybe that boy had a point when he said your luck would improve if you were closed on Shabbos. Won't you be tempting fate if you went back on that now? How do you know it won't bring you bad luck?*"

Shocked by the notion, he forced himself to think rationally. Are you getting fanciful in your old age? he asked himself, desperate to justify himself and stick to his decision. But he couldn't shut out that little voice. It kept popping up, making him unsure what to do. Perhaps, he found himself considering, I can persuade them to put in extra hours during the week. They certainly seemed to work with more enthusiasm since I gave them Shabbos off.

He thought about his Jewish workers. They went home so cheerfully every Friday afternoon, calling "good Shabbos" to each other as they left. Suddenly he found himself envying them. They didn't spend a boring aimless day each week, as he did. Their day was filled with something spiritual, which was just what he suddenly decided he was lacking.

That, he realized with a shock, was what was wrong with his life. It was empty—completely devoid of anything spiritual.

All of a sudden, he knew what he wanted. He felt a strange desire to hear the uplifting sound of someone making *kiddush*! If only it could be his grandfather. But that was not possible. Grandfather was no longer alive. But what about Mr. Wollinger?

Hardly aware of what he was doing, he pushed away his breakfast plate and stood up. Going straight into the hall, he put on his hat and coat and picked up his car keys from the hall table.

No! he thought suddenly. I can't go by car. They won't tolerate that! Replacing the keys, he wrapped a scarf round his neck and prepared to walk out into the cold March air.

It turned out to be milder outside than he thought and within half-an-hour he had reached his destination. As he turned into the street and began to approach the house, he was aware of men coming out, just as they had done when he had been there before. Slowing down his pace, he waited till he was sure everyone had gone before going up to the front door. This time it was firmly closed. Mr. Colman hesitated for a moment before knocking… bracing himself for the ordeal he would surely have to face.

It was Doniel who opened the door for him, staring at him in surprise. However, before Doniel had time to say anything, Mr. Colman blurted out, "Have I missed *kiddush*?"

It took Doniel a moment to collect himself. Trying not to show his utter amazement, he answered as calmly as he could, "No, Mr. Colman. Actually, you're just in time."

Doniel led his employer towards the dining room, where the scene was exactly as it had been the time before. Reb Yechiel gaped for a moment when he saw who it was, but one look at Doniel's face told him everything. With a smile of welcome, he nodded towards Mr. Colman and proceeded to make *kiddush*. Harry Colman, enveloped by a feeling of warmth, almost felt as though he were listening to his grandfather. He knew instinctively that he had been right to come. If anyone could teach him how to become a religious Jew, it was this man and his family.

The Wollingers soon assessed the situation. They behaved as if his presence was the most natural thing in the world.

Sitting at the table with the rest of the family, he began to enjoy the food he was served. The slice of plaited loaf, which they referred to as *challah*, was extremely tasteful. Just like his grandmother's, he told himself, although he couldn't possibly remember the taste after all those years!

But the thing that mostly filled him with nostalgia was the steaming plate of *cholent* that was placed before him.

It was delicious and it really did bring back memories. As he ate it, he felt as though he was that young boy again, seated at his grandparents' table.

What was it that was so special about this dish? he wondered. Why did the taste have this effect on him? And suddenly he knew.

It tasted… of Shabbos!

# A Measure
# of Courage

There was no getting away from it. I, Sheindy Kaplowitch, was the biggest coward on earth. Not only did *I* know it, but my family and friends were aware of it too. My mother had long ago stopped sending me to the park with my younger siblings. They would invariably return home complaining that I wouldn't let them climb to the top of the climbing bars and that I embarrassed them by yelling loudly if they went a bit high on the swings.

At school, I was subjected to a fair amount of good-natured teasing, which I didn't really mind. But I did feel uncomfortable when I knew they avoided trips to go rowing or climbing because… "Sheindy will be too scared to join in!"

It was awful always being afraid. I could never relax and

enjoy myself. I constantly expected dangers to be lurking round the corner. Why couldn't I be carefree, like the other girls? And why did I have this terrible fear of heights? I could never stand on the top rung of a ladder—or look down from the window of a high building—without getting a dreadful, sinking feeling. If only I had just a little bit of courage! Nobody knew how much the complete lack of it made me suffer!

And nobody knew what I went through the day the school building caught fire.

It happened on a Sunday afternoon, which was fortunate, really. I shudder to think what the consequences might have been had the place been full of pupils and teachers! We had decided to spend the afternoon there, four of my classmates and I, as well as our art teacher, Miss Kaufman, to work on a project we were doing for a competition.

We were having a terrific time, working away in the arts-and-crafts room on the top floor of the building. The large, wooden table was littered with pencils, and various colored paint sticks, as we outlined and painted the lettering and pictures Miss Kaufman sketched for us. We were so engrossed in our work that we were quite unaware of the time until Miss Kaufman glanced at her watch.

"Girls!" she exclaimed, "it's quarter-past-five! I think we should call it a day. We can finish it off next week."

Amid groans of disappointment, we began to tidy away our utensils. Suddenly Simi Deutsch, in the act of arranging the paint sticks neatly in the box, looked up and sniffed.

"Do you smell that? I can smell burning!" she announced ominously. All at once, we all could smell it. Miss Kaufman ran to the door and opened it. A cloud of black smoke flowed into the room. She closed the door abruptly, her face white!

"The staircase is on fire!" she cried.

This time I was not the only one to panic.

"What shall we do?"

"Where can we go?"

All the girls seemed to be shouting at once.

It was Yitty Shultzberg, the class daredevil, who was the first to spring into action. Running to the window, she pulled it up and leaned out.

"We can't jump out," she declared, her words sending shivers down my spine. "We're too high up. But there's a ledge out there that leads to the fire escape…"

Before anyone had time to think, she had lifted her leg and begun to climb out of the window.

"Yitty!" I screamed. "Don't! You'll fall!"

I wanted to run to the window and pull her back, but someone—I don't know who—restrained me. Yitty's face appeared at the window. "Come on, all of you, it's quite safe. There's a water pipe running along the wall to hold on to. I'm going to run to the next house and call the fire-brigade!" A moment later, Yitty vanished. Simi leaned out of the window.

"She's done it!" Simi informed us. "Yitty is on the fire escape. Come on, we've all got to do the same," she said urgently. And, to my dismay, she too climbed out of the window. Channy Berens followed next, then Dina Lehmann.

Now Miss Kaufman and I were the only two left. But I was sure of one thing. No way would I be able to climb out of the window! I turned to face my teacher. To my absolute horror, I could see that flames were already licking the bottom of the door!

"Quick, Sheindy!" Miss Kaufman cried, propelling me towards the window. "We've got no choice! The fire is coming closer!"

Responding to the urgency of her tone, I forced myself to lift one leg over the sill. But the feeling of sheer terror that engulfed me made me tremble all over and I drew back immediately.

"I can't!" I wailed hysterically. "I'm scared! Please, don't make me go!"

"But you're in more danger here!" Miss Kaufman argued, her voice choked with emotion. "Please, Sheindy, please try to make the effort!"

I knew she was right. It was getting harder to breathe as the room filled with smoke. In spite of that, I could not bring myself to do it! I seemed frozen in place. How could I explain to Miss Kaufman that the thought of balancing myself in such a precarious position so high up frightened me more than the fire that was advancing menacingly towards us. At the back of my mind, I clung to the hope that the fire-brigade would still arrive in time to rescue me, though I knew it was a slim chance. Stiffening, I pulled away from the window.

"Please, Miss Kaufman," I pleaded, "you go out. Please don't wait for me. I *can't* do it! I just *can't*!!"

"No, Sheindy," the teacher said firmly, though her voice trembled, "I'm *not* going out and leaving you here!"

Could I let someone else risk her life because of my fear? Even if I was terrified, was I so selfish as to put Miss Kaufman at risk? Gritting my teeth, I willed myself not to think of the danger as I heaved myself out of the window.

I cannot begin to describe my feelings during that unnerving experience! I had a moment of sheer panic as I groped with my foot for the ledge. It's gone! I thought. It isn't there! But no, I was standing on it! My legs feeling like jelly and my hand trembling, I grabbed the water pipe and clung to it desperately, suppressing a sob. I could feel tears pricking my eyes but I blinked them away, heeding a warning light in my head, telling me that I mustn't cry! Tears would blind my vision and I wouldn't even be able to see where I was going! The very thought made me shudder!

Somewhere behind me, I heard Miss Kaufman give a cough and exclaim hoarsely, "Ooh, the smoke!" I did not dare turn round to see if she, too, had climbed out.

The ledge seemed a mile long as I edged my way forward. Once or twice I missed my footing and my heart lurched in fear, but I managed to steady myself with the help of the water pipe.

Don't look down, I kept repeating to myself, knowing what the sight of that steep drop would do to me. But my eyes did occasionally stray downwards, increasing my terror. Unable to stop myself, I began to sob loudly and I could hear Miss Kaufman behind me, uttering words of encouragement.

Making my trembling way along the ledge, it seemed like an eternity later when I found myself at last within inches of the fire escape! But, horror of horrors, the water pipe had suddenly come to an end! How was I going to get across? There was nothing for me to hold on to! I clung to the end of the water pipe, too petrified to move!

Down below, I could hear Yitty's voice announcing, in a loud, triumphant voice, "The fire-brigade will be here soon!" Then she called up to me, "Bravo, Sheindy! Get on to the fire escape, quickly!"

"I c-can't!" I called back, my voice shaking. "It's too far!"

"Okay," Yitty's voice floated up, "don't worry. I'm coming to help you!"

Soon she was level with me on the fire escape, reaching her hand out towards me. But I felt too frightened to lean forward. Yitty had to stretch right over to reach me before I let her pull me to safety.

My heart lurched again in that dreadful moment as I was pulled across. I felt as though I was suspended high up, in mid-air! My feet were jelly and my heart seemed to be pounding louder than I had ever heard it before. Could I do this? Would I just fall to my death?

At last, I was standing firmly and squarely on the fire escape, so overcome with relief that I clung to Yitty, blubbering like a baby! Yitty gave me an encouraging pat before pushing me aside to help Miss Kaufman off the ledge. Then, as we heard the welcome sound of the fire engine approaching, we ran down the steps of the fire escape, into the waiting arms of our cheering friends.

"*Boruch Hashem*! *Boruch Hashem*!" they kept repeating as they hugged us.

My memory is a bit blurred regarding what happened after that. I was vaguely conscious of a lot of people milling around; of screaming sirens and bustling activity; of gasps of horror and a woman shouting in a high voice, "The roof has caved in!" But to me it seemed as if it was all happening miles away. I was shaking and could not stop myself from sobbing hysterically. I was aware of a fireman speaking in a concerned voice to my friend Simi, who was bending over me solicitously.

"Is she alright? Should I call an ambulance?"

"No, no," Simi assured him, "she's not been hurt. She's just in shock, I think."

"Mmm," the fireman muttered knowingly, "it often happens. Nasty things, these shock reactions. She ought to see a doctor..."

Shrugging his shoulders in a dismissive way, he ambled off. In spite of the state I was in, the vague idea flitted through my mind that he was a bit disappointed that I wasn't injured. Perhaps he had been looking forward to putting his first-aid skills into practice.

The incident seemed to calm me down somewhat. However, before I had time to think, I was bustled into someone's car and driven home, with Simi sitting beside me, gently holding my hand and every now and again saying comforting things.

Before I knew it, I was home and Simi and I were walking toward my mother. The sight of her worried face absolutely ruined whatever composure I was gathering and brought on a fresh bout of hysterical sobbing. I didn't even hear what Simi was telling her. In a daze, I just heard her say to me, "you'll be okay," and Mummy thanking her as Simi left.

Everything after that is just one hazy blur in my memory. I vaguely remember my mother taking me upstairs to bed… the doctor coming… Mummy bringing me a cup of cocoa and giving me a tablet to swallow. I think she tucked me in and spoke in a soothing tone—but even that is not lucid in my mind.

When I awoke the next morning, I was relieved to notice that the shaking, quaking feeling that had overtaken me the day before had gone completely. Actually, I felt quite refreshed. My first thought was "*Boruch Hashem*, nothing terrible happened to me after all!"

I washed *negel vasser* and was about to get up, full of the joys of life, when suddenly, like a cold shower pouring over me, a terrible feeling of shame and embarrassment went through me!

Why, oh why had I behaved so idiotically? I had made such a fool of myself! Of course I had been scared. Who wouldn't be? And perhaps, because of my irrational fears, I had it worse than the others. But in the end, since I had to climb out of the window all the same, why couldn't I have done it with dignity… instead of howling and wailing like a two-year-old?

Until now, my classmates had accepted my cowardice good-naturedly. Now they would definitely look down on me… especially because I had risked Miss Kaufman's life as well as my own.

I dealt with my feeling of mortification by getting back into bed again and covering my face with my quilt. I did not want to face anyone! I felt I couldn't even face my mother, who must have been acutely embarrassed when she heard how I had disgraced myself. She must be so ashamed of me! My brother and sister never behaved like that. My eleven-year-old sister Tzippy was an expert swimmer and had won a few medals already (while I hardly dared to let go of the bar at the shallow end!), and my brother Moishy rode his bike with such confidence, doing things I would never *dream* of doing!

"Good morning, Sheindy," my mother's hearty voice came to me from the door. "Feeling better today?"

I just buried my face in my pillow and shrugged my shoulders.

"Still groggy?" Mummy's voice sounded deflated and not a little concerned. "Oh well, give yourself time. You don't have to get up yet, in any case. I just received a message that there will be no school till they've found some temporary premises, so you can stay in bed a bit longer if you want to."

Suddenly I *did* want to get up. It was such a relief to learn that there would be no school for a while! At least I would not have to face the other girls for the time being and could keep my shame to myself a little longer.

Of course I should have realized that my classmates—with plenty of time available while school was closed—would all come along to "see how poor old Sheindy is".

The first one to arrive was my best friend Simi. Recognizing her shape through the frosted glass of the front door, I beat a hasty retreat up the stairs, having first whispered frantically to my mother, "Say I'm asleep!"

Mummy gave me a quizzical look, but I could hear her obeying my instructions, all the same.

After Simi there was a continual stream of visits and telephone calls from the girls in my class, all wanting to know how I was, but I continually avoided speaking to them. If anyone called round or phoned, I was officially either asleep or had gone out!

My mother kept eyeing me searchingly, concern on her face, but she said nothing for a while. However, after passing on my excuses for a few days, she could stand it no longer.

"What's the matter with you, Sheindy? Your friends are all worried about you. It's so thoughtful of them to keep enquiring about you. Why are you behaving so churlishly?"

Stung by her disapproving tone, I felt bound to explain.

"I'm so embarrassed!" I blurted out. "They all think I'm just a silly baby—I *know* they do! They all look down on me now because I made all that fuss!"

Mummy smiled, a look of relief crossing her face. At least the reason for my strange behavior was now clear to her… even if she didn't agree with it.

"Silly girl!" she said patronizingly. "Of course they don't look down on you. I think they all understand that you *can't* help the way you are!"

Thank you! I thought sullenly. That doesn't made me feel any better. Quite the opposite, in fact. I said nothing but my resolve to keep out of sight was even stronger now.

The situation continued for another few days, after which the girls grew tired of their unsuccessful attempts to contact me and finally left me in peace.

However, the time came when I could dodge my schoolmates no longer. Two weeks after the fire, we received notification that premises had been found to house the school while our building was being restored. We were asked to report there the following Monday morning.

"I know where that is," my mother said, perusing the letter. "It's on the other side of the park. It's a lovely area — all tree-lined streets and some big, Victorian houses. It might take you a bit longer to get there, but you can cut through the park if you're in a hurry."

I left in good time on Monday morning, just in case I'd have trouble finding the place, and though I did intend to take a short-cut through the park, I changed my mind when I saw some of my friends going in through the park gates. I still did not feel ready to come face to face with them. Fortunately, I didn't meet anyone as I made my way down the streets surrounding the park and I still got to my destination in time.

I joined the throng of girls outside the gates of the new location, waiting for Mrs. Lederman, the headmistress, to arrive and let us in. Trying not to be noticed by my own classmates, particularly the ones who had been there during the fire, I mingled with some girls from a lower class. But Yitty Shultzberg spotted me.

"Hi, Sheindy! How are you?" she called across, her voice loud enough to draw everyone's attention to me. I wished I could sink into the ground! My friends began to gather round me, asking me if I had recovered from the ordeal. They told me how they had come round — or telephoned — but hadn't been able to get to me. This was precisely what I had been dreading! But, strangely enough, there didn't seem to be anything mocking or patronizing in their manner. I felt grateful for the spate of time that had obviously dimmed their memory of my immature behavior.

Somewhat relieved, I joined in the general subject of conversation, which was an appraisal of the new building we would soon be entering.

"It looks nice…" someone commented. "What was it used for before?"

"I think it was some sort of college…" another girl volunteered the information.

"It's not very big, though…"

"No. I expect we'll be a bit cramped…"

"Well, it's only temporary…"

The buzz of conversation was interrupted abruptly by the arrival of Mrs. Lederman, a large bunch of keys in her hand. The sudden hush caused by her appearance lasted only a moment. In the wave of excitement that followed, everyone began talking at once, bombarding the headmistress with questions and comments. Holding up her hand authoritatively, she waited for the noise to subside before unlocking the large black wrought-iron gates. Impatiently, we all pushed our way through them and followed Mrs. Lederman up to the house. It certainly looked like an impressive building! Leading up to a beautiful oak front door were five wide steps, flanked by two low stone walls that curved outwards with a carved design. We stood waiting eagerly as Mrs. Lederman mounted them and selected another key from the bunch. Flinging the door open wide, she ushered us all in with a smile and a flourish.

The square entrance hall was really quite large, but as soon as it was filled with teachers and pupils, it suddenly seemed to shrink! Expecting to be led straight to our various classrooms, we were quite surprised when the headmistress unlocked another door and beckoned to us to enter the room.

"Come into the dining room," she said. "We will use this as our Assembly Hall."

The room, which had obviously once been two rooms that had been made into one by knocking through the dividing wall, looked enormous, with its high ceiling and wide windows. The dining tables and chairs had all been stacked into two alcoves on either side of an ornate marble fireplace, leaving enough room for the hundred and fifty girls to stand in the rows that were quickly organized by the teachers, even though we filled up the entire center area.

Mrs. Lederman mounted an overturned wooden chest and began to speak. She welcomed us all to the new temporary accommodation, expressing her appreciation that something had been found so quickly and assuring us that we would soon be back in our old school building as work had already begun on it.

"But the main thing to remember," she went on, her voice low and serious, "is to show our gratitude to Hashem for saving us from disaster. Remember that the fire, which was caused by an electrical fault, could have broken out any time, but, praised be Hashem, it did *not* happen on a school day! And even those few people who were in the building at the time were, *boruch Hashem*, saved!

"Now I want to say a word of praise to one girl whose bravery and prompt action helped save the lives of four of her classmates and a teacher, as well as preventing even more damage to the school building. Because of the swift way she climbed out of that top-floor window, ..." A gasp rippled through the crowd at this point, even though the entire school already knew the details. "... the fire-brigade came in record time. Yitty Shultzberg, you deserve a medal for your heroism. I'm sure the teacher and the girls concerned will be grateful to you forever! A round of applause for Yitty, girls!"

Everyone looked toward Yitty, who was standing amidst her friends in the middle of the room. The applause was tumultuous and I joined in heartily for a moment, forgetting my own shameful behavior.

Mrs. Lederman waited for the clapping and cheering to subside before continuing.

"There is also another person whose courage deserves commendation," she said.

Oh, no, I thought with a sinking feeling, as I felt color rush to my face, she's going to mention the way Miss Kaufman—at risk to her own life—had refused to abandon one cowardly pupil! Even though she would surely not mention my name, everyone would know immediately to whom she was referring. My humiliation knew no bounds!

"It is not always a fearless person who is courageous," the headmistress was saying. "On the contrary, it is easier for them... though their bravery is to be praised. But the person who has a fear and overcomes that fear... that is a truly brave person! Sheindy Kaplowitch, we all know that you are terrified of heights. It is *not* your fault and actually it is not an unusual problem. Climbing out of that window, high up on the top floor, must have been a terrible ordeal for you. Yet you did it! And you did it not only for the sake of your own safety. You did it because Miss Kaufman would not climb out unless you did. That showed true courage! I think, girls, that Sheindy deserves a big round of applause. Her courage is, in a way, greater than everyone else's!"

Was I dreaming? Could all this clapping and cheering really be for me? For my... COURAGE? I was blushing in embarrassment. But I was suddenly grateful for Mrs. Lederman's words. All eyes were on me as the girls clapped and I felt a softening inside myself. Maybe I had been mistaken in measuring myself against girls without a fear of heights. Maybe, after all, I did have a measure of courage. According to Mrs. Lederman, I had quite a large chunk of it!

Which is not bad at all... for a coward like me!

# Apple Pie Order

It was lying on the table when Mrs. Heineman came into the kitchen with her shopping… a beautiful, crusty round apple pie, liberally dusted with icing sugar and sealed in polythene wrapping.

Mrs. Heineman put her shopping bags on the table and stared at the pie for a moment. Then she called out to the cleaner, who was vacuuming in the next room. "Mrs. Pike! Mrs. Pike! Please come here a minute!"

It took a few more "Mrs. Pikes" before her voice was heard above the noise of the vacuum cleaner.

"What?" Mrs. Pike asked, appearing in the doorway.

"Where does this pie come from?" Mrs. Heineman asked.

Mrs. Pike shrugged. "Dunno," she said. "A young girl came

with it, askin' for you. When I said you was out she said, 'can I leave this 'ere?' And off she went."

"I see," said Mrs. Heineman, trying not to show Mrs. Pike that she was utterly baffled. Mrs. Pike went back to her work in the living room and Mrs. Heineman remained staring at the apple pie for quite a long time, wondering what to make of it.

Who could have sent it? It was obviously meant for her, because the girl who had brought it had asked for her by name.

The realization burst into her brain like a thunderbolt!

Of course! Who else could have sent it but Bayla Myers? Bayla had been an expert at baking apple pies, and would often send her one, in the days when... a lump came to her throat... they had been close friends. This one looked almost exactly like one of Bayla's apple pies, except that Bayla used to bake them in a round baking-tin and send them to her on a plastic plate, with a doily underneath. Now, it seemed, she had adopted the modern method of baking them straight into disposable foil tins. But why had Bayla sent her one? She and Bayla had not spoken to each other for ten years now, ever since that bitter quarrel they'd had.

A feeling of anger suddenly rose up inside Nechama Heineman. Spite! she decided. That was what was behind Bayla's strange gesture! Bayla had obviously sent it to show her what she was missing and to remind Nechama of the friendship she considered *Nechama* to have destroyed!

What nerve! It was Bayla who had stopped speaking to *her*! Well, she could keep her silly apple pie! She didn't want it!

Mrs. Pike came in just then, interrupting her thoughts. "I've finished now, Mrs. H.," she said, untying her flowered apron.

"Oh... er... yes," Mrs. Heineman answered in a preoccupied manner, picking up her purse to pay Mrs. Pike. She got the money out and handed it to her.

"It looks real good, that apple pie," Mrs. Pike commented, eyeing it admiringly. "I wouldn't mind someone sending *me* one like that!"

On a sudden impulse, Mrs. Heineman grabbed the apple pie and thrust it into Mrs. Pike's hand.

"Here!" she cried, "Please take it! I-I'm not keen on apple pies, and neither is my husband, so you might as well have it."

"Are you sure?" Mrs. Pike asked, gaping in surprise.

"Yes, yes!" Mrs. Heineman said hastily, afraid of the chance to change her mind. "Please enjoy it with your tea!"

"I will!" Mrs. Pike declared gleefully, hurrying to the front door with her prize. "I'll be off then," she said. "Thanks a lot, Mrs. H. See you on Friday."

No sooner had Mrs. Pike gone when Nechama became overcome with regret. What had she done? Perhaps it wasn't even from Bayla. But then, if it wasn't from Bayla, who was it from? And, since she didn't know, how could she or Shaul eat it in any case? She couldn't be sure of the *kashrus*. Stupid, she thought, she should have looked underneath. Bergstein's, the local kosher bakery, sometimes sealed the polythene wrapping closed at the bottom with a label, complete with name and *hechsher*. But why should someone buy a cake at Bergstein's and send it to her? No, it must have been Bayla. Her apple pies looked professional enough.

But had she been right, just giving it away? Nechama's anger was suddenly subsiding and she reasoned that the apple pie probably wasn't sent out of spite after all. One couldn't call Bayla a spiteful person. In fact, she was basically quite good-natured. That was the thing Nechama had liked about Bayla. She was always trying to be helpful. It was this trait in her character that had caused the trouble between them. She had gone a bit too far that time, poking her nose into something that didn't concern her.

Nechama sat down at her kitchen table, a feeling of desolation sweeping over her. It had been such a good friendship! She began to reminisce, remembering how it had all started.

Eleven-year-old Nechama Seltser lay back in her hospital bed, feeling utterly miserable. Visiting time at the hospital was over and her parents had just left, leaving her to wallow in her loneliness. Her throat still felt sore, making it difficult to eat and drink. Her mother had brought some ice cream, begging her to eat it, even though it was also painful to swallow.

"It's only one day since you had your tonsils out," her mother had said soothingly. "It'll get easier every day, you'll see. The ice cream and the ice cubes they give you will take the soreness away eventually. So be good and eat it like a good girl."

It was alright while her mother was there, fussing over her, but now she was at the mercy of the nurses, who, though extremely kind, didn't have much time for her. Why were they so strict about visiting times? If only her parents could stay longer, she thought, full of self-pity. She didn't know what to do with herself now. She had plenty of books to read, but they somehow didn't seem interesting.

"Hullo," a cheerful voice said, beside her bed. She turned her head round to see a girl of about her age looking down at her. She was wearing a light blue dressing gown and her curly, chestnut-colored hair was tied back with a blue ribbon. Nechama stared at her, taking in her blue-green eyes, her pointed chin and her small nose that tilted slightly upwards.

"Hullo," Nechama replied, her voice a little weak, "who are you?"

"My name's Bayla Silver," the girl replied. "I had my appendix out three days ago… on Shabbos, of all days! I was rushed in with acute appendicitis," she explained, "so it was an emergency. What have you had? I saw them wheel you back yesterday afternoon."

"I had my tonsils out," Nechama told her.

"Oh, I bet your throat feels sore. They'll probably let you get up tomorrow morning. What's your name?"

Nechama told her, a little croakily.

"Pleased to meet you, Nechama!" Bayla said amicably. "I'm so glad there's another *frum* girl here! We're so lucky to be in the hospital at the same time!"

Nechama nodded her agreement.

"Oh, I'm sorry, Nechama! It probably still hurts you to talk," Bayla's tone was sympathetic. "I'll go back to my own bed now. Tomorrow, when you're feeling better, let's spend all day together!"

The two girls really got to know each other during those few days of their stay. Nechama learnt that poor Bayla was an orphan, her parents having been killed six years previously in a car crash. She waved away Nechama's expression of sympathy, telling her that the uncle and aunt that she lived with were amazingly good to her. They came to visit her at visiting time and Nechama could see that this was true.

Thanks to her new friend, the days in the hospital passed quickly. In some ways, Nechama didn't want them to end. It would mean that they must part company. Bayla lived in the area where the hospital was situated but Nechama's home was in a district quite far away. They would keep in touch, they told each other, but it wouldn't be easy.

Remembering all this now, thirty-five years later, Nechama recalled the fun they'd had in that hospital ward. One incident suddenly came back to her. At the far end of the ward there had been a bunch of lockers for each of the patients to keep their belongings. Once, the ward sister—who was a real battle-axe—opened Bayla's locker and saw how everything was stuffed inside in a most untidy manner. She had tut-tutted disapprovingly and told her to tidy it up.

"On this ward," she had said sternly, "we like to have everything in apple pie order!"

The two girls had giggled hysterically as soon as she was out of earshot.

"Apple pie order!" Bayla had exclaimed, eyeing her locker ruefully. "I wouldn't mind if this locker *was* filled with apple pies!"

*Apple pies*! Nechama Heineman gasped. Why had that memory come back to her just now? She stared at the spot on the table where the apple pie had been before she had given it away so rashly, and she willed herself to stop her reminiscences. But the painful memories refused to go away. They just came pouring into her mind as if a floodgate had opened up in her head!

She remembered the time Bayla had phoned her, full of excitement, and told her that she would soon be moving to

Nechama's neighborhood, as her uncle was opening a grocery shop in the area.

"Isn't it terrific?" she had cried. "And what's more, I'll be coming to your school! "

"Oh, my! That's incredible!" Nechama had exclaimed enthusiastically. "Maybe we'll even be in the same class!"

"Oh, I do hope so! I must admit, going to a new school is a bit scary."

"Don't worry, I'll look after you," Nechama had promised.

She recalled how she had looked forward to taking Bayla under her wing. Being somewhat reserved, Nechama tended to stay in the background a little and she was therefore not one of the most popular girls. Taking charge of someone in the class would definitely make her feel important.

But, as it turned out, Bayla hadn't needed her protection for long. Bayla's naturally extroverted nature soon helped her settle down and fit in, with everyone clamoring to be her friend. She and Nechama still remained best friends, however, although their roles had gradually become reversed. It was Bayla who had assumed the leadership, drawing Nechama closer into the circle.

Their friendship continued right through their school years and beyond. They went together to seminary and when they returned Bayla soon found a job as a kindergarten teacher. Having a wonderful way with children, she was a success. Nechama, feeling she was not cut out for teaching, had taken a secretarial course at the seminary and then worked in the office of the school where Bayla taught.

Then, within two weeks of each other, they both got engaged. Shaul Heineman, after learning in yeshiva for twelve years, had started working for a real estate agent, hoping to eventually start his own business. Bayla's *chosson*, Yisroel Myers, was still learning in a *kollel* and Bayla planned to stay at her job so that he could continue learning as long as possible.

As the ensuing years scrolled through Nechama's mind, she had a picture in front of her of hard-working Bayla, looking after her family of little ones while still going to work. She was always smiling and she never seem to tire of doing mitzvos within the community, as well as constantly cooking and baking, which she did to perfection. Nechama sighed as she remembered how Bayla would send her one of her professional-looking apple pies on various occasions, such as Purim or on her birthday.

Nechama often found she had to suppress a pang of jealousy where Bayla was concerned. Bayla seemed to be managing her busy life with such ease, whereas she, Nechama, could just about cope with looking after her son and daughter and helping Shaul in his business. Why should *I* envy *her*? Nechama would think guiltily, aware that she had much more, at least materially, than her friend. Shaul had a good business while Yisroel Myers had constant *parnossoh* problems.

Eventually, bowing to the necessity of supporting his ever-growing family, Yisroel had accepted that he would have to work and had taken over Bayla's uncle's grocery shop. Then a large supermarket had opened nearby, and the competition forced him to close the shop. After that he had tried various jobs—Nechama was not quite sure what they all were—but he didn't seem to be in them for long. Bayla never grumbled, but she sometimes looked quite worn out.

At this point in Nechama's reverie, she realized she had come to the point she would much rather not think about.

The quarrel!

Her husband Shaul's business was going through a bad patch. Although usually an easy-tempered man, he was beginning to worry about it. Then, one day, he came home and told his wife that he had received an offer that might solve his financial problems. A big-time property-dealer named Carl Handler had offered to buy out his business, with Shaul remaining on and running it as part of his company, for a good wage.

Nechama thought this was a terrific proposition and advised her husband to accept it. It was a surprise to her when Bayla paid her a visit a few days later, telling her that she had heard about the deal and advising the Heinemans to steer clear of Carl Handler.

"Please, Nechama, take my advice," she had begged. "He's not a straightforward person! He could ruin Shaul altogether. I know what I'm talking about!"

"What do you mean? How can you know?" Nechama had asked, her tone disbelieving. "What do you know about the business world?"

"I don't," Bayla admitted. "But I know about this man. Yisroel used to work for him and he had a strange feeling that there was something shady about his business. In the end, he went bankrupt and Yisroel was out of a job."

Her words cut into Nechama like a knife. She didn't want to accept the seed of doubt Bayla was planting in her mind. It was as if Bayla was pulling the rug away from under their feet, threatening their whole livelihood.

"I see!" she said in a strange voice that, even to her, didn't seem to belong to her. "Just because your husband can't stick to a job and can't support you, you want to stop *us* from being successful too!"

No sooner were the words out of Nechama's mouth than she realized she should never have said them. What had gotten into her? She knew she ought to apologize, there and then, but something—probably the worry about the threat to their *parnos-soh*—stopped her.

Thinking about it now, Nechama knew she would never forget the look of utter shock and incredulity on Bayla's face. Bayla just stood there and stared at her friend for a moment, white-faced. Then she had turned round abruptly and walked out.

All this had happened ten years ago and the two women had not exchanged one word since then. Nechama knew she had been terribly wrong saying what she did, but for some reason she could not bring herself to telephone Bayla and apologize. Nechama had waited for an opportunity to come face to face with her friend, when she would quickly say she was sorry.

However, when Nechama did meet Bayla at a *kiddush* one Shabbos morning, Bayla had immediately turned away, avoiding any kind of contact. Feeling snubbed, Nechama had been furious. Well, if Bayla's dodging me, she thought, I'll keep out of her way too!

The years went by and, instead of feeling their bitterness softening with time, the two women became more entrenched in their resentment. They went their separate ways, hardly aware of each other's existence.

And now, suddenly, out of the blue, Bayla had sent Nechama an apple pie!

Why? Nechama wondered. She had already ruled out spite. That was just not part of Bayla's make-up. It was definitely a peace offering Bayla had sent her.

Nechama was overcome with a tremendous guilt feeling! *She*

should have been the one to hold out an olive branch, not Bayla. She had said some unforgivable things and she couldn't really blame Bayla for turning her back on her.

To make things even worse, her friend had been quite right to try and warn Shaul about Carl Handler. It was less than a year later when they had found out with whom they were dealing. As a result, Shaul had very nearly found himself without a livelihood. It was only the *chessed* of the Ribono Shel Olom that had saved him from joining the ranks of the unemployed. An acquaintance of his — someone who was in the same line of business — had realized that Shaul's expertise would be an asset to his firm and had offered him a partnership.

Thinking about all this, Nechama was suddenly aware of an overwhelming desire to renew her old friendship with Bayla. If only they could talk to each other again in the easy, unrestrained manner of the past! She had been so wrong not to apologize!

She suddenly knew for sure what she had to do. She had to respond to Bayla's magnanimous gesture and pluck up the courage to contact her and beg her forgiveness.

She thought about the apple pie and was filled with regret for giving it away so impulsively. She pictured Mrs. Pike proudly showing it to her family with a gleeful, "Look what Mrs. H. gave me!" and then sitting down with them to enjoy it, making ecstatic noises over it. The fanciful thought suddenly crossed her mind that her friend's apple pie certainly did not deserve to be eaten without a *brochoh*!

What would Bayla think if she knew what she had done? She resolved not to mention the apple pie, even though she knew she ought to have the good manners to thank her for it. Hopefully, Bayla would realize that she had received it and wouldn't find it necessary to ask her about it.

Like someone in a daze, Nechama Heineman walked across the room to the telephone and dialed her friend's number, amazed how well she still remembered it!

Ten minutes later, Bayla Myers replaced the receiver, a bemused look on her face. She couldn't believe it! The thing she had been hoping for for the last ten years had actually happened! Nechama had contacted her, taking the first step towards a reconciliation!

So many times, Bayla had been tempted to pick up the phone and try to patch things up, but she had refrained, fully aware that she had nothing to reproach herself with. If she were to make the first move, Nechama might never really see how wrong she had been. True, Nechama had probably resented Bayla's interference, but she should have realized that Bayla had meant well and that, knowing all that she did, she could not just stand back and allow Nechama's husband to make a move that could ruin him. There had been absolutely no need for the scathing remarks Nechama had made, especially the comments about Yisroel, who always had tried so hard but didn't seem to have much luck. Bayla had been so hurt! And yet, she had long ago forgiven her friend. She was only waiting for her to apologize.

And now, at last, Nechama had made the first approach. Bayla could not help wondering what had prompted it, but what did it matter? She had done it and it had surely taken a great deal of courage. Nechama was now on the way to her and Bayla found herself looking forward to the meeting with relief and anticipation.

It had indeed been an emotional affair, the reunion between the two friends. Anyone witnessing the scene would have found it hard to believe that these two women, hugging each other and weeping profusely, were both approaching fifty!

They were both so overcome that they had hardly been able to speak at first. Eventually, their tears spent, they had looked at one another, each one noting the other one's red-rimmed eyes and they had both spontaneously burst out laughing. Then they had talked and talked until, at last, the barrier that had built up between them had been completely removed. They agreed to never again let misunderstandings come between them and they arranged an evening to spend together, doing the things they had always enjoyed, just like old times.

Aware that her eyes were still a bit red, Nechama bade her friend goodbye and hurried out, before Bayla's children came home from school.

With a light-hearted step, Bayla went back into her kitchen to resume the baking she had begun. The pastry was lying on the board and the unpeeled apples were waiting on the draining board.

You know what? she said to herself as she began to peel them. I'm going to do something I haven't done for a long time. I'm going to send Nechama an apple pie for Shabbos!

The telephone rang at Bergstein's, in the kitchen area behind the shop. Golda Bergstein hurried to answer it, leaving her new assistant, young Shoshana Grossman, to mind the shop.

"Is this Bergstein's?" a brisk female voice asked.

"Yes. Mrs. Bergstein speaking."

"This is Devora Heineman," the voice informed her.

"Oh yes, Mrs. Heineman. What can I do for you?" Mrs. Bergman asked politely, while at the same time thinking, that's funny. I always thought Mrs. Heineman's name was Nechama.

"Mrs. Bergstein, what happened to the apple pie I ordered? It's already five o'clock and it hasn't come. Am I still getting it?"

"Are you sure it didn't come?" Mrs. Bergstein asked, puzzled. "I'm positive we sent it out." She began to flip through her order book as she spoke. "Yes. Here it is! Mrs. Heineman. One apple pie."

"Well I didn't get it!" Mrs. Heineman declared plaintively.

"I can't understand it." Mrs. Bergstein sounded worried. "Shoshana! Come here a minute!" she called.

The girl appeared immediately. "Shoshana, didn't you deliver an apple pie to Mrs. Heineman today? It's ticked off in my book, so it must have gone out."

"Yes, I did!" Shoshana replied, sounding worried. "Mrs. Heineman wasn't in so I left it with the cleaner. Shouldn't I have?"

Mrs. Bergstein gave her a reassuring nod and repeated her words to the irate woman on the phone.

"Well, that doesn't make sense! I've been in all day—and I haven't *got* a cleaner! I do my own cleaning!"

Looking perplexed, Mrs. Bergstein turned to Shoshana, who seemed ready to burst into tears. "Are you sure you took it to the right house, Shoshana? Which number in Crawley Avenue did you go to?"

"Number sixteen, as you told me!" Shoshana declared, her lip trembling.

Mrs. Heineman, hearing every word, could be heard through the earpiece, calling frantically, "I don't *live* in Crawley Avenue! I live in Fairbank Road!"

Suddenly everything became clear to Mrs. Bergstein. The pie had gone to the wrong Mrs. Heineman! This Mrs. Heineman was quite a newcomer to the district and she didn't really know her. Hearing the name "Mrs. Heineman" she had assume it was Nechama Heineman, who was one of her customers, and she hadn't bothered to jot down the address… an awful mistake, she realized now.

"I'm terribly sorry, Mrs. Heineman," she said into the phone. "There has been some mistake. Are you desperate for the apple pie tonight? We have some in the oven now but they'll be too hot to send out just yet."

"Well, I would have been, but, fortunately, my visitors have been held up and will be coming tomorrow night instead."

"Right!" Mrs. Bergstein said, relieved. "I'll send you another one first thing in the morning. And please, Mrs. Heineman, accept my sincere apologies." Mrs. Bergstein wrote down the correct address and hung up.

"So," she said, almost to herself, "it went to Nechama Heineman instead. That's strange. I wonder why she didn't send it back. Perhaps she's been out all day and hasn't come home yet. Or maybe she thinks her husband — or someone — bought it without telling her. In any case, I can't ask for it back now…" She was suddenly aware of Shoshana looking at her tearfully.

"Oh, Mrs. Bergstein!" the girl cried. "I made such a mistake! I'm awfully sorry!"

"Shoshana! Please don't apologize. It wasn't your fault at all! It was my mistake. But it doesn't really matter. Mrs. Heineman will get another one tomorrow — and a fresher one at that — so there's no harm done!"

Little did Mrs. Bergstein know how true her statement was! There certainly was no harm done. Quite the opposite, in fact!

# The Initiation

ehudis regarded her two sleeping children and smiled. They looked so peaceful and innocent, it was hard to believe they had been so boisterous and full of mischief only an hour ago, turning her kitchen upside down! Now that they were sound asleep, she could get the place straightened again.

She went downstairs and surveyed the scene of chaos in front of her. Toys were scattered everywhere, not to mention the pots and pans that had been pulled out of the cupboards! She began to pick things up mechanically, going through her usual daily routine, until the place began to look normal again.

Then she made herself a cup of tea and sat down with it, forcing her mind to settle on a subject she had been pushing off thinking about for the last few days. Tonight was the deadline. She had to decide what she was going to do, as she had to give her answer by tomorrow. Should she take that job or not? It was so hard to make up her mind!

Why was she such an indecisive, insecure person? If only she had a little more self-confidence! That had been her problem ever since she was a child. She could never make up her mind about anything. She hemmed and hawed for ages before making a choice. And even then, once she managed to make a decision, she would never be sure it had been the right one.

When she was growing up, her parents would often make decisions for her. Shimon, her husband, had a different attitude. He believed in boosting her confidence by forcing her to decide things for herself. And that was why he refused to advise her when she begged him to tell her whether she should take this job.

Basically, it was the ideal job—precisely what she was looking for. The hours suited her, it was near her home and there was a day care center where she could leave Yitty and Mendy. And her secretarial skills were not bad.

But it seemed there was more to being a secretary in this small Jewish primary school than just office work. According to the school's principal, her duties included public relations as well. Apart from chasing up school fees, organizing times of meetings and the like, she would be expected to iron out little internal problems such as disagreements or misunderstandings between staff or petty complaints from parents and children. She wondered if she would be any good at public relations.

Her family and friends were not terrifically helpful. Even her mother, who thought she ought to take the job, did not seem overly positive about her abilities.

"I'm sure you won't have too much of that sort of thing to do," was her mum's "encouraging" comment.

Her sister, perusing the advertisement, had pointed out the words, "must be able to use own initiative." She didn't actually say anything, but Yehudis knew she was thinking, "Well, that counts *you* out!"

Shimon told her that, until one tried, it was impossible to know what one could do. "But you must decide this for yourself," he had said.

The trouble was that she *couldn't* decide! She had intended to nag Shimon tonight, over supper, to tell her outright what to do, but it didn't look as if there would be time for that, after all. Shimon had sprung the news on her that there was an emergency staff meeting that night at the *cheder* where he taught and he wouldn't be home till late. Yehudis knew what that meant. He would come in just in time to grab a hurried meal and rush out again for the late maariv minyan. After that, they would both be too tired to discuss it properly. Yehudis gave a frustrated sigh. What should she do?

The ringing of the telephone interrupted her thoughts. It was Mrs. Katzman, her mother.

"Well?" she wanted to know. "Have you decided yet about the job?"

"No... not really," Yehudis replied falteringly. "But I don't have to give an answer till tomorrow morning."

"Well, I think you should take it," her mother said firmly. "And I think you should ring the principal tonight. I know you! You'll leave it till too late and then someone else will get the job. Then you'll be sorry!"

"Y-yes... maybe. But, ..." Yehudis stammered. Perhaps her mother was right. Should she take her advice?

"Not 'maybe'!" Mrs. Katzman insisted. "Do it now! Are you going to?"

"I might." Yehudis wished her mother would not pressure her so. How could she be so sure it was the job for her?

"Okay, then. I'll leave you to it. Bye… and good luck!" Mrs. Katzman hung up abruptly.

Perhaps she's right, Yehudis thought. I will be upset if I lose the job. I suppose I'd better phone Rabbi Weiss or I might have *charotoh.*

However, in her heart, Yehudis did not feel convinced and so she didn't pick up the phone and dial immediately. I'll get supper ready and finish tidying up first, she told herself, putting a casserole into the oven. Then, after rinsing out her teacup and sweeping up some crumbs from the floor, she poured the contents of the garbage bin into a black plastic bag and tied it up, ready for Shimon to take out when he got home. No, she decided, he'll be too tired. I'll do it myself.

Taking the bag outside, she threw it into the bin and hurried back inside. Being outside in the dark always made her a bit nervous. She was about to close the back door when she was conscious of something stopping the door from closing. Thinking she must have dropped something on her way out, she look down and saw, to her absolute horror, that there was a man's foot in the doorway! The man attached to the foot was pushing his way into the house. When she looked up, she saw that he was pointing a gun at her!

She froze in terror and wanted to scream, but the scream would not come out.

She just stood there, gaping.

"Get inside!" the man hissed, waving the gun menacingly.

Too frightened to resist, Yehudis had no choice but to obey.

She felt the urge to scream again, but something seemed to stop her. What was it? Why couldn't she let out a loud, piercing scream? Maybe one of the neighbors would hear her and come to her rescue. But she soon realized what was holding her back. It was her natural maternal instinct. Her children would be in danger if she woke them. Mendy would start crying and Yitty would surely climb out of her cot and come downstairs.

Oh no, she prayed, please don't let them wake up! Let them be safe!

Trembling like a leaf, she backed into the kitchen, with the man following her. In spite of her fear, she took in the man's appearance. He looked quite young, probably no more than eighteen or nineteen at the most. His brown, curly hair was tousled and his somewhat spotty face looked grubby. His dark, shifty eyes seemed to dart about the room and Yehudis had the impression that he was nervous.

"Sit down!" he barked.

Not daring to turn her head away, she felt her way round to a chair and did as she was told. She wondered whether the intruder would sit down too, but he preferred to remain standing.

Yehudis could hardly believe this was happening to her, in her cozy little kitchen, with its blue and white décor. Even the cute kitchen clock, in the shape of a teapot, didn't look so cheerful now. She had always felt so safe here, but the presence of this nasty-looking man had completely taken away that feeling!

"Okay," he said gruffly, "give me the keys to the safe!"

"Th-the s-safe?" Yehudis stammered. "What safe?"

"Come on! Don't try that one on me! You know very well what safe! The one where all the jewelry is!"

"Jewelry?" Yehudis repeated stupidly. "The safe with the jewelry? I don't know what you mean!"

"Of course you do!" the man insisted impatiently. "Come on, give me the keys... or tell me the combination numbers... or whatever..."

So, Yehudis thought, he's after jewelry. She began to pull at the rings on her fingers. It broke her heart to have to part with her precious wedding and engagement rings, but her life—and that of her children—was more important!

"I haven't got much jewelry," she said, "but you can take my rings... and this necklace if you must—and then, please, go away!" Her voice was pleading.

"Hah!" the man gave a short laugh, taking her offerings all the same and stuffing them in his pocket. "You're not fobbing me off with that! It's the real stuff I'm after! The lot your husband takes home from the shop every night. Don't tell me he doesn't keep it in a safe!"

"I have no idea what you're talking about!" Yehudis cried plaintively. "My husband hasn't got a shop. He's a teacher!"

"Oh yes?" the man snarled sarcastically. "Well, he ought to teach you not to tell lies, then. You know as well as I do that your husband owns a jewelry shop and takes some of the merchandise home every night in a black briefcase. Kev followed him home the other night and he marked the house with an X so I'd find it. ..."

While he was rambling on, Yehudis suddenly understood. The man who owned the jewelry shop was her next-door neighbor, Mr. Mossberg! She had seen him herself quite often, getting out of his car and hurrying into the house holding a black leather briefcase. Telling this crook that he had mistaken the house for a different one was extremely tempting. It would let her off the hook immediately! But she knew she could never do that. She would never forgive herself if any harm came to her neighbors, the Mossbergs. Perhaps he would realize, in any case, that he had made a mistake and go away eventually... taking her rings and necklace with him, she thought ruefully. The one thing that worried her was if he decided to search for the safe and go upstairs where her two little darlings were asleep. The thought made her start trembling again.

"I ought to search the house," he said, as though reading her thoughts, "but I can't do that and keep the gun pointing at you at the same time. Pity I've got nothing to tie you up with. I'll have to wait till Kev gets here. And he wanted me to have the haul ready for him." He clicked his tongue in annoyance.

"Who's Kev?" Yehudis couldn't help asking.

"He's my... er... partner. He'll be here soon and he won't stand for any nonsense, so you'd better just hand over the key to the safe."

"I haven't got it!" Yehudis declared truthfully. "Why don't you go away!" Her voice rose hysterically.

"There's no need to yell!" the man said crossly. "If you haven't got it, your husband must have it on him. Don't worry! We'll get it off him as soon as he comes in!"

Yehudis felt her panic intensify. What would happen to Shimon when he came home? Somehow she would have to warn him before he came into the house. But this man and his accomplice were obviously prepared for that. What if they... *chas v'sholom*! She shuddered, not letting herself dwell on the terrible thought.

The telephone rang, making her jump.

"Let it ring!" the man snapped, giving the gun a jerk to remind her that she had no choice.

The persistent ringing sound grated on her already taut nerves. She wondered who it was. Possibly it was her mother, wanting to know if she had phoned Rabbi Weiss. A grain of hopefulness passed through her mind. Mummy would wonder why she was not answering, knowing she would never go out and leave the children on their own and, with any luck, she would send someone to investigate. On the other hand, Yehudis thought dejectedly, she might think little Mendy had woken up and she wasn't answering because she was busy rocking him to sleep.

Presently the ringing stopped, leaving an eerie silence in its place. The only sound in the room was the ticking of the clock, conveying—it seemed to Yehudis—an ominous message.

Staring at her captor, it struck Yehudis that there was something odd about him. Something didn't quite fit. In spite of his aggressive manner, he seemed nervous and edgy. He was even perspiring slightly. Then there was the way he spoke. He didn't have that rough-and-ready, common way of speaking she imagined experienced crooks would have.

Unable to bear the loaded silence in the room, she bravely decided to make some sort of conversation. Tentatively, she commented on her observation.

"You don't speak like a crook normally speaks," she pointed out.

"And how many crooks have you spoken to?" he asked sneeringly.

"Well, none really," she said, adding *"Boruch Hashem"* in her thoughts. "But you don't sound like one would expect. Your way of talking seems much more educated."

*"Educated!"* he repeated with a snort. "Who wants to be educated? That's what caused all the trouble!"

"What do you mean?" Yehudis asked softly, hoping to keep him talking for a while. Maybe some sort of salvation would turn up in the meantime.

"What business is it of yours?" the man snapped.

"None at all," Yehudis replied, surprised herself at the calmness of her manner. "I just feel bad for you. You seem nice but sort of unhappy."

"So what if I am! It's nothing to do with you!"

"No, I know it hasn't got anything to do with me." Yehudis still managed to keep that soothing tone in her voice. What was happening to her? she wondered. "But it sometimes helps to talk about it. What's your name, by the way?"

"Steve," he answered curtly. "And you'd better stop your chattering! I don't want to talk to you about my problems!"

Realizing she had no choice but to obey, Yehudis sat still, her lips pursed. But she continued eyeing Steve with a look of concern. She couldn't help wondering what had made a boy from an obviously decent home turn to a life of crime.

It was the sympathetic look Yehudis was giving him that suddenly loosened Steve's tongue. Sympathy was something he rarely encountered and he found himself involuntarily responding to it.

"My dad's an accountant," he finally told Yehudis, playing with the gun in his hand. "He wanted me to be one too, but it wasn't what *I* wanted! I hated math! I hated all lessons really. The only thing I liked about school was sports. Dad was forever ramming education down my throat and he tried to make me go to college when I left school. No way! I'm going to be a professional football player! You don't need college for that!"

Yehudis was quiet for a minute as she gathered her thoughts.

"But, Steve, if you don't mind my saying, it looks to me as if you'll end up in prison instead," Yehudis commented. "And once you've got a criminal record, none of the football clubs will take you on. What made you get involved with this kind of thing in the first place? It's not for someone like you!"

"Why not?" Steve sounded defiant. "It's easy money, isn't it? It'll help me achieve my ambition."

"Who says so? What if your parents find out what you're doing?"

"They won't. They don't even know where I am. I ran away from home ages ago and I do just as I please."

He was trying to sound smug and self-satisfied, but Yehudis wasn't fooled. He was so young! She figured he was probably only eighteen years old.

"Kev says we'll make thousands on this job and he knows what he's talking about!"

"Who is this Kev?" Yehudis wanted to know.

"Kev? He's what you might call 'an experienced crook'." Steve told her with a slight smirk. "They'll never catch him. He's much too clever!" Yehudis thought she detected a note of bitterness in his tone.

"How did you get mixed up with a man like Kev?" she asked.

"Well, I was living rough when I left home. Kev found me and sort of pulled me out of the gutter. He's been really great. I've been working for him ever since."

"Steve, I hope you don't mind me saying this, but I think that you're making a mistake working for this man. Take my advice and give it up before it's too late!" Yehudis' voice was pleading. "Go back to your parents. I'm sure they'll understand and—"

"No!" Steve cut in sharply. "Stop lecturing me, lady! Kev will be here any minute and he'll be livid."

"Where is he then?" Yehudis asked, hoping to sow seeds of mistrust in Steve's mind. Obviously this Kev had Steve completely under his thumb. "Why is he leaving you to do this on your own?"

"Never you mind where he is! He's got another job to see to

first and I was supposed to have the takings from this house ready for him. It's your fault that I don't have everything ready! You won't cooperate!"

His face took on a belligerent look and he began to wave the gun about menacingly. "Don't force me to use this!" he said through clenched teeth.

A fresh wave of terror swept over Yehudis. This Kev he was talking about might be more frightening but, in her opinion, Steve was more dangerous. He was young and inexperienced and his fear of the man who was controlling him might drive him to do anything in desperation. His finger was on the trigger. It would only take a second! Quaking inwardly, she shut the horrendous notion out of her mind and decided to keep trying to talk Steve into abandoning this path he had chosen.

The telephone rang once more, cutting into her thoughts.

"Ignore it!" Steve ordered.

Yehudis bit her lip and clenched the hand that was itching to pick up the receiver. She found herself wishing it would stop ringing, but it just went on and on, seemingly forever. Eventually, after a very long while, it did stop, only to start again a moment later.

The sound was beginning to unnerve Steve too. "You'd better answer it," he told Yehudis. "But I'm warning you! Don't let on that there's anything wrong! Any foreign language or cryptic clues and you're dead! You hear me? No funny business! Whoever it is, act naturally!"

Act naturally! Yehudis thought. How does he expect me to do that? With a trembling hand, she picked up the receiver.

"Hu-hullo?" she said shakily.

"Yehudis?" Shimon's concerned voice came over the line. "Are you alright? Why didn't you answer for so long?"

Aware of the stern expression on Steve's face and the gun being held more tightly in his hand, Yehudis pulled herself together. She had better do as he said. How frustrating! Rescue was almost within her reach and she couldn't make use of it! Desperately, she racked her brain for some way of getting a message across.

"Yes, I'm fine," she told her husband. "How's the meeting going? Is it finished yet? When are you coming home?"

"Oh, it won't be long now. I just slipped out for a moment to phone you because you didn't answer before. Kids up playing, are they?"

"The twins?" Yehudis said, grasping a sudden idea that came to her. "No, they're fast asleep, though they were rather naughty before."

"Twins?" Shimon sounded puzzled. "What twins?"

Another flash of inspiration hit Yehudis. Ignoring his question she said, "Oh, by the way, Mr. Mishtara phoned before. He asked that you phone him as soon as you can. He says it's urgent."

"Mr. Mishtara? Who's that?" Shimon asked, completely baffled.

"Yes, goodbye then," Yehudis said, sounding airy and cheerful with great effort. "Don't be too late. Your supper will be burnt!"

She hung up quickly, saying a silent prayer. Please, Hashem, make him get the message!

Shimon clicked off his mobile phone and stared at it, perplexed. What had got into Yehudis? Had she taken leave of her senses? An alarming thought came to him, filling him with concern. Could all this worry about the job have had some adverse effect on Yehudis' mind? It wasn't possible! True, she was a terribly insecure, indecisive person, but she was basically sensible and level-headed. Then what could have made her talk all that gibberish, not even answering his questions properly? Twins! Yitty and Mendy *were* only fourteen months apart, but they weren't twins! And what was all that nonsense about a Mr. Mishtara? He'd never heard of the man. And Yehudis had spoken as if it was someone he knew. Wait a minute! *Mishtara*! It rang a bell! To his surprise, a picture of Eretz Yisroel rose up in his mind. It must be someone he had met while they were there. *Mishtara… Mishtara…* he struggled to remember. And then it came to him in a flash! Of course, *Mishtara* was the Hebrew word for police in Eretz Yisroel! *Police!!* Realization gripped him suddenly. Yehudis was sending him a message! She was in some sort of trouble. Someone had broken in! He had better call the police immediately!

Hastily, he clicked his mobile on again and, with a shaking hand, punched in the emergency number.

After Yehudis hung up, she glanced apprehensively at Steve, hoping he hadn't realized anything was amiss. He nodded approvingly. "You must really have been scared to put on such a good act," he said gloatingly. "Your husband, was it?"

"Yes, it was," Yehudis replied, resisting an urge to tell him to mind her own business.

"When is he coming home?" Steve wanted to know.

"Any minute now," Yehudis lied, hoping to frighten him. "He's on his way home."

"Good!" Steve said. "Kev should be here too, by then. We'll get the key off him alright!"

"What makes you think he'll hand it over?" Yehudis asked with false bravado.

"We won't give him much choice!" Steve told her menacingly, once again brandishing his gun.

Yehudis' heart sank. What had she done, luring Shimon into danger? What if he hadn't understood the bit about the police? After their phone conversation, he would surely realize something was wrong and would hurry home — possibly by himself. Oh, if only she could somehow prevent him from coming in! Perhaps she could still convince Steve he was on the wrong track.

"Look," she said, her tone desperate, "you're just wasting your time. My husband hasn't got a jeweler's shop, I tell you!"

"I don't believe you! If it's not him, it must be someone else in this street. Kev might have mixed up the house, but he wouldn't make a mistake with the street. So if that's the case, why don't you tell me who it is? The fact that you don't proves that you're lying!"

How can one explain to a non Jew that a Jew would never betray another Jew? Yehudis reflected. But how could she convince him that she was telling the truth?

"I wish you'd put away that gun!" she said, beginning to feel unbearably strained. "You're not going to shoot me anyway!"

"Who says I'm not?"

"You'd be a fool to do such a thing," Yehudis said, trying her reform tactics once more. "Committing murder could get you put away for the best part of your life. By the time you'd come out, you'd be too old to *play* football, let alone be a professional."

Steve's face muscles tightened. Yehudis could see she had hit a sore point and it made her nervous. It's no good antagonizing him, she told herself. There's no knowing what he might do.

If only Shimon would turn up already! How long would she be able to keep this up, playing for time and keeping Steve talking?

She sighed deeply, trying to think of something to say, but her mind had gone blank. Once again, the sound of the ticking kitchen clock conveyed an ominous message. She sighed again.

Steve didn't miss the sigh.

"Scared, are you?" he asked.

Yehudis detected a hopeful tone in his voice. She realized he wanted her to be afraid of him. But she didn't want him to think he had too much power. What should I do? She thought. Admit I'm scared — or deny it?

The answer she gave him was a shrug of her shoulders.

"I think you are afraid," Steve said proudly. He loved having this power over someone else. "You won't come to any harm if you cooperate. Now, tell me where the key to the safe is."

"I already told you, Steve, I really don't know!" Yehudis sounded weary and exasperated.

"Suppose I believe you?" Steve said. "That would mean that we *have* got the wrong house. If you know what's good for you, you'll tell me which is the right one!"

Yehudis shook her head, her mouth pressed tightly shut. Looking extremely cross, Steve leaned forward, holding the gun closer to Yehudis with a menacing expression.

Suddenly his head shot up, obviously alerted by something. "Was that a car?" he asked, his tone apprehensive. "It seems to have stopped near here. That must be Kev, at last!" Steve stood up and backed towards the back door.

"I'll open the door and let him in. Then we'll wait for your husband to arrive!" His tone was ominous.

Moving back slowly, he reached the door and, with his free arm, pulled it open behind him.

"What took you so long, Kev?" he asked plaintively, without turning round. "She wouldn't give me the key, but her hus—" He stopped in mid-sentence when he felt something hard and metallic prodding into his back. At the same time, a firm voice barked, "Drop that gun!"

The gun fell out of Steve's hand immediately and the look on his face was one of utter astonishment. Yehudis, too, was surprised see a burly police sergeant in the doorway, poking a gun into Steve's back. Two more policemen arrived on the scene, seconds behind the first officer, grabbing hold of Steve and clapping handcuffs onto his wrists. Behind them, she could see Shimon pushing his way forward.

"Yehudis! Are you alright?" he asked, coming straight in, a look of deep concern on his face.

"Yes, perfectly!" Yehudis replied, her voice full of relief. "Oh Shimon, *boruch Hashem*, you got the mess—"

She was interrupted by a commotion outside the door. Two more policemen were holding another man, who was struggling to free himself. He was wearing a crash helmet that hid his face.

"We found him outside, sir, prowling around the back of the house," one of the policemen explained.

"Ah, an accomplice I presume," the sergeant said, going up to the wriggling man and roughly pulling up the crash helmet to reveal his face. "Well, well! If it isn't Kevin Jones! So we've caught up with you at last!"

Yehudis stared. So this was Kev! He wasn't at all as she had imagined. She had pictured him as a towering giant, striking fear into a person's heart. This man was slightly built, with ginger hair and freckles. He had a pointed nose and thin, twisted lips.

"Steve, you idiot!" he shouted, glaring furiously at Steve. "You've gone and botched it!"

"I did not!" Steve protested. "It was you! You took so long getting here! And I'm not sure if you didn't mark the wrong house. It's all your fault!"

"Okay, okay! You can fight it out in jail!" the sergeant said. "Take them away!" he told his officers. "And if they've left a car here, search it. I suspect they're behind the Mossberg jewelry shop job I've just received a call about."

Yehudis couldn't help feeling a little sorry for Steve. He looked so dejected as they led him away. If only his parents had handled things better, he might not have got into this mess. Still, it served him right. He deserved to be punished.

It was quite late by the time Shimon and Yehudis sat down to their meal. After the criminals had been led away, the police sergeant had stayed behind to get a full, detailed report from Yehudis. He had been particularly interested to know how Yehudis had conveyed the message to Shimon without the criminal being aware of what she was doing. When they had explained it to him, he had been highly impressed.

"That was incredibly ingenious!" he had exclaimed. "What initiative! I take my hat off to you, Mrs. Verber!"

Yehudis could hardly believe her ears! Someone was actually congratulating her on her *initiative*!

By the time he had written down her statement and left, Shimon had to rush out to catch maariv. While he was out, Mrs. Katzman had phoned. "I'm just off to bed," she told her daughter, "but I have to know. Did you phone Rabbi Weiss?"

"No, I've been too busy," Yehudis said, deciding there was time to tell her mother what had happened another time — not when she was on her way to bed! "But I'll phone him first thing tomorrow," she promised, suddenly realizing that she had actually made a positive decision — by herself!

"Good," her mother said. "I'm so glad I persuaded you. Well, good night, Yehudis. Sleep well."

Now, as Yehudis served up the rather dried-up casserole, both she and Shimon felt they did not have much appetite to eat. They were still distraught from the evening's experience. But their main feeling was one of relief that, *boruch Hashem*, everything had turned out well.

"That message was a really brilliant stroke, Yehudis!" Shimon told her admiringly. "What made you think of it? And how did you have the courage and the presence of mind to think at all, with a gun pointing at you? I'm really impressed... not to mention ashamed because I took so long to work it out!"

"Well, let's say I passed the 'initiative test'," Yehudis said with a laugh. "That's why I really feel I *could* do that job after all. So I'm going to accept it."

"Good for you!" he husband said. "I'm sure you'll make a terrific success of it!"

Yehudis settled the children in the school day care and made her way to her office. She had been at her job for two months now and she was really enjoying it. There were still times when she didn't feel too sure of herself, but she kept her doubts to herself, giving the impression that she was more self-assured than she actually felt. It gave her self-esteem quite a boost to feel that other people had confidence in her.

The horror of her unnerving experience was beginning to fade in her mind, although she was still petrified to go outside in the dark, but she hoped that would eventually wear off, too.

The two crooks were now behind bars. Kevin Jones, long sought by the police, had been given quite a long sentence, taking all his other thefts—as well as one assault on an elderly man—into account. Before he had arrived on the scene, he had raided Mr. Mossberg's shop, helping himself to an enormous amount of the stock. Steve's sentence was considerably smaller, as he had not done much. Even the fact that he was in possession of a dangerous weapon was not held against him, as it turned out that the gun hadn't even been loaded!

In spite of her anger at the way he had frightened her, Yehudis felt a certain gratitude towards Steve. It was odd to think about it, but if not for him, she would most probably have turned down this job. She had already decided that it was probably not for someone as indecisive as her!

She let herself into the office and hung up her coat. It was a pleasant office with its light wood furniture and cheerful, colorful décor. The filing system was orderly and a large window let in plenty of daylight.

Yehudis sighed with contentment. She was not even fazed by a note on her desk asking her, yet again, to sort out a disagreement between a certain member of the staff and the school cleaner, who was once more threatening to leave because of it.

When she had been interviewed by Rabbi Weiss, he had asked her whether she had had any public relations experience. She had honestly answered "no." But a letter she had received this morning made her wonder whether that was strictly true. It was a letter from Steve, written in prison.

In the letter, he had apologized for the aggravation he had caused her. Having a lot of time to think there, he could now see how right she was. A life of crime was not for him! When he came out of prison, he would put all that behind him and try to live a different life. He hoped his parents would forgive him for the disgrace he had brought upon them and would help him to rebuild his life. He thanked her for her understanding and for making him see the error—and the folly—of his ways.

So, Yehudis realized, she *had* done some public relations work, after all. Amazing, she reflected, what a good teacher experience is! And doesn't all this show that whatever happens is *gam zu l'tovah*?

# Out of the Blue

The parcel arrived a few days before Pesach. Recognizing her mother's handwriting, Mattel Kurtzig's hands trembled as she began to open it. An unbearable wave of nostalgia swept over her as she thought longingly of her parents and indeed of her life in Lvov, before she and her family had so brutally been wrenched from it.

This was their first Pesach here in Siberia, and Mattel fervently hoped it would be their last. Surely this war that they had so unexpectedly been thrust into could not last long, and they would soon be reunited with their loved ones—free, once more, of the torturous life they now had to endure.

As she deftly tore the brown wrapping paper, her mind went back to that Friday night when they had been ordered from their homes and herded into a cargo train—packed like sardines—to make the long journey to Siberia.

She remembered the weeks before that when they had been faced with an agonizing dilemma. Should they—or should they not—get Russian passports and become Russian citizens?

Shortly after Germany invaded and took over Poland, the Germans made a pact with Russia in which a part of Poland would belong to Russia. People were told that it would be advisable for them to take Russian citizenship. Many *yidden* in the towns of Galicia, including Mattel's parents and her parents-in-law, took advantage of the offer, convinced it would be safer for them. But many hesitated, reluctant to be under Russian rule, aware of that country's harsh regime.

Mattel's husband, Feivel, was one of those who vacillated. Time and time again Mattel begged him to follow the example of their parents, but he just could not make up his mind. There were too many arguments for and against taking such a step, making it impossible to decide.

And then, all of a sudden, it was too late!

There had been such wailing and crying as their relatives had stood by helplessly, watching them being led away. Their eyes seemed to say, "Why didn't you listen to us?"

Thinking of them now, Mattel pictured them all, carrying on with their everyday life, while she and her husband and children were here, in freezing Siberia. Although virtually prisoners, they were not brutally treated, but life was extremely hard for them here. It was colder than she ever imagined and their living accommodation in the barracks—where they were forced to remain—was cramped and uncomfortable. The meager food rations they were allowed were barely enough to sustain them and the men were forced to work hard, driven by harsh taskmasters.

I suppose I should be grateful, Mattel thought, as she removed the layers of wrapping paper, that we can at least receive parcels from time to time. She knew her mother would have loved to send her enough food to last her for a long while, but didn't dare make the package too big for fear that it would not get through at all.

Mattel knew what the parcel would contain this time and she had already scrubbed the table clean before opening it, making sure it was free of *chometz*. She stood looking down at the matzos in front of her and her eyes filled with tears. *Boruch Hashem*, they would now be able to celebrate Pesach properly and have a *seder* with proper matzos, even if they would have to be extremely sparing with them.

The parcel also contained a bag of raisins, which she would be able to boil up to make wine for the *arbah kosos*. Feivel would be incredibly pleased about that.

Wrapping the parcel up again, she picked it up and put it into a corner of the room, covering it with a cloth so that it would not come into contact with *chometz*.

It was not long before the children came rushing in, their cheeks rosy-red from playing in the snow. Eyeing them affectionately as they rubbed their hands to get them warm, Mattel could not help a tinge of sadness. The brisk outdoors had surely stimulated their appetites and there was so little for them to eat!

As they huddled together on the bench by the small table, she split each child's meager portion of bread. Then she brought the pot of potatoes to the table and spooned a small mound onto each plate, aware of the looks of disappointment on their faces. They had long ago stopped complaining, but she knew just how they felt.

To cheer them up, she told them about the matzos. Their eyes lit up at once. As they gazed with awe at the bulge under the cloth in the corner, Mattel warned them not to touch the matzos while there was still *chometz* in the house. She put her two daughters, Chaitchi and Liebele, in charge, telling them to make sure the two younger boys, Srulchik and Shiyale, did not go anywhere near it.

The children were fast asleep on their thin straw mattresses when Feivel returned from work at last. He came in, looking utterly exhausted, his hands chapped and blistered from cutting down trees all day in the cold forest. Tossing a bundle onto the floor, he sank onto a chair with a sigh.

Mattel picked up the bundle, which contained some off-cuts of wood they were allowed to take home. She used these to fire the stove that warmed them up and served as a cooker at the same time. Looking at her husband with concern, she dished up the remaining mashed potatoes and placed the plate in front of him. Then she told him about the parcel of matzos and raisins.

"*Geloibt is Der Eibeshter!*" he cried, his face lighting up with pleasure. "We can have a proper *seder* after all!"

Feivel Kurtzig shivered as he trudged through the snow on his way to work. He knew there was another grueling day ahead of him, but somehow his step seemed a little lighter than usual. Tomorrow night he would be sitting with his family, conducting a *seder*. True, it would be nothing like the *sedorim* they were used to, with a clean white tablecloth spread on a table that was laden with beautiful dishes. Feivel sighed as he visualized all the gleaming silver in his mind's eye... the candlesticks, the *seder*

plate, the collection of *kiddush* cups and the ornate *Kos shel Eliyahu Hanavi*.

Ah, well… he told himself with a vigorous shake… it's no good hankering for those things now. Until a few days ago, he had thought they would have to conduct a *seder* without even the bare necessities… no *matzos* and nothing to drink for the *arbah kosos*. At least now they would have these items, and for that he was grateful!

At last he reached the workplace, a clearing at the edge of a forest where logs were lying on the ground, ready to be bundled together and loaded onto barges. Some of Feivel's fellow workers were already at work, though the majority had not turned up yet.

"You're late!" a rasping voice barked behind him. Feivel turned round to face Oleg Brassilov, the Commandant in charge of the unit. He was tempted to point out that hardly any of the others had arrived yet, but one just did not answer Brassilov back. Once the Commandant decided he didn't like someone, he would make that man's life a misery, driving him relentlessly. So far Feivel had managed to keep a low profile and because of that he had often managed to avoid working on Shabbos. Once, on Friday afternoon, he had deliberately dropped a heavy log onto his foot, enduring the excruciating pain and noting, with satisfaction, that his foot was swelling up. Brassilov had sent him home, declaring that he would not be much use while he was limping and telling him not to come back for two days. He even gave him a stick to hobble home with!

Then there was the time he had succeeded in getting away with another daring plan. That Friday morning, Mattel had cooked a pot of oats and water for the family and it gave Feivel an idea. Pouring some of the hot mixture into a cloth bag, he made his way to the local doctor. Just before going in he placed the bag up his shirt sleeve, just under his armpit. It felt quite hot and he hoped it would not cool down too much before it was his turn to see the doctor.

It was quite chaotic in the doctor's office. Mothers were there with small children who cried a lot and some of the adult patients seemed to be moaning too.

The doctor, an elderly gentleman with a grey goatee beard, seemed decidedly harassed, moving around from one patient to the next. When he approached Feivel, he looked at him inquiringly.

"I-I'm not feeling well," Feivel told him in a feeble voice.

The doctor tut-tutted sympathetically and gave him a thermometer, telling him to put it under his arm while he attended to another patient. This was just what Feivel wanted. Making sure the thermometer was touching the warm bag he held it there tightly till the doctor came back, putting his hand out for Feivel to hand it to him.

"Your temperature is rather high," the doctor said after examining the thermometer. "Let me look in your throat."

Needless to say he could not find anything wrong with Feivel, but he told him to stay off work for at least three days, in view of his high temperature. "I will give you a sick-note to show the Commandant when you go back," he said.

Relieved that, once again, his plan had worked, Feivel knew he could not use any of these tactics again without arousing suspicion, but he tried every week to avoid working on Shabbos. He had befriended a rather unintelligent Polish gentile, whom he often persuaded to cover up for him and do the jobs that were proper *mechalel* Shabbos while he busied himself doing work that was not actually a *melochoh*. Thus he managed to avoid *chillul* Shabbos as much as possible.

Now, on the day preceding *erev* Pesach, he worked diligently, thinking of the approaching *Yom Tov*. He knew that his wife was busy at home, scrubbing and cleaning and making general preparations with her limited resources. When he had left home, she was already boiling up the raisins in water. It wasn't exactly the wine he was used to but, *boruch Hashem,* at least they had that. It would certainly serve the purpose, enabling them to say *Borei p'ri hagofen.*

Feivel was relieved when it was finally time to go home. His hands were sore from wielding a heavy axe and he was exhausted. Bracing himself for the long, tedious trudge, he was just shrugging himself into his coat when the Commandant's grating voice called out, "Attention, everybody! I have to make an announcement. I have been told to send a contingent of twenty-five men to go and work in another place for a week. Those of you that I indicate stand here to the right and wait. The rest of you can go."

He began to pick men out at random, signaling to them to stand at the side. Feivel prayed fervently that he would not be chosen. What would happen if he were sent away for a week? There would be no *seder* that they had all been looking forward to. The children had prepared some questions and explanations and even little Shiyale had been taught to say the *Mah Nishtana.* They would all be so disappointed! Wishing he could avoid being seen, Feivel tried to hide behind a tall, broad man standing in front of him but he was spotted by the Commandant.

"Hey! You with the black beard and the grey hat!" he called out, pointing directly at Feivel and indicating, with a flick of his thumb, that he should join the men standing at the side.

With a sigh, Feivel obeyed and stood with the others, his shoulders drooping dejectedly.

Brassilov completed his selection and sent the others away. Feivel watched them longingly, wishing he could be one of them. He dreaded telling his family the bad news.

"Right!" The Commandant turned to the men who stood awaiting further instructions. "You can all go home now, but tomorrow morning at seven a.m. you are all to gather at, ..." describing a point not far from the barracks, "where a wagon will pick you up and take you to the other workplace. Is that clear?"

There was a general murmur of assent and, after a nod from Brassilov, the men began to walk away.

Plodding wearily home, Feivel was hardly aware of the cold. His mind was on the distressing situation he found himself in. His family had endured so much in the last few months and now they would have to suffer yet another blow! Apart from his own bitter disappointment, how could he bear to witness their anguish and their tears as he was forced to leave them for the whole of Pesach?

He was half way home when he made a decision. He would not go!

Don't be a fool! an inner voice told him. You know what the punishment is for failure to show up for work. You will end up in prison, which will be much worse!

Nevertheless, Feivel's mind was made up. He *would* go to work—but at the usual workplace—not one that was a long, long way from his home!

It was a little later than usual when Feivel set out for work the next day. He wanted to be sure to avoid the crowd who were setting off to the new location. He took his time davening, praying for *hatzlochoh* in his daring scheme. After that, he sat down to finish eating *chometz* and burnt the few crumbs he had saved for the purpose of *biur chometz*. He bent over the stove and said *kol chamiroh* with intense feeling. Then he took a few cooked potatoes for his lunch and he left to work.

When Feivel arrived, he was relieved to note that Brassilov was inside his own little hut eating his breakfast, and had not noticed him. Feivel slipped hurriedly into the woods and began chopping down a tree, throwing watchful glances towards the entrance of the wood, in case the Commandant appeared. Later, when Feivel saw the Commandant approaching, he quickly pulled his grey woolen hat as far down over his face as he could and kept himself out of sight as much as possible.

It was about midday when Feivel suddenly felt a hand on his shoulder and he was pulled roughly backwards.

"Ha!" the Commandant cried, turning Feivel round to face him. "What are *you* doing here? You were supposed to go to the other place!"

Feivel did not know what to say—or how to react. In a flash of inspiration he decided to feign stupidity.

"Oh... er... was I? I didn't know..."

"You didn't know?" Brassilov shouted, slapping Feivel on the forehead. "Where are your brains? Of course you knew! You just didn't want to go!" He gave him a rough shake, sending him staggering backwards. "But don't think you'll get away with it! Oh, no! You'll go there, whether you like it or not!"

He continued to rant and rave while he dragged Feivel to the clearing outside the wood. "Go home!" he shouted. "I don't want you to work here! But I'm warning you! You will not get out of going to the other place. It's too late for you to go there today but early tomorrow morning *I* will personally come and fetch you myself! Go! I don't want to see you here, you cheat!" With a wave of his hand, the Commandant dismissed him.

At least, Feivel told himself as he walked home, I will be there for the first *seder*!

The *seder* was in full swing and Feivel threw himself into it with enthusiasm, even though the children's radiant faces were like a knife in his already heavy heart. He had decided not to tell the family what would happen the next day until the *seder* was over. He didn't want to spoil it for them.

The two boys, Srulchik, who was six, and four-year-old Shiyale, were asleep when he broke the news to Mattel and the girls. Their tears tore at his heartstrings and he was unable to offer them any words of comfort.

True to his word, Brassilov thumped loudly on the door early the next morning. Feivel was ready for him and, with a solemn nod in Mattel's direction, he slipped outside quickly, hoping the noise had not disturbed the children.

Without speaking, Brassilov began to lead the way. They walked together in silence, away from the barracks, until they came to a road that had been cleared of snow. Feivel knew that another group of prisoners, some of them fellow Jews from his own part of Poland, had been employed to clear the path by shoveling away the snow—a task even more back-breaking than chopping trees.

It was quite a long walk along this road and when they came to the end of it, Brassilov stopped.

"This is as far as I go with you," he barked. "Now you are on your own. Don't think you can turn back as soon as I've gone. I will find out if you do that!" His voice sounded menacing and Feivel knew that he meant what he said.

Pointing far into the distance, Brassilov told Feivel to keep walking straight ahead, giving him a few landmarks to follow.

"Now go!" he roared, giving him a hearty push. "And mind you walk briskly or you won't get there before dark! Go on, march!"

Feivel was about to begin walking when both he and Brassilov were startled by the sound of a galloping horse.

They turned round just as the horse came level with them. The rider was tall and erect, with broad, square shoulders and a small pointed beard. He was wearing the uniform of a high-ranking military official and his horse was obviously of a superior breed.

"Why are you shouting at this man?" he asked Brassilov in a cultured voice.

Feivel was fascinated to see how the Commandant seemed to shrink in his presence.

"Oh… er…" he stuttered, "he has been trying to dodge work and I am sending him off there at once!"

"And where is this place, may I know?" the stranger asked sternly. When Brassilov told him he cried out, "What? Are you mad? How can you send him off there on his own? The way is dangerous! He might get lost or be attacked by a bear! If anything happens to him, you will be held responsible and I wouldn't want to be in your shoes then!"

Then the stranger whipped his horse into action and rode off.

There was a stunned silence for a few moments, and then Brassilov turned to Feivel, a bewildered look still on his face.

"Well, go on!" he snapped. "What are you standing here for, staring like an idiot? Go home!"

Feivel didn't need to be told twice. Turning on his heel, he began to run home as fast as he could, fearing Brassilov might have second thoughts and come after him.

He couldn't believe his luck and he immediately began to express his gratitude to Hashem by saying the psalm of thanksgiving—*Mizmor l'sodah...*

It was several weeks later, by which time he had gotten to know Brassilov better and found him less intimidating, that Feivel plucked up the courage to ask him about the mysterious stranger who had suddenly appeared out of the blue.

"Who was that man?" he wanted to know.

"I don't know," the Commandant told him, bafflement in his tone. "According to his uniform, he was one of the higher ranking officers and I thought I knew them all. But that one, I must admit, was a complete stranger to me. I had never *ever* seen him before then! And I never saw him after that!"

Sixteen months after they had been taken to Siberia, the Kurtzigs were told that they were free to go wherever they wished in Russia. Things were a little easier after that, although they still faced many hardships. Food was scarce and disease was rampant. Feivel and his family managed to survive, unlike some of their acquaintances. Contact with their families in Poland had been completely broken off and they had no idea what had become of them. It was only after the war ended and they were allowed to leave Russia that they learned of the fate that had befallen them.

How ironic, Feivel reflected, as he mourned for his parents. When we were led away *we* had been the object of everyone's pity and yet we were the ones who managed to stay alive!

For a while, the family traveled around, from pillar to post, until they eventually settled in England. Life became pleasant at last, although Feivel never forgot those years in Russia, especially the episode with the mysterious stranger. In his later years, as his children and grandchildren came to sit at his *seder* table, he would recount the story to them. The grandchildren were fascinated and always referred to the incident as 'the time Zeide met *Eliyahu Hanavi!*'

*This story is based on a true incident,*
*although the characters and some of the situations are fictitious.*

# Distant Cousins

*a novella*

# 1

ady Cornelia Davenport stood at the bottom of the ornate oak staircase in the wide, luxurious hall of her home, twisting her fingers nervously. If only Lavinia and the doctor would come out already! She would have liked to accompany the doctor upstairs but she had to remind herself that she was only Amanda's grandmother and must not be too pushy just because her daughter's family was living in her house. It was an excellent arrangement really, with Lavinia's husband Reginald, a high-ranking officer in the Royal Navy, being away from home so much. However, she had to be careful not to interfere in her daughter's life.

But now, with Mandy being so ill, it was hard to stay in the background.

The sound of a door opening on the landing caught her attention. Looking up apprehensively, she saw Dr. Gregory and Lavinia coming down the stairs, talking earnestly.

"Perhaps if you could get this cousin to come and see her," the doctor was saying, "it might bring her out of her delirium."

Cousin? What did he mean? Lady Cornelia wondered.

"But doctor, we don't even know where she is!" Lavinia declared, her voice tearful. "I wish Mandy had never been told about it!"

"Nevertheless, it might save Mandy's life," Dr. Gregory's tone was grave. "I would move heaven and earth to find this cousin, if I were you. Ah, good afternoon Lady Davenport," Dr. Gregory said, raising his hat, as the countess came out of the shadows. "I hope a solution to this worrying business will soon be found."

With a promise to come again in the morning, the doctor took his leave.

"Lavinia!" Lady Cornelia called in a loud whisper, as soon as the doctor was out of the house. "What was Dr. Gregory talking about? What cousin?"

"Oh, you heard, Mother?" Lavinia said, giving a deep sigh. "That stupid woman! Why did I ever ask her to come back here to be Mandy's nanny!"

"You mean Dorothea Carstairs? What has she done? She's always been a good nanny to Amanda—and to you and Mi—" She stopped abruptly.

"Yes!" Lavinia exclaimed with feeling, "and once she left because we didn't need a nanny anymore, you told her all about Michael and everything that happened when she came to visit us. I never dreamt—when I decided to employ her as Mandy's nanny—that she would do something like this!"

"But what *has* she done?" Lady Cornelia asked, bewildered.

"She told Mandy that she has a cousin that she never met!" her daughter retorted crossly. "You know how Mandy keeps going on about how unfair it is that she's the only girl she knows who hasn't any cousins? Well, two weeks ago, when she was getting over the measles… or so we thought…"—there was a sob in Lavinia's voice as she spoke—"Mandy repeated her complaint once again and Nanny Carstairs said… maybe without thinking… 'Well, you really have a cousin, but you don't know anything about all that.'

"Mandy, of course, wanted to know what she meant, but by then Nanny Carstairs realized she had said too much and refused to tell her, even though Mandy begged and begged. And now," the desperation mounting in Lavinia's voice, "ever since Mandy's become so ill with this measles complication, she doesn't stop shouting that she wants her cousin to come to her!"

"Oh, no!" There was panic in the voice of the aristocratic old woman, which was unusual, as her emotions rarely showed. "What shall we—"

The loud chiming of the doorbell interrupted Lady Cornelia.

"Oh, I hope that's Reginald," Lavinia said. "I telegraphed him to apply for leave and come home quickly!" She turned and was about to go to the front door when Rivers, the butler, came hurrying towards them.

"Captain Faraday has arrived, Madam," he announced, addressing Lavinia. "He is just bringing his things in from the carriage."

Lavinia hurried away to greet her husband and Rivers withdrew, leaving Lady Cornelia standing alone in the hall, deep in thought.

She hardly ever thought of Michael nowadays. She had

accepted all that had happened with the proverbial English "stiff upper lip" and had determined to banish Michael from her thoughts for good. And she had nearly succeeded. If memories of her only son did enter her mind—usually accompanied by a pang of sorrow—she strove to suppress them.

But now everything suddenly came back to her so vividly, taking her back to that fateful day, eighteen years ago. ...

*Sitting on one of the high-backed elaborately carved wooden chairs in the drawing room in Wakebridge Hall, she stared, dumbfounded, at her son Michael, who was standing in front of her.*

*"Am I hearing you right, Michael? You... you want to convert to Judaism? Whatever for?"*

*"I've already explained it to you, Mother," the Michael replied, somewhat impatiently. "As I've said before, in my opinion it's the only true religion! In any case, nothing else will satisfy me!"*

*"But I still don't understand why you have to go away," his mother protested. "Even if you followed this hare-brained idea and became a Jew, ..." she said, wincing slightly, "there is no reason why you have to withdraw from society altogether. Who needs to know about it? Look at your friend Jeremy Selwyn. His family is Jewish, aren't they, but his father is a prominent physician and Jeremy is well on the way to following in his footsteps."*

*"Yes, I know, Mother, and I must admit that it was Jeremy who first made me aware of the Jewish people. But Jeremy isn't religious and I'm not interested in that attitude. I want to live the way a Jew is meant to live! For quite some time now I have been visiting a religious community in London and have learnt a lot about their laws and their way of life. And that is the way I want to live my* life!"

*"So...?" Lady Cornelia began.*

*"So," her son went on, "I can't live that life as the heir to the tenth Earl of Wakebridge!"*

Remembering that conversation so clearly now, Lady Cornelia gripped the banister rail tightly, allowing all the other memories to come flooding back.

She had always been so proud of her Michael. He had served in the army during the war and won a medal for bravery, fighting on in spite of being wounded. And then, only four years after the war ended, just when he was doing so well at university, he had stood in front of her and dropped this bombshell!

She recalled her husband Cedric's vehement reaction, furiously declaring that his son would make him the laughing-stock of the House of Lords and threatening to disown Michael if he went through with his plan. Michael had gone away after that, leaving behind an empty silence.

They heard nothing for three years. Then, a short letter arrived one day from Michael himself, telling them that he had been abroad for the last few years, studying Jewish law and that he had now returned to London and married a Jewish girl from the community there. Lord Davenport had received this news in his usual aggressive manner, tearing up the letter and declaring that in no way were they to acknowledge this Jewish daughter-in-law!

Thinking about all this now, Lady Cornelia could not remember exactly how it had come to them, but a year or so after his marriage they had somehow received news — in June 1953, she recalled — of the birth of Michael's daughter. The whole subject being taboo in their household, there had been little discussion about it.

Then, some time after that — Lady Cornelia couldn't remember how long after they had heard about the baby — a telegram had arrived telling them that Michael had died after contracting pneumonia. Lady Cornelia was stunned. How could it have come to this? Her baby Michael dead! The anguish Lady Cornelia had felt at the time was still crystal clear in her memory, though she had been forced by her husband to keep her feelings to herself. Cedric would not allow her to grieve, insisting that, as far as they were concerned, Michael had died seven years ago!

It had been extraordinarily hard for her. Unable to discuss her heartbreak with the rest of the family, she had felt terribly alone. It was hardly surprising, therefore, that when Dorothea Carstairs, her children's old nanny, paid her a visit and enquired after her erstwhile charges, Lady Cornelia had found herself pouring the whole story out. Little did she dream that the old nurse would betray her confidence like that!

What was one to do now? Her beloved grandchild was gravely ill and the one thing that might give her solace had put them all in a quandary! Lady Cornelia stood for a few moments, turning the problem over in her mind. By the time Lavinia came back in with her husband, both looking strained and worried, she had made a decision.

"I think," she said, when they came up to her, "that we really should get this girl to come and see Amanda."

"Yes, I agree," Captain Faraday declared.

"But, Mother," Lavinia argued, "we don't know where she is! We'll never find her! It's like looking for a needle in a haystack!"

"Nonsense!" her mother protested. "Anybody can be traced!"

"Oh. You mean you're going to get the police on to it?" Lavinia looked hopeful.

"The police?" her mother exclaimed. "Most certainly not! Your father would be furious! No, I was thinking more on the lines of a private detective. That is what we need. The services of the best private detective we can get!"

# 2

Malka Sternfeld tried to ignore the ringing of the doorbell. She just had to get the ironing finished while little Dovi, who was just a year old, was playing quietly with his toy bricks for a change. But there was something so persistent about the sound, as it chimed for the third time, that she felt she had no choice. With a resigned air, she placed the iron onto the sideboard, out of Dovi's reach, and went to answer the door.

The man who stood at the door was a complete stranger. A little smaller than average height, he wore a brown trilby hat and a fawn-colored trench coat and he carried a brown leather portfolio under his arm. A pair of piercing blue-green eyes peered at her from under unruly thick eyebrows. A small, brown moustache rested over thin lips, from which a lighted cigarette dangled somewhat precariously. Removing the cigarette, he stubbed it out on the outside wall and raised his hat.

"Mrs. Sternfeld?" he said, speaking with a slightly nasal voice. "My name is Hamish McDermott..." He held a card towards her. "May I have a word with you?"

Mrs. Sternfeld was about to say a curt, "I'm sorry; I'm busy," and close the door firmly in his face, but something on his card caught her notice. Under his name were the words "private investigator." What could a private investigator possibly want with her? Puzzled and bewildered, she stammered, "W-what do you want?"

"I'm here on behalf of Lady Cornelia Davenport. Does that name mean anything to you?" His look was searching.

She paled immediately. Of course she knew who that was! When she had married Michoel, she knew he was a *ger* and that he had an aristocratic background. He had changed his name to Davis and had severed all connection with his former family, only writing to them once to let them know that he had married. When Miriam was born, he had sent them a message, via an acquaintance, with no indication of where he was living and what he now called himself. He had been so determined to live his life as a steadfast, Torah-observant Jew, and he made sure nothing would happen that might interfere with this. When, two years after Miriam's birth, he had contracted pneumonia and been taken from her so quickly, she had felt, in spite of her own grief, that she ought to let his parents know and had sent them an anonymous telegram. That, she had thought, was the last time she would have anything to do with them.

What had happened now to make them contact her? And how had they found her? Even if they had discovered Michoel's name and his whereabouts, how had they connected a Mrs.

Malka Sternfeld—as she was called since she had re-married six
years ago—with the widow of their late son?

"May I come in, Mrs. Sternfeld?" Hamish McDermott's voice
seemed to come from somewhere far away. "I have something
rather important to discuss with you."

"Oh… er… yes, of course," Mrs. Sternfeld replied, her tone
flustered. Little Dovi had meanwhile crawled out of the kitchen
and was playing about at her feet. Scooping him up in her arms,
she beckoned to Mr. McDermott to follow her and she led him
into the living room.

"Take a seat," she said. "I won't be a moment. I would just
like to call my husband."

Normally she would never have disturbed Leibel while he
was working. Even now she thought twice about it, knowing he
was busy with something urgent. In his capacity as a *sofer*, he was
checking a client's tefillin and he had promised to bring them to
shul with him when he came for maariv, which didn't give him
much time. All the same, this seemed to be an urgent matter,
Malka reasoned, as she sped along to her husband's workroom at
the back of the house.

As they listened to Mr. McDermott, the Sternfelds began to
feel apprehensive, although they had no idea at first what all this
was leading up to. However, by the time he had finished and had
stated the reason for his mission, they were filled with dismay.
Mrs. Sternfeld, at a loss for words, just sat looking appalled and
her husband took charge of the situation immediately.

"I'm afraid it is quite impossible!" he declared emphatically.

Mr. McDermott looked taken aback. "But Mr. Sternfeld," he said, "how can you possibly refuse, under the circumstances?"

"Believe me, I do sympathize with Lady Davenport and her family, but I cannot allow my daughter to be subjected to such a traumatic experience!"

"Er... pardon me saying so..." There was an almost imperceptible smirk on the detective's face as he spoke. " But the girl is not, strictly speaking, your daughter..."

"Yes, she is!" Mrs. Sternfeld butted in quickly. "My husband legally adopted her and has every right to say what should happen to her. In any case, I am her mother and I totally agree with him!"

"No one is trying to take her away from you," Mr. McDermott persisted, anxious to persuade these people so that he could present the girl to Lady Davenport, and successfully complete his assignment. "It'll only be until — "

"Mr. McDermott," Mr. Sternfeld interrupted, his eye quickly sweeping over the visiting card lying on the table, "please let me explain. There are too many problems involved if a Jewish girl goes to stay in the home of a non-Jewish family. Besides which, she doesn't know much about her... er... ancestry..." he said, uttering the word hesitantly, "and I'm afraid It might be too much of a shock for her."

Unwilling to give up when success was almost in his grasp, the private detective tried as best as he could to bring them around. However, realizing eventually that they were adamant, he stood up with a resigned air and informed them that he would pass their answer on to his client. Gathering up his papers and his card, he bade them a curt "good afternoon" and left.

"Leibel, what are we going to do?" Mrs. Sternfeld cried, as soon as the door closed behind their visitor. "They'll be back in no time — I'm sure they will!" There was panic in her tone.

"You're right, Malka," her husband agreed, sighing. "Once they know our address, nothing will keep them away."

"But what shall we do? We can't just move away, lock stock and barrel, in one day, with five children and all!" Her voice rose to a hysterical pitch, causing Dovi to squirm on her lap and begin to whimper. Instinctively, she patted him comfortingly.

"No, of course we can't. But we don't really have to. It's Miriam they're after and if they can't find her they'll give up."

"But they will find her!" Mrs. Sternfeld cried, almost in tears. "They have already! She lives here!"

"Yes, that's true," Mr. Sternfeld said somberly. "That's why I've been thinking. ... Hard as it is for us, we will have to send her away for a little while."

"Oh, no!" Mrs. Sternfeld cried out. Her first reaction was one of shock and she immediately rejected the idea. But the more she thought about it, the more she realized he was right. "But where could she go?"

"I don't know," her husband replied. "Let me think. ..."

Mrs. Sternfeld's eye strayed towards the clock on the mantelpiece. "You'll have to think quickly!" she said nervously. "Miriam will be home from school soon! I really don't want her to know anything about all this."

"I think," Mr. Sternfeld commented, trying to sound calm for his wife's sake, "that we will have to tell her something. Maybe not all the details, but enough to make her understand why we are sending her away."

Mrs. Sternfeld's reply to this was to shrug dejectedly. She glanced at her husband anxiously while he sat pondering. "I know," he said after a while, "what about my sister Elke? I'm sure she'll be glad to have her. And Gateshead is far enough away to make it difficult to find her. What do you think?"

Mrs. Sternfeld nodded, if somewhat reluctantly. At least Miriam would be with family and not with strangers, she told herself, deriving some comfort from the thought.

She had a high regard for her sister-in-law, Elke Jacobson. Twelve years Leibel's senior, Elke had virtually brought him up, together with another two brothers and a sister. At the beginning of the war, their father had been arrested in Romania, where they had lived, and was never seen again. Their mother had managed to escape to Vienna and from there to England with all her children. However, being already a frail person, she had not survived long and Elke had been left to care for her siblings, continuing to do so after her marriage. Now a warm-hearted yet determined woman of forty-nine, three of her own four children were married and her eighteen-year-old son was studying in yeshiva in Eretz Yisroel. If Miriam had to be sent away, she couldn't go to a better person. Elke had time on her hands and she would be grateful for the company.

While Leibel was out of the room, putting through a long-distance call to his sister in Gateshead, Malka Sternfeld sat and reflected. Why had this cropped up now, just when life at last seemed normal? When Michoel had passed away so suddenly, she had felt as if it was the end of the world. Left all alone with a small child, she had no one to turn to. But eventually the pain had eased and, after a while, she had met Leibel and married and settled down to a happy life again. Little Miriam had grown up in a calm and secure atmosphere, with a father and mother and four siblings, just like any other Jewish child, and was now a well-balanced thirteen-year-old. How would her daughter react now? Mrs. Sternfeld wondered. Would her world suddenly be turned upside-down? If only she could protect her somehow from the shock that was coming her way!

*3*

iriam Sternfeld walked through the still unfamiliar streets of Gateshead, accompanied by her old friend, Esther Milberg, whose family had moved here from London three years previously. She had spent a pleasant afternoon at Esther's house, picking up the threads of their old friendship, and now Esther had walked her back to Aunt Elke's house.

"Here you are," Esther said, when they arrived at the gate. "I'd better hurry home before it starts getting dark." She began to walk away, waving as she went.

"'Bye, Esther," Miriam called to her. "Thanks for seeing me home. I'd surely have got lost if you hadn't!"

"Pleasure," her friend called back. "Don't worry, you'll soon get to know your way round. Goodbye, Miriam! Don't forget to give Mummy's regards to your aunt."

As Miriam watched Esther go, a wave of desolation swept over her. She stood looking at the front door, reluctant to go inside. She liked Auntie Elke and would normally have enjoyed staying here for a visit, but there was something strange about the way she had been sent off so quickly and, although they had assured her it was only for a short while, she couldn't help but fear that her visit might go on indefinitely.

Sighing deeply, Miriam tried not to wallow in homesickness, but it was no use. She missed her parents and her siblings too much. She had always known that Leibel Sternfeld was not really her father, but he was so good to her that she loved him like a father. However, she could not help being absolutely shocked by what she had been told two days ago. Her real father had not always been Jewish! Not that that really mattered. He had become a Jew—and a deeply religious one at that. It was the thought of having non-Jewish relatives that had shaken her. And to make it worse, they were looking for her—though she couldn't imagine why.

"Miss... er,,, Sternfeld?" A man seemed to step out from the shadows, startling her. Too shaken to answer, she just stared at him as he confronted her. Who was he? And how did he know her name?

"Hamish McDermott at your service," the man introduced himself hastily, bowing slightly.

"W-what do you want?" Miriam stammered, finding her voice at last.

"I have a matter of grave importance to speak to you about. I called on you in London the other day but you were not available. Please hear me out, now that I've found you. If you don't, a young girl might die because of it." McDermott spoke in a sinister voice, hoping to shock her into staying and listening. His tactics had the desired result. Miriam stared at him, making no move to run into the house.

"I don't know if you are aware of it," McDermott said, snatching his chance, "but you have a cousin—a young lady by the name of Amanda Faraday, who is dangerously ill. She is only semi-conscious and has bouts of delirium in which she is constantly calling for her only cousin… namely, yourself. The doctor thinks it might help bring about a recovery if she were to see you."

"But… but… who is this cousin? I don't know anyone with that name!" Miriam sounded bewildered.

"She is the granddaughter of the Earl of Wakebridge. Apparently your late father was her mother's brother, the Earl's only son. It was the Countess, Lady Cornelia, who asked me to find you. Naturally the family is desperate…"

Neither of them noticed the front door opening and were both startled by the voice of Elke Jacobson calling out. "Miriam! What's going on? Why aren't you coming in?"

The private detective gave an audible sigh of exasperation and Miriam, swinging round, said, "Oh, Auntie Elke!" looking and sounding utterly confused.

It did not take long for Mrs. Jacobson to realize that her interference was required. Putting the latch on the front door, she advanced down the path, a determined look on her face.

"What is the matter?" she demanded, addressing the man. "Are you looking for someone?"

"Not any more!" McDermott replied airily.

Ignoring her, he turned to Miriam and handed her a card. "Here is my card," he said. "Don't take too long thinking it over.

Remember, the matter is extremely urgent. I will call on you later on this evening."

"You will do no such thing!" Mrs. Jacobson declared firmly. "Come inside quickly, Miriam! You really shouldn't talk to strangers, you know." Swiveling her niece round, she marched her up to the house, shutting the door firmly once they were inside.

Hamish McDermott stood watching them, his lips pursed. Stubborn people, these Jews, he reflected. But I can be too! Shrugging his shoulders, he drew a packet of cigarettes out of his pocket and, selecting one, he began to light it with his lighter as he turned and walked away.

Once they were inside the house, Mrs. Jacobson closed the front door firmly and turned to face Miriam. Gone was her aggressive manner as she regarded her niece with a look of concern, noting the bewildered expression on the girl's face.

"Miriam, dear, what has that horrid man been saying to you? You look so worried!"

"Auntie Elke, is it true?" Miriam blurted out. "Is it true that my father, *olov hasholom*, was the heir to an *earl*?"

Mrs Jacobson's heart sank. Obviously Leibel and Malka hadn't told her that part of the story, which meant that they didn't want her to know about it. What was she supposed to do now?

"Is that what he told you?" she asked, hedging.

"Yes," Miriam said. "Is it true?" she persisted.

Mrs. Jacobson had to think quickly. She knew she had no right to give Miriam any information without permission from her parents, but how could she check with them now? Just saying she would need to check with her parents would give the game away in any case. At the same time, lying to the girl would not be right either.

Adopting the evasive line again, she said, "And if it is… what difference would it make to you? Would you regret being deprived of that kind of life?"

"No, of course not!" Miriam replied emphatically. "Not in the least! But if it is true, then I'm worried about it—"

"—Worried? Why?" Mrs. Jacobson eyed her niece searchingly, not quite understanding the look of anxiety in the girl's clear blue eyes.

"Don't you see, Auntie Elke? That girl the man told me about is extremely ill. If I refuse to go to her and she… if something happened to her… it would anyway make a *chillul Hashem*. But if she belongs to an influential family, they could make trouble for *all* the *yidden*!"

Mrs. Jacobson could not help a slight smile at this piece of reasoning and at Miriam's earnest expression. "I don't think it's quite like that nowadays," she said, trying not to let her amusement show. "Present day English aristocrats are not as powerful as, for instance, the Polish *porutz* used to be in olden times."

"All the same, don't you agree that I've got to go?" Miriam persisted. "How can I refuse without making a *chillul Hashem*?"

"Mmm. I do see your point of view," her aunt agreed. "But it's a problem. Your late father, *olov hasholom*, I am told, was always so particular to distance himself from his family. I'm sure the last thing he would want is for you to become involved with them."

"I know. But there's someone who is ill."

"Yes, that does rather complicate things," Elke Jacobson eased herself onto a chair by the kitchen table and sat looking thoughtful for a few moments. Presently she stood up and said, "I had better talk it over with your parents straight away, before that man turns up again."

Placing a loaf of bread onto the breadboard on the table, she took a soup bowl out of the cupboard and began to ladle some hot soup onto it from a pan on the stove. "Here you are, sweetie," she said affectionately. "Wash and have some soup while I go and phone." Giving Miriam an encouraging smile, Elke began to move towards the door. "*Ess gezunterheit,*" she said and went out, closing the door behind her.

It was quite obvious that Aunt Elke wished to speak to her brother and sister-in-law in private and, much as she was tempted to sneak up to the door and listen, Miriam knew it would not be right to do that. Restraining her urge, she sat still at the table and obediently ate her soup.

After what seemed an amazingly long time to Miriam, Mrs. Jacobson returned to the kitchen, a thoughtful look on her face.

"Your parents understand your concern about causing a *chillul Hashem,*" she said. "They are worried about that too. But they still feel they can't let you go. ..."

"But why?" Miriam could not conceal her bewilderment. "I don't understand. ..."

"You're a Jewish girl," Mrs. Jacobson explained. "It wouldn't be right for you to go into a non-Jewish home all by yourself. ..."

"But why must I go by myself?" Miriam asked. "Why can't Mummy come with me?"

"You're right, really. Your mother feels she ought to accompany you, even though it would be awkward for her to go into a house where she would normally not be accepted. But she has a baby only a year old, as well as a three-year-old and two other young children. How can she go away and leave them... especially when you're not there?"

"Yes... I see..." Miriam said, understanding the problem. "But what about Daddy? Can't he take me?"

"That's also not easy just now," Mrs. Jacobson replied, shaking her head. "He's got a lot of work on at the moment. He has to finish two sets of tefillin in time for bar mitzvahs in a few weeks time and he just can't let the people down. So that's it, I'm afraid!" She gave a resigned shrug.

But Miriam refused to give up.

"Auntie Elke," she said desperately, "can't you think of someone who could come with me? I can see why Daddy and Mummy don't want me to go, but I'd never forgive myself if someone died because of me!"

The earnest, sincere expression on the girl's face, and the pleading look she was giving her, made Mrs. Jacobson realize how much Miriam was relying on her to sort out the situation and it gave her an idea. Better not say anything yet, she told herself, resolving to speak to her husband first.

"Uncle Yehuda should be home soon," she told her niece. "Perhaps he will be able to come up with something."

Later on that evening, they were facing Hamish McDermott once again. His arrival on their doorstep had been no surprise to them but McDermott himself, half expecting to have the door slammed in his face, had been quite amazed when the formidable woman who had chased him away earlier had asked him in.

He sat opposite them at the sitting room table, wondering what their reply was going to be.

"It has been decided…" Mrs. Jacobson said, hesitating a little, "…against our better judgement, let me tell you—to let Miriam go. *But*… with certain conditions!"

"Sure! Fire away!" McDermott said enthusiastically, quite confident now that the fee Lady Cornelia had promised him would soon be in his pocket! The affluent Davenports would surely be prepared to meet this woman's monetary demands, however high they might be.

"First of all," Mrs. Jacobson began, "please make it clear to your client that my niece will not be staying at... er... what did you say the place was called?"

"Wakebridge Hall," the private detective replied, a note of reverence in his voice. "It's in the village of Wakebridge, near Huntington, in Cambridgeshire. You will like it, I'm sure," he said, addressing Miriam.

"I doubt Miriam will have much time to like it," Mrs. Jacobson commented, before Miriam had a chance to reply. "Once she presents herself to the poor girl who is ill and hopefully brings her out of her delirium, surely there will be no reason for her to stay."

McDermott shook his head, a doubtful expression on his face. "I don't know anything about that. My job was merely to find the young lady and bring her to Wakebridge. However, it seems to me that a fleeting appearance won't solve the problem. It might even make it worse. Imagine what it would be like for Miss Faraday... the sick girl... if her cousin just pops her head in—so to speak—to say 'hello' and then disappears again. No, I don't think Lady Cornelia will agree to that!"

His comments were followed by a few moments' silence, during which Mrs. Jacobson turned the matter over in her mind, while Miriam just sat eyeing her, a worried look in her eyes.

"In that case," Mrs. Jacobson said, after a while, "they will have to find a small flat somewhere nearby for us to stay in."

"Us?" McDermott regarded her questioningly.

"Yes. I shall be accompanying my niece. Her parents are adamant that she is not to go alone and, as neither of them can go with her, I have offered to do so. Please explain to the Earl and his family that she will not be able to eat anything in their house—except fruit, perhaps. You understand that she keeps the Jewish dietary laws. Also, it would not be advisable for her to spend the whole day there, so they will have to agree to her only coming in the afternoon. Apart from everything else, she is missing quite a lot of schooling and I have promised her parents to do a bit of studying with her. I used to be a teacher..." she added, by way of explanation.

Looking somewhat skeptical, Hamish McDermott stood and picked up his briefcase, tucking it under his arm in a business-like way. "I shall contact my client as soon as I am back at my hotel," he said, "and I will pass on your message. I don't know what she will say, but since this is a matter of grave urgency, please be ready to leave first thing in the morning, when I will call to give you instructions for your journey if Lady Cornelia finds your terms acceptable."

He gave a stiff bow, replacing his hat on his head. Mrs. Jacobson saw him to the door and watched for a few moments as he walked down the path with a resolute step.

$\sim$ 4 $\sim$

From her seat beside Aunt Elke at the back of the black Rolls Royce, Miriam watched the chauffeur unlock the large elaborately designed wrought iron gates of Wakebridge Hall and fling them wide open. Staring at the sight ahead of her, she was overcome for a moment by the strange sensation that she had been transported into a make-believe fantasy world. The scene she was looking at was something she had hitherto only seen in pictures. The well-mown lawns on either side of a broad, paved drive resembled soft green carpets as they stretched across a wide expanse of ground. In the center of one of the lawns, a fountain spurted out a fine spray of water onto a stone-walled lily pond, while the other lawn displayed an array of colorful flower-beds.

Gazing beyond this attractive sight, Miriam could see the house itself, its splendor almost taking her breath away! It must be a few hundred years old, she thought, taking in the pillars supporting a porch over the wide front door and the rounded turret-like brickwork and large curved windows on either side of the door.

It was difficult to believe that she was actually about to enter this impressive building!

And yet, overawed though she was, she was not looking forward to going inside.

It had been a long and tiring journey from Gateshead to this village in Cambridgeshire. They had had to change trains twice, and by the time they arrived at Wakebridge's quaint little railway station, she and Aunt Elke were quite exhausted.

They had been met at the station by a rather pompous man with a handlebar moustache. He was wearing a maroon, gold-trimmed jacket and a flat cap to match, which he raised slightly on approaching them. He introduced himself as Morley, the chauffeur at Wakebridge Hall.

"I have been told to take you first to your flat in the High Street and then bring the young lady straight to the Hall," he told them, as he picked up their suitcases, grimacing at their size and weight.

"What… already?" Mrs. Jacobson exclaimed, not bothering to explain that the reason for the excessive amount of baggage was because they had to bring dishes and plenty of food with them. "My niece is extremely tired from the long journey. Can't it wait until tomorrow?"

"I'm afraid not," the chauffeur replied. "Under the circumstances, you understand, no time can be wasted."

"Yes… I see…" Mrs. Jacobson agreed. "Miss Sternfeld… er… my niece…" she said, hastening to make herself clear as she noticed the man's puzzled look, "is naturally a little nervous. However, we will do as you say and come at once."

"Er… pardon me, madam…" Morley said, his tone clipped. "My instructions were to *only* bring the young lady!"

"Excuse me, instructions or not," Mrs. Jacobson retorted assertively, "my niece is *not* going without me!"

The determination in her tone belied her feeling of apprehension. Weary after the long journey, she hoped her statement would not involve her in a lengthy argument. However, she would not give in!

Last night, she had had another telephone conversation with her brother and he had told her that on no account was she to allow Miriam to go unaccompanied into the house and be alone with those people. If they refused to accept this condition, she and Miriam would have to turn round immediately and return home!

Morley pushed back his cap and scratched his head, looking perplexed. What should he do now? He was used to obeying orders and now he was in quite a predicament. Lady Cornelia had told him specifically just to bring the girl, but if he insisted on doing that he might end up coming back without her at all.

After a few moments, he gave a resigned shrug and began to walk off towards the car with the suitcases, putting them down from time to time to stretch his arms and giving an exaggerated puff every time he picked them up again. Mrs. Jacobson and Miriam followed him, not quite sure what was happening.

As soon as they reached the shiny black Rolls Royce, the chauffeur opened the car trunk and lifted the luggage into it, making a great show of checking the sides of the car to make sure the cumbersome suitcases had not scratched them at all. Only when he had closed and locked the trunk did he usher his passengers into the car.

Miriam might have enjoyed the drive through the winding lanes of this picturesque village, were she not so unbearably tense and apprehensive. What had she let herself in for? Everything seemed so unreal! Was she dreaming or was this really happening?

Before long, they had reached what was undoubtedly the High Street. Both sides of the curved street were lined with shops, mostly in the quaint style of Victorian times, while one or two shops had obviously been modernized. Morley stopped the car outside a pretty, "Olde Worlde"-type flower shop and got out. Taking a key out of his pocket, he unlocked a door at the side of the shop and went to open the trunk of the car.

"If you will, please wait in the car," he told his passengers. "I will take the luggage upstairs, then take you straight to the Hall."

Now, as they sat waiting for Morley to come back into the car, Miriam grasped her aunt's hand, a sudden wave of panic coming over her. She felt so far away from everything that was familiar to her... her family, her friends, her usual surroundings. It was almost as though she had been taken to another planet! Understanding her feelings, Aunt Elke gave her hand a reassuring squeeze.

Soon, Morley returned and they continued their drive through the town and then the beautiful countryside. Now, as they drove down the drive towards the house, the building seemed to grow bigger and more imposing! Miriam trembled a little as they arrived right in front of the steps leading up to a wide mahogany door. Morley hooted the horn and got out of the car. The door was suddenly opened by a tallish man with grey-ing hair that was brushed neatly back. He wore pin-striped trousers and a dark grey waistcoat over a white shirt, with a black bow-tie at the neck. Was this the earl? Miriam wondered.

Morley hurried up the steps towards him and spoke to him quietly. The man tilted his head to one side and scratched his ear, looking as perplexed as the chauffeur had done before. Then he too gave a resigned shrug and held the door open with a little affected bow.

Morley returned to the car and opened the side door.

"Here we are, Miss," he said, addressing Miriam and point-edly ignoring Aunt Elke. "Welcome to Wakebridge Hall! Rivers, the butler, will take care of you now. I have to go and pick up His Lordship from the golf course. He must be getting a bit impatient by now!" He touched his cap and, slipping back into the driving seat, he turned the car round and drove off.

Feeling a little disoriented, Miriam watched him drive away and then turned back to face Rivers, who stood at the top of the wide marble steps, beckoning to them to come up. With some trepidation, she allowed Aunt Elke to lead her as they followed the butler into the house.

"Wait here, please, while I tell Her Ladyship that you have arrived," Rivers said and hurried away, leaving them standing in the hall.

If she found the outside of the house impressive, Miriam was almost bowled over by the luxury of the wide hall she was stand-ing in. Fully fitted with a deep, soft carpet in purple with black swirls, it was tastefully furnished with an intricately carved, mir-rored hall-stand near the door and two armchairs covered in a thick material with a delicate floral design, that stood by one wall, on either side of an onyx occasional table. Large ceramic pots with leafy plants were placed here and there and at the far end, the staircase with its intricate balustrade seemed to sweep down, curving round to reveal the last three steps.

Miriam's feeling of unreality was further enhanced by the elegant elderly woman who was walking towards her. Of average height and slim build, she wore a silk, emerald green robe, and her silvery, immaculately styled hair was swept away from her face into a neatly coiled bun at the back of her head.

Miriam did not need to be told that this was Lady Davenport. She resembled so closely the mental picture that Miriam had had in her mind. As she was looking at Lady Cornelia, she tried to remember what her aunt had told her about addressing her. She had never spoken with royalty before. She knew that as an earl's wife, Lady Cornelia was also a countess. Could she then address her as Countess Davenport? She would have to ask her aunt later.

Lady Cornelia's reaction at the first sight of Miriam, however, was quite the opposite. The girl was not what she had expected at all! Demure-looking, with fair hair held back in two plaits, her navy raincoat open to reveal a high-necked blue and white checked blouse and a navy skirt, she was so utterly different from the girls Amanda associated with… boisterous types with up-to-the-minute hairstyles and flashy clothes. This girl seemed positively dull in comparison.

The fairly tall, broad-shouldered woman who had accompanied the girl looked equally out of place amidst the elegance of Wakebridge Hall. As the countess disdainfully eyed her beige belted coat, her brown felt hat and the large bulging handbag she carried, she felt considerably irritated. Why did she have to come too? It was nothing but a nuisance! Of course, at the same time she understood not wanting to let a young girl stay with total strangers by herself. In any case, she told herself, with Amanda's life at stake, she could not afford to be choosy. However, there was no reason why she should have to acknowledge the woman's presence.

As Lady Cornelia came towards Miriam, her hand outstretched, she felt a momentary sense of shock. This girl she was regarding so disapprovingly was Michael's daughter! Her own granddaughter, in fact! How could she be expected to accept that?

And yet, when she reached her and looked into her candid blue eyes, she found herself inexplicably drawn towards her. There was something appealing about this honest-looking, unsophisticated girl. She grasped her hand and had some difficulty resisting a sudden urge to bend forward and kiss her.

"Good afternoon and welcome... er... Miriam... that is your name, is it not? I am Lady Davenport."

"Pleased to meet you, Lady Davenport," Miriam replied dutifully.

"Thank you so much for coming," Lady Cornelia said, uncharacteristic warmth in her voice. "I know it wasn't easy for you, but you do understand—"

She stopped in mid-sentence as one of the downstairs doors opened and Lavinia Faraday walked into the hall. "Oh, here is my daughter, Lady Lavinia—Amanda's mother," she explained.

"Miriam is here, Lavinia," she announced. "Shall we take her straight upstairs?"

Lavinia walked toward them and eyed Miriam with a guarded look, barely concealing her dismay. Was this frumpy-looking girl really her niece—her brother Michael's daughter? In her mind, she rejected the relationship and wondered whether the whole thing had been a waste of time and money. How would Mandy react to someone she had so little in common with? What if she were disappointed at finding that the cousin she was dreaming about was not what she expected? Could it make her *worse* instead of curing her? Well, it was too late to worry about that now. The girl was here already. But who is that woman with her? she wondered, looking at her mother quizzically. Lady Cornelia's reply was an almost imperceptible shrug. Mrs. Jacobson—realizing she was somewhat in the way—crossed the hall and sat down on one of the armchairs, taking her embroidery out of her bag.

Attempting to quell her misgivings, Lavinia led the way to the staircase. Miriam and Lady Cornelia followed her and, as they climbed the stairs, Miriam looked down at the hall, casting a longing glance at her aunt. The higher she went, the further away Auntie Elke seemed to be!

They reached the top of the stairs and Miriam had an impression of more grandeur as she briefly surveyed the upstairs landing, with its many doors. Paintings hung on the walls and a few more ceramic pots, filled with silk flowers and leaves, stood here and there. There was too little time to take it all in properly as Lavinia hurried to one of the doors and opened it, beckoning to Miriam to enter.

Miriam stood back to allow Lady Cornelia to precede her, feeling apprehensive as she followed her in. The room, she noted, was quite colorful. The walls, decorated with an abstract-patterned wallpaper in orange and green, displayed various poster-like pictures of people. Miriam wondered vaguely who they were. Her eyes strayed towards the bed in the center of the room. The multi-colored heavy bedspread was neatly folded back and, propped up slightly on large pillows, lay a girl with fair curls clinging to her forehead and framing her face. She was quite pale and her eyes were closed but she kept throwing her head to and fro, mumbling incoherently.

So this was Amanda, Miriam thought, overcome with concern as she watched the girl's mother bend over her. After a moment, Lavinia straightened up and signaled to Miriam to come closer. Feeling a little nervous, Miriam allowed Lady Cornelia to take her hand and lead her towards the bed.

"Mandy, darling," Lavinia spoke tenderly, "your cousin is here. She has come to see you."

Mandy stopped her head-tossing and her mumbling and lay extremely still for a while. Then her eyelids opened and she glanced around at the three people standing by her bed, until her gaze settled on Miriam. She stared at her for a few moments, while Lady Cornelia and her daughter looked on with bated breath. What would her reaction be? they wondered fearfully.

And then, to their surprise, a contented smile hovered about her lips.

"Hello," she said weakly. "Are you really my cousin? What's your name?"

"Yes, I am your cousin," Miriam replied, "and my name is Miriam."

"Miriam," Mandy repeated faintly. "That's a nice name." She went on eyeing her for a few minutes, and then, with the smile still on her face, she closed her eyes.

"You're tired, sweetie," her mother said, plumping up the pillows and smoothing the duvet gently. "Go back to sleep now. Miriam will come again tomorrow."

"Can't she stay?" Mandy whispered. "I don't want her to go away!"

As calmly as she could, Lavinia explained to her daughter that there was no point in Miriam staying now as Mandy was too tired to talk to her. Lavinia repeated her promise that Miriam would return the next day. Mandy nodded slightly and closed her eyes again, a satisfied and relaxed look on her face.

They tiptoed softly out of the room and Lavinia closed the door quietly, heaving a deep sigh.

"I think it has done the trick," Lady Cornelia said optimistically, and her daughter nodded. "Let's hope so," she said.

Miriam followed them towards the staircase, trying her best to stifle a yawn. The journey had been so tiring and the events that had followed had been so overwhelming that she suddenly felt completely drained.

Lady Cornelia, walking in front of her, turned round and noticed how tired Miriam looked. "You poor child!" she exclaimed. "You must be exhausted! And you haven't had anything to eat. Come downstairs and sit down and I will send for some tea and cake. We could all do with some!"

"Oh, no!" Miriam cried hastily. "I can't… I mean, I mustn't—" she broke off, not sure how to explain her refusal.

"Oh yes," Lady Cornelia said, suddenly remembering that the girl was not allowed to eat anything in their house. "I have been told about it. But surely you can make an exception, once in a while, can't you?"

Too weary to start explaining, Miriam just shook her head.

Lady Cornelia nodded resignedly. She would never understand this way of life.

She would have liked to sit down and talk to this girl for a little while and learn more about her, but with this relative sitting and waiting for Miriam, she did not feel able to do that. She wished Morley would return already so that he would take them to the flat.

To her relief, it was only a few moments later that the front door was suddenly flung open and an elderly man strode in, with the chauffeur behind him. Fairly tall and broad, he had a red face and a large white moustache. Miriam realized that this intimidating-looking man was Lord Davenport. Rivers, the butler, came forward and took his hat and cape, hanging them up on the coat-stand.

The Earl nodded to his wife and eyed Miriam quizzically.

"Cedric," Lady Cornelia said, "this is Miriam. She's Michael's daughter."

"*Whose* daughter?" Lord Davenport's tone was cold and the word he stressed seemed loaded with meaning. With a dismissive shrug, he turned away from them and walked over to a cabinet in the corner, pouring himself some whisky in a heavy crystal glass.

Lady Cornelia turned to Miriam apologetically, despair in her eyes. "Morley will take you home now," she said, keeping her voice steady with effort. "Goodbye, Miriam. We'll see you tomorrow, then?"

"Yes, of course," Miriam promised, as she and Mrs. Jacobson followed Morley to the door.

They were fairly quiet on the way, hardly daring to express their views with the chauffeur sitting in front of them. At last, he pulled up outside the flower shop, getting out of the car to open the door for them.

Mrs. Jacobson unlocked the door at the side of the shop and she and Miriam wearily climbed the stairs to their flat. The little hall was completely filled with suitcases and they had to climb over them to get inside. Then they stood and surveyed their surroundings.

In spite of being rather small, it was actually quite a cozy flat. The hall was decorated with a pretty floral wallpaper. An ornate gilt-framed mirror hung on the wall and a coat-stand stood in one corner. There were two small bedrooms and a neat living room that also served as the kitchen. Blue and white checked curtains hung on either side of a curved lattice window, under which there were two easy chairs. A wooden table and four chairs stood by one wall, next to a small sideboard, while the other side featured a stove, a stainless-steel sink and a compact unit with cupboard space underneath.

Miriam longed to sink onto one of the easy chairs but Aunt Elke informed her that, tired as they were, they had to *kasher* the kitchen and cover the surfaces before they could unpack their crockery and have something to eat.

They set to work at once, *kashering* the stove according to the instructions Mr. Jacobson had given his wife and pouring boiling hot water onto the sink before covering it with aluminum foil. It was only when they had covered all the surfaces and spread an oil-cloth onto the table, which they had already lined with paper, that Aunt Elke took out the cups, saucers, plates and cutlery. From another bag, she drew out a loaf of bread, placing it on the table with a bread knife and a small salt shaker. The flat was already beginning to look a bit more like home!

"Come on," Aunt Elke said, her tiredness having apparently disappeared. "Let's wash and have something to eat."

Miriam felt her tension gradually ebbing away as she and Aunt Elke sat together cozily, discussing the day's events as they ate.

It was now almost a week since they had come to Wakebridge, and to Miriam the time seemed to drag. The mornings hadn't been too bad. She and Aunt Elke had filled in the time davening and enjoying eating breakfast together, then going over Miriam's schoolbooks to make up for lost time. It was the afternoons that bored her. She spent two tedious hours every day sitting at Mandy's bedside, desperately searching for things to talk about. Sometimes Lady Cornelia or Lady Lavinia would come in for a few moments, but they seemed more interested in making sure Mandy was not becoming overtired than they were in making conversation with Miriam.

Miriam was beginning to feel less intimidated by her strange surroundings, but she was becoming impatient to go home. She missed her parents and her siblings and she longed to see them again. If only her contact with them were not so limited! There was no telephone in the little flat and she had to rely on the public telephone in a booth at the other end of the street. Sometimes it was occupied and she had to stand around waiting for her turn. Then there were times when two or three people were waiting to use it, fidgeting impatiently, and she had been forced to cut her conversation short.

How long was this situation going to last? she wondered. Mandy, though still terribly weak, seemed to be improving. Two days ago, however, when Miriam had tentatively mentioned going home, Mandy had immediately become hysterical, and had ended up lying back on her pillows, her eyes closed, breathing heavily. Her mother came rushing in, looking frantic with worry and had sent a maid to call the doctor immediately. Miriam could not help the feeling that Mandy's outburst was her way of getting what she wanted and she had the impression that Lady Cornelia, who had also arrived on the scene, thought so too. The old lady said nothing, but she stood looking on with pursed lips.

Having calmed her daughter down somewhat, Lavinia turned to Miriam and begged her to assure Mandy that she was not going away. A little afraid that it might have been a genuine relapse, Miriam had not dared to refuse and had done as she had been asked. Mandy had relaxed then, but she had not perked up entirely. She lay on the pillows, looking listless. The doctor had arrived and had made his pronouncement.

"She has not fully recovered yet," he said, "and it is important to keep her as calm as possible."

Miriam was beginning to feel trapped. She wondered if she

would ever get away. Today was Tuesday and she and Aunt Elke had hoped to be home again for Shabbos, even though Uncle Yehuda had promised to come down for Shabbos if they were still there. Things had been really difficult last Shabbos. Lady Cornelia and her daughter had adamantly refused to excuse her from coming and when she told them that she and her aunt would have to walk there and back they had eyed her with distinct disapproval.

Now, as she made her way upstairs, she wondered how Mandy would be today. Yesterday, only a day after her bout of hysteria, she had been sitting in an armchair and had seemed quite lively and talkative.

Half expecting Mandy to be sitting in the chair again, she was disappointed to find her in bed. However, she seemed quite animated and her face was a rosy pink.

"Some of my friends came today," she told Miriam excitedly. "It's a shame you weren't here to meet them. They're a lively bunch! We had a jolly good time!"

"That's nice," Miriam said, glad that she *hadn't* been there. She had a feeling she would have very little in common with Mandy's friends and she certainly had no desire to meet them. "But aren't you tired now?"

"Yes, I am, a bit," Mandy admitted. "But never mind. I can sleep later. What shall we do today?"

"What would you like to do?"

"Do you know how to play Scrabble?" Mandy asked.

"Of course I do. I play quite often with my friends at home," Miriam told her. "Do you want to have a game now?"

"Yes, I would. You'll find the Scrabble in the bottom drawer of the chest of drawers."

Miriam fetched the game and took it over to the bed. They

played for half-an-hour, until Miriam, waiting for Mandy to take her turn after she had made her own move, realized that her companion was fast asleep, her head lolling to one side. Having all those visitors has tired her out, Miriam told herself. I'd better let her sleep.

Carefully removing Mandy's back-rest, she laid her back gently. Then, as noiselessly as she could, she tidied away the Scrabble and crept out of the room.

On her way downstairs, she could see Aunt Elke, bending over her Tehillim, oblivious to her surroundings. She had obviously not noticed her niece coming down and Miriam knew she could not call out to her here. She was about to walk towards her when she met Rivers, coming out of one of the rooms.

"Are you looking for anyone, Miss?" he asked solicitously.

"I… er… I was wondering if Mr. Morley could take us home now," Miriam stammered shyly. "Miss Amanda has fallen asleep —she's very tired today—so there's no point in me staying…"

"I'm afraid Morley's not here yet," Rivers told her. "He's driven down to London to pick up His Lordship from the House of Lords. He was expecting to be back to take you home at the usual time, though." His tone implied that Miriam's desire to go early was a bit of a nuisance. "We had better ask Her Ladyship what to do. She's in the drawing room."

Leaving Miriam standing in the hall, he went up to the drawing room door and knocked, going in when he heard Lady Cornelia's "come in."

Aunt Elke had meanwhile become aware of Miriam's presence and had put away her Tehillim and come towards her, an inquiring look on her face.

At that moment, Lady Cornelia and the butler emerged from the room.

"What's the problem, Miriam?" Lady Cornelia asked. "Is Amanda alright?"

"Yes, she is fine," Miriam assured her, "but she's fallen asleep. She was awfully tired while we were playing Scrabble. She told me some of her friends came to visit this morning..."

"Yes, they did," Lady Cornelia said, her lips set in a disapproving line. "Noisy lot! I'm not surprised she was tired."

"I hope I was right to leave her sleeping..." Miriam said tentatively.

"Of course you were. Very sensible of you. But I'm afraid you can't go home just yet. Morley's not back from London for another half-an-hour, at least."

"We could go home by bus," Miriam said. "We're not really used to being driven about in a car, in any case."

An amused smile crossed Lady Cornelia's face. "I know you're not," she said, "but you're not in a big town now, my dear child. This is a small village, where buses only run every few hours!"

"Perhaps we could call a taxi," Mrs. Jacobson suggested, speaking for the first time.

Lady Cornelia winced, feeling irritated once again. Although she hadn't planned it, she realized that this situation would be a perfect opportunity for her to talk to Miriam a bit and get to know her better. But how could she do that with this woman present?

The suggestion the aunt had made did not meet with her approval either. They were not in the habit of calling taxis to Wakebridge Hall. They had a perfectly good car, and an excellent chauffeur. Furthermore, Lavinia had her own car... although that did not help at the moment, as Lavinia was out. A taxi being called to the Hall—and to pick up two strange

there! On the other side of the street she could see the pony and trap they had come home in the previous day, with the same horseman in the driver's seat.

"Miriam," Lady Cornelia said at once, "I've come to take you for a drive round the village. How about it?"

"Oh... er... I-I don't know," Miriam stammered, nonplussed. "I would have to ask my aunt. But she's not in just now."

"Oh, that is a pity," Lady Cornelia said, sounding disappointed. "It's quite a pleasant drive and today is such a beautiful day. This is really a lovely village. I was looking forward to showing you round it."

"I'm sorry," Miriam said lamely, not knowing what else to say.

It occurred to Lady Cornelia that perhaps it was not such a disappointment after all. Since the aunt was not at home, she would still be able to have her talk with Miriam — without the girl being distracted by the countryside scenery.

"May I come in?" she asked gently.

"Oh... yes, of course!" Miriam replied hastily, hoping she hadn't appeared rude. Holding the door open wider, she allowed Lady Cornelia to precede her up the stairs, then led her into the living room.

"You *have* made it look cozy!" Lady Cornelia declared, her eyes sweeping round the room. She noted the foil coverings everywhere in the kitchen but refrained from commenting. It was obviously something to do with their religion and having it explained to her would only drive home the fact that Miriam was out of her reach!

Miriam offered Lady Cornelia a cup of tea, which she politely refused. Nevertheless, Miriam placed a plate of Aunt Elke's biscuits in front of her, as well as another plate with fruit.

Watching her, the countess felt a surge of affection sweep over her. This well-mannered girl had such depth of character—much more than Amanda, who was rather self-centered and selfish. Of course, she dearly loved her young granddaughter but she could not help comparing them. And besides, Miriam was also her granddaughter! Involuntarily, she sighed. How unfair it was! Here was this pleasant, intelligent girl standing right in front of her, yet there was an immense distance between them! Lady Cornelia was suddenly overcome by a desire to draw Miriam close.

"Miriam," she said softly, gazing intently at the girl as she sat down opposite her. "Amanda is not my only grandchild. I am your grandmother too, you know."

Miriam looked down, not sure what to say. A wave of panic engulfed her—a feeling that a net was closing around her! She must try to get out of it before it was too late!

"Lady Davenport..." she began, struggling to find the right words.

"Can you not call me 'grandmother'?"

Miriam looked up at her, a pleading look in her eyes, but could only shake her head.

"I know," Lady Cornelia said, trying to sound understanding, "it's all a bit too sudden for you. Naturally you need time to get used to the idea. But stay with us a little longer. Don't rush away too soon. We need to get to know each other. ..."

"But I can't!" the words came rushing out at last. "I miss my parents and my sister and brothers. And my aunt has to get back home too. As soon as Mandy is well enough we've got to go!"

"Yes, I see," Lady Cornelia said, determined to keep trying. "But at least promise you'll come back to us from time to time. You know you'll always be welcome at Wakebridge Hall."

"Thank you," Miriam said, remembering her manners, "but

you must understand that I wouldn't really be able to stay in your house."

"Why not?" Lady Cornelia persisted. "I could order kosher food for you from London and you wouldn't be expected to stay here over your Sabbath. You could come during the week. Think about it, Miriam. You could have your own room there. You can even choose the way you would like it to be decorated…"

A sudden picture flashed through Miriam's mind of her bedroom, back home in London, a room that she shared with her five-year-old sister Deenie. The walls, badly in need of a coat of paint, had scribblings all over them and the chest of drawers was supported on one side by the two previous years' telephone directories because a foot had broken off. Then, before she knew it, she was picturing an attractive room in Wakebridge Hall and she found herself trying to decide on a color scheme. Blue and yellow, perhaps? Or maybe peach and lilac?

A shock wave suddenly washed over her, making her go hot and cold. Ribono Shel Olom! What was she thinking of? She could not believe she was actually considering the idea!

Was the *yetzer hara* working on her already? It wasn't even as if she secretly desired to have a room in that grand house. She missed her admittedly shabby bedroom at home and longed to be back there. Then why had she allowed herself to have those thoughts, even for a moment? Overcome with guilt, Miriam wished she could ask her visitor to leave. Of course, she could not do anything so ill-mannered and she certainly didn't want to give this aristocratic lady a bad impression of *yidden*!

To her relief, she could hear Auntie Elke plodding up the stairs and letting herself into the flat a moment later.

Mrs. Jacobson's eyebrows shot up in surprise at the sight of Lady Cornelia.

"Good morning," she said, her tone questioning.

"Good morning," Lady Cornelia replied, standing up. "I came to ask Miriam if she would come for a drive round the village with me. Would you allow her to come?"

"I'm afraid not," Mrs. Jacobson said firmly, hoping she didn't sound rude. "Miriam has been missing quite a lot of school work being here and I promised her parents that she wouldn't fall behind with it."

"I see," Lady Cornelia said stiffly. What a strict person! she thought to herself. In some ways she admired Mrs. Jacobson for her strength of character and her dedication, but at the same time it increased her resentment. That woman was standing between her and her granddaughter!

Bidding them "good day," Lady Cornelia left the flat. Climbing into the carriage, she instructed Hopkins to take her home, now considerably strengthened in her resolve to bring Miriam around somehow!

Aware that her aunt was eyeing her questioningly, Miriam hurried off to her bedroom, calling over her shoulder that she was going to fetch her school books. Her mind was in such a state of confusion that she just could not face Auntie Elke at that moment. What was happening to her? Had she made a mistake coming to Wakebridge at all? Was the atmosphere of wealth around her starting to influence her? No, she told herself. It definitely was not! Then why had those thoughts occurred to her? The nagging voice of her guilt feeling went on and on in her mind. If only she could drive it out!

Miriam knew one thing. She must get away as soon as possible, in case, *chas v'sholom,* the *yetzer hara* really did get hold of her! Was this why her parents had not wanted her to come here? Even Aunt Elke had been against it. It had been Miriam herself who had persuaded them all. Perhaps she had been wrong after all. But she had only meant it for the best!

Aunt Elke had been so unbelievably kind, coming all this way to look after her and protect her from all the bad influences. What would Aunt Elke say when she told her about her conversation with Lady Cornelia and all her mixed-up feelings? She would surely be most disapproving and would probably reprimand Miriam sharply.

She imagined her aunt giving her a stern lecture and realized suddenly that she could not bear the thought. It was bad enough that her own conscience was doing that to her already! No, she decided, it would be much better if Auntie Elke knew nothing about it!

Pulling herself together, she brought her books to the table and, with a determined air, sat down. Mrs. Jacobson gave Miriam a puzzled look, wondering why she made no reference to Lady Cornelia's visit. Obviously, the countess had said something to upset Miriam. However, she refrained from asking her about it. No doubt Miriam would tell her about it when she was ready to, she reflected, unaware of the torment raging in the girl's mind.

Still feeling tense, Miriam climbed the stairs of Wakebridge Hall that afternoon and knocked on the door to Amanda's room. She had found it extremely difficult to concentrate on her lesson earlier and she could tell her aunt was aware that something was wrong.

"Perhaps we should give lessons a miss today," Aunt Elke had suggested. "You seem a bit tired."

"No, no," Miriam had protested. Having more time to brood was the last thing she wanted! "I don't want to get behind with my school work," she had declared and bent over her textbook, determined to give it her full attention, though the effort exhausted her.

Now, as she went into Mandy's room, she struggled to overcome her weariness.

Mandy, in complete contrast, seemed livelier than ever! Wearing a pretty floral dressing gown, her fair hair brushed up and tied on top of her head with a blue ribbon, she was sitting by a small table, on which the Scrabble game was already set out.

"Hi!" she greeted Miriam cheerfully. "Sorry I fell asleep in the middle of the game yesterday. It must have been such a bore for you!"

"Not really. I could see you were tired. You must have been a bit too lively with your friends."

"Maybe," Mandy agreed. "But Mummy and Grandma seemed to be worried about me."

"Were they? How do you know?" Miriam asked, surprised. Lady Cornelia hadn't seemed unduly concerned when she spoke to her.

"Well, they came creeping in… ever so quietly." Mandy mimicked their movements mischievously. "I was still feeling a bit dozy and couldn't be bothered to open my eyes, so I pretended to be still asleep."

"Did you? That was a bit naughty!" Miriam could not help smiling at the girl's audacity.

"Yes, I know!" Mandy chuckled. "But it was fun. They didn't know I could hear what they were saying and they talked about you."

"About me?" Miriam exclaimed, alarm bells ringing in her mind.

"Yes, Grandma was saying she hoped to persuade you to stay here, or at least come here from time to time. Mummy said you never would because she said that you're too committed to your religion. But Grandma says she was sure she could change all that with a bit of gentle persuasion…"

Miriam was horrified! Could Lady Cornelia really have said that?

"Mandy," she began, determined to make her position clear, "it's not true! She would never be able to do that!"

But Mandy was hardly listening to her. She was busy trying to remember the exact wording of the conversation she had overheard.

"They talked about Uncle Michael... your father," she went on. "Grandma said she blamed Grandpa for being so heavy-handed. If not for that, Uncle Michael might not have gone away and she would have worked on him gradually to make him give up the whole idea."

"He wouldn't have!" Miriam declared emphatically. "And I'm also not going to change!"

"Don't say that!" Mandy said plaintively. "I don't want you to go away *ever*!"

"Look, Mandy," Miriam spoke firmly, "you'll have to accept the fact that I *will* be going... and soon! I can't stay here long. It's too difficult for me."

"But why? What's so difficult here?" Mandy asked petulantly.

"Well, for one thing I'm missing school! I can't miss too much, you know! Plus I really miss my sister and brothers and my Mum and Dad. Mandy, there are so many reasons it's difficult for me here! You know, I live so differently than you live. It's also impossible to find kosher food here and awful to spend Shabbos without my friends or family."

"It's not fair!" Mandy said sulkily. She sat pouting for a few moments, but then her face brightened. "Well I'm not giving up hope that you'll change your mind. Grandma said that a Mr. McSomething-or-other told her that your family lives quite simply and she's sure you won't be able to resist the tempting offers she intends to make you."

Miriam's heart sank. Oh, no! she cried inwardly. Is this going to happen again? Am I going to end up having more fights with my conscience?

Suddenly she realized there was only one thing she could do. She must get away from here as quickly as possible. There was nothing really to keep her there. She had done what she could for Mandy—and had hopefully avoided causing a *chillul Hashem*— but she felt no bond with the girl she had helped, in spite of the fact that she was her cousin.

The realization suddenly hit her that Mandy was her only true cousin, since her mother was an only child. There were plenty of cousins on her stepfather's side and though they were not actually blood relations she felt extremely close to them. But Mandy, as well as Lord and Lady Davenport and Lady Lavinia, her own father's parents and sister, seemed to belong to another world—a world that her father had left. Although she did not remember her father at all, she was grateful to him because it was a world she was happy not to be a part of!

She would pluck up her courage before leaving the house and tell Lady Cornelia that she would not come back. It would not be easy, she knew, but it had to be done!

She ought to start by telling Mandy, she decided. However, before the words had a chance to come out, she was struck by the thought that it would not be a good idea. Mandy might have another fit of hysteria, causing a general panic and Miriam might, once again, be trapped into promising to stay. No, Mandy had better not know of her intentions.

"Come on, Mandy," she said with forced cheerfulness, "let's have that game of Scrabble now."

"Okay!" the younger girl said enthusiastically, "and *I'm* going to win this time!"

Her mind in a turmoil, Miriam could hardly concentrate on the game. It soon became obvious that Mandy was winning and, quite unaware of her companion's preoccupation, she threw herself into the game with gusto, looking triumphant when they counted up the score.

Before she had a chance to suggest another game, Miriam yawned and stood up.

"I'm really tired," she said. "Do you mind if I go now? It's almost time in any case."

Mandy nodded indulgently, still basking in the glory of her success. "See you tomorrow," she said.

Stopping herself from saying 'maybe,' Miriam went out and hurried down the stairs to tell Auntie Elke about her intention. She couldn't tell her, here in this house, what she had heard, but she hoped her aunt would come with her and back her up.

However, before she had a chance to cross the hall, she encountered the butler.

"Are you ready to go home?" he asked. "Would you like me to find Morley?"

"Yes, soon," Miriam replied. "But I would like to have a quick word with Lady Davenport... or Lady Faraday... first."

"I'm afraid they are both out," Rivers told her. "And so is Lord Davenport. They have all gone to attend a banquet and will not be back for two hours."

Miriam was not sure whether she was relieved or disappointed. In some ways the temporary reprieve from her ordeal was welcome. She was not looking forward to the interview, even with her aunt's support. On the other hand, now it was still hanging over her head. She would have preferred it to be over already.

Rivers went off to summon Morley and, before long, Miriam and Mrs. Jacobson were on their way back to the flat, where they could discuss the situation in private. All of a sudden Miriam was overcome by a desire to pour her heart out to her aunt, telling her of her predicament.

Mrs. Jacobson sat listening silently as Miriam recounted the conversation she had had with Lady Cornelia that morning, as well as what Mandy had told her she had overheard. When her niece had finished, she said, "Miriam! Why didn't you tell me about this before?"

Miriam gazed at her aunt for a moment, a flush appearing on her face. Then her eyes filled with tears and suddenly, without warning, she began to cry, putting her head down on her arms. Mrs. Jacobson left her seat and sat down next to Miriam, putting her arm across the girl's shoulders.

"Miriam, darling, tell me what's the matter," she said gently.

"Oh, Auntie Elke, I'm too ashamed to tell you!" Miriam sobbed.

"Ashamed? Why? What have you done?" Aunt Elke asked, alarmed.

All at once the words began to tumble out. Miriam told her about her feeling of guilt over her momentary thoughts and how frightened she was that it would happen again.

"You silly girl!" Aunt Elke said, smiling encouragingly at her. "It's nothing to feel guilty about! We can't always help the thoughts that cross our minds and it doesn't necessarily mean that we feel that way. You should have told me how you felt straight away! Now just forget about it. You've got the right *kavanah*, and that's all that matters!"

Miriam looked up at her aunt with an expression of relief and gave her a teary smile.

"You are quite right, though, about having to get away from there," Mrs. Jacobson said, her tone practical. "I think you will have to tell them straight away, tomorrow."

"Y-yes," Miriam said, her nervousness returning.

"I know you would like me to be with you when you talk to them," Aunt Elke said, aware of her niece's tension. "But if I am they will say that I am forcing you to do this. I really think it's best if it comes from you yourself, however difficult it will be for you. I will be nearby, in any case, and I can always come and help you out, but I'm sure you're brave enough to carry it through without me!"

# 8

"Miriam! What's the matter with you?" Mandy asked crossly. "You've not been listening to a word!" Mandy was reading out loud some of the get well cards she had received during her illness and she suddenly became aware of Miriam's detached expression.

"Yes, of course I'm listening, Mandy," Miriam protested, though, in truth, her mind was miles away. She was thinking of the difficult interview awaiting her and she fervently hoped her courage would not fail her. It had been different yesterday when, still in a state of shock from what she had heard, she was ready to charge straight into battle. Now, after some time had elapsed, she was extremely nervous, even though she still felt the same.

"Well, you don't *look* as if you're listening!" Mandy complained. "What's the matter with you?"

Pulling herself together, Miriam made a sudden decision. She *would* tell Mandy that she was leaving. Even if the girl became hysterical or threw a tantrum it could not do her much harm. She was obviously much stronger now and unlikely to lapse back into her former state of delirium. Even the most doting parent would not be too concerned.

"Mandy," she said tentatively, "I want to tell you something…"

"Yes? What is it?" Mandy said, looking interested.

"The thing is… er… please don't be upset… but you see—"

"—You're going home," Mandy stated in a matter-of-fact tone.

Miriam stared at her. This reaction was the last thing she had expected. "You… you don't mind?" she asked, surprised.

"No. Why should I? You have to go back to school eventually! However, as soon as I'm completely better, I'm coming to join you."

"Who said you are?" Miriam asked, nonplussed.

"Nobody," Mandy told her calmly. "No one knows yet. I only decided myself last night."

Miriam was far from delighted at the notion and realized that she must talk Mandy out of it at once. "I don't think it's a good idea," she said, feeling her way carefully. "You'll feel awfully out of place."

"Why?" Mandy asked directly. "Because you and your family are Jewish and I'm not?"

"Yes, that mainly…"

"Well that won't be a problem for long," Mandy said dismissively, "because I've decided to do just what my uncle did and become Jewish!" She made the statement with a flourish.

"No, Mandy!" Miriam cried, aghast. "You can't! Forget the idea!"

"But why? I thought you'd be so pleased!" This time it was Mandy's turn to look taken aback. "People usually *want* other people to take on their religion."

"Well it's different with Jewish people!" Miriam declared emphatically. "Look, Mandy, let me try to explain it to you."

She attempted to put Mandy in the picture, explaining how committed to the Torah a Jew must be. And she started to detail all the mitzvos that needed to be followed.

"But your father took it on," Mandy argued. "It was possible for him, so why wouldn't it be possible for *me*?"

"For one thing, you're too young," Miriam told her. "For another thing, your mother would never allow it!"

"I'm not a baby!" Mandy cried. "I'll be twelve next month! I know Uncle Michael was older than that, but he was still quite young."

"Well, he was old enough to know what Judaism was all about... and he meant it all sincerely. He really made a commitment. He gave up all this! You're only interested because you want to come with me. That's not a good enough reason to change your religion!"

"I can see you're trying to put me off because you don't really like me!" Mandy said sulkily, a disgruntled expression on her face.

"Oh no, Mandy, you know that's not true!" Miriam protested. "I'm only telling you what the rabbis will tell you in any case."

They argued and argued until they were interrupted by a knock, and a maid put her head round the door.

"Mr. Morley said to tell you he can take you home whenever

you're ready," she told Miriam. "He's waiting in the car."

"Oh," Miriam jumped up hastily. Morley might be ready, but she wasn't! There was still something for her to see to. The maid withdrew and Miriam walked towards the door.

"Goodbye, Mandy," she said, turning to face her.

Mandy shrugged, the sullen look still on her face. "Goodbye, Miriam," she said grumpily. "Don't think you've made me change my mind. You can't tell me what to do!"

Miriam sighed and, with one last wave, went out of the room.

Lady Cornelia, who had apparently been out riding and looked her usual immaculate self in a tweed suit with a royal blue sweater, was standing at the foot of the stairs when Miriam came down. Was she waiting for her, Miriam wondered, or did she just happen to be there? Whatever it was, Miriam was glad she did not have to go in search of her.

Miriam took a deep breath. She would need courage for this conversation.

"Lady Davenport, could I speak to you a minute?"

"Still determined not to call me 'grandmother'?" Lady Cornelia commented with a rueful smile. "Well, Miriam, come into the drawing room and say what you have to say."

Lady Cornelia led the way into the room and, as she followed her, Miriam glanced in Aunt Elke's direction. Her aunt was sitting in a large Queen Anne chair in the hallway. She smiled at her and made a gesture with her hand that Miriam interpreted correctly to mean, *"hatzlochoh rabboh."* Miriam smiled back at her and went into the drawing room, leaving the door slightly ajar.

The room was wide and spacious, with an ornately patterned Persian carpet resting on a highly polished parquet floor. A beige leather three-piece suite filled the room, with a marble coffee table in the center. Various large oil paintings adorned the walls and two tall windows, curtained in a deep pink and beige velvet, flanked a beautiful marble fireplace, the mantelpiece of which displayed an array of photographs. Miriam's eyes strayed toward them for a moment, wondering if there were any pictures of her father amongst them, though her common sense told her it was most unlikely.

Lady Cornelia waved her towards an armchair and, sitting down opposite her, looked at her expectantly. Miriam opened her mouth to speak, but her mind suddenly went blank. The words she had rehearsed over and over again in her head seemed to have disappeared. Instead she burst out, "Mandy just told me now that she wants to become Jewish!"

Lady Cornelia blanched visibly. She stared at Miriam, dismayed. Oh no, not again! "So this is what you've been stuffing into her head," she said accusingly. "I would never have brought you here if I'd known!"

"No!" Miriam protested. "It's not like that! I've spent the whole afternoon trying to talk her out of it!"

"Oh, come on!" Lady Cornelia smiled cynically, "You can't fool me! Isn't that what religious people always do—try to convert people?"

Miriam found herself repeating the argument she had had with Mandy, explaining the whole concept to Lady Cornelia. This time, however, her explanation did not fall on deaf ears. After a few moments Lady Cornelia began to appear convinced.

"I see," she said thoughtfully when Miriam had finished. "So what are we going to do?"

It suddenly occurred to Miriam that here was an opportunity to come out with what she had originally intended to say. Perhaps Lady Cornelia would accept it now without arguing.

"It would be better if I went away at once," she said quietly, eyeing the old lady apprehensively.

"You mean today? … Straight away?" There was distress in Lady Cornelia's voice. She sat gazing at Miriam, fighting an inner battle. Although the girl did not really resemble her father, there was something about her that reminded her of Michael. Perhaps it was the candid look in her eyes — or maybe the earnest expression on her face. Whatever it was, it seemed to be tugging at her heartstrings in an unnerving way. She didn't want her to go away. She had grown fond of her and she wanted her to stay — perhaps even more than Amanda did. On the other hand, she could not face the thought of going through all that agony once again. She had lost her son that time… and now here was one of her granddaughters who did not really belong to her. How could she bear to lose Amanda as well?

"You are right," she said resignedly, giving a sigh. "It would be better if you went. But how can you be sure Amanda will give up the idea then? Amanda is quite strong-willed. Who knows what she would do? She might even decide to run away from home and follow you."

"Oh," was all Miriam could say, looking somewhat deflated. The thought had crossed her mind, too, but she had pushed it away, thinking only of her chance to break free.

"There is only one way," Lady Cornelia went on, regarding Miriam searchingly. "If she were to be angry with you, she might abandon the whole notion."

"She is a bit cross with me now," Miriam said, "because I tried to talk her out of it."

"No, that's not enough. I'll have to make her really dislike you. Leave it to me. I will tell her something to make that happen. I hope you will forgive me for the lies, though."

The idea did not appeal to Miriam at all. It was true that she longed to break away from Mandy and her family but she did not relish the thought of being disliked. The idea caused her acute embarrassment! All the same, she knew Lady Cornelia was right. That was the only way and she had no choice but to nod in agreement.

"Well, goodbye then, Miriam, my dear… and thank you once again for all that you have done." She extended her hand and Miriam took it. Lady Cornelia clasped her hand firmly for a few moments, overcome by a desire to lean forward and embrace her. However, her natural reserve prevailed, preventing her from doing so.

"Morley will be getting impatient by now," she said, somewhat stiffly, ushering Miriam out of the room and walking her to the door. Mrs. Jacobson was already standing up and, seeing that they were both making for the front door, went to join them. Lady Cornelia stood aside to let Mrs. Jacobson go through the door, then, with another quick shake of Miriam's hand, allowed her to go out, too.

Lady Cornelia stood and watched as Miriam went down the steps and let herself into the car, waving once more as the chauffeur drove her away — out of her life forever. Her heart was bursting with pain, but she controlled the tears that threatened to spill forth, just as she had controlled them all those years ago when Michael had left. She knew now that she would never have persuaded Michael to stay — and strangely enough, after Miriam had explained things to her, she understood that her son had been compelled by a force stronger than any hold she might have had over him. She had had no choice but to let him go, just as she now had to give up all claims on his child. Accepting that fact, she told herself, might help her to bear the pain.

It was then that she suddenly remembered the necklace she had bought for Miriam. She had waited for her to come downstairs that afternoon, intending to give it to her. It was a beautiful piece... a heart-shaped gold locket, delicately engraved, on a golden chain. Inside the locket, there was a picture of Amanda and she had meant to suggest that Miriam place a picture of herself in the other half. It was too late now. She could not give it to her anymore.

Turning away from the door, Lady Cornelia returned to the familiar surroundings of Wakebridge Hall, determined to carry on her life as if nothing at all had ever happened to disturb it.

Once they were in the privacy of their flat, Mrs. Jacobson turned to her niece, eager to discover how she had fared. But one look at the girl's face told her there was something wrong. Instead of looking relieved, Miriam seemed to be upset.

"What happened, Miriam?" she asked. "Didn't you manage after all? Do you want me to go back and speak to Lady Cornelia?"

"No, it's alright. I told her—" Miriam began, but her aunt interrupted her.

"Then what is the matter?" she persisted. "Has she said something to upset you? How dare she!" Her voice suddenly became angry and she began to move towards the door in an agitated manner. "I am going to have a word with her!" she declared belligerently. "She had no right. ..."

"No, Auntie Elke, it's not like that! Lady Davenport was amazingly nice about it, really."

"Then why are you upset?" Aunt Elke calmed down and took off her coat. "Come and sit down and tell me exactly what happened."

Aunt Elke filled up the kettle with water and placed it on the stove, and then put a plate of biscuits on the table. As soon as the kettle began to whistle, she prepared two cups of tea. Then she sat down opposite Miriam, listening as Miriam gave an account of her conversation with Lady Cornelia. She nodded sympathetically when Miriam told how hurt she was by the idea of Mandy thinking badly of her. As soon as Miriam had finished expressing her feelings, Aunt Elke said, "But Miriam, you know yourself that it's the only solution. Lady Davenport had the right idea. You don't want to be forever plagued by Mandy, do you?"

"No, of course not," Miriam agreed.

"Well, then, can't you see that it was *gam zu l'tovah* that she had that idea? It gave you the perfect way out. So forget all about it now and look forward to going home!"

"Yes, you're right!" Miriam said, brightening up suddenly. "*Boruch Hashem*, we are going home at last! I can't wait to see Daddy and Mummy and the kids! Can we go tonight?"

"No, darling, it's too late. We've got a lot of packing to do first."

"But tomorrow is *erev* Shabbos!"

"I know," her aunt assured her, "but the journey to London won't take so long. It's much nearer than Gateshead—in the other direction."

"But what about you? How will you get home in time for Shabbos?"

Aunt Elke smiled. "Ah," she said, "I might not be going home. I'm thinking of going to telephone your parents now and ask if I can come for Shabbos. I'm sure they'll agree. And Uncle

Yehuda will love coming down from Gateshead for Shabbos. How does that idea appeal to you?"

In reply Miriam jumped up and hugged her aunt tightly. "Oh, Auntie Elke, it's a wonderful idea! I'm so excited! I don't know how I'll ever be able to thank you for everything you've done!"

They spent the next few hours packing away all their belongings, including Aunt Elke's pots and pans, laughing and singing together as they worked.

"Do you know what we're going to do?" Aunt Elke said when they had finished and were preparing to go to bed. "Before we leave tomorrow morning, we're going down into that quaint little flower shop to buy your mother an enormous bunch of flowers for Shabbos!"

# 9

*M*iriam settled in back home very quickly. She had not even realized just how much she had missed her family until she saw them all again! Her homecoming had been wonderful, and the warm, happy atmosphere of their little home was a welcome relief after the cold austerity of the luxurious Wakebridge Hall.

As soon as they found a quiet moment, she recounted to her parents all that had happened to her. After that, it was never mentioned again. She never forgot that strange episode in her life, but it had its own place in her mind and did not interfere with her everyday existence.

The only time it left the realms of fantasy and seemed more

like reality was when, two months after she had come home, she received a letter from Lady Cornelia. It came on beautiful, silky cream, delicately scented writing paper with the Wakebridge Hall letter heading on top. In it, the aristocratic old woman had thanked her again for saving Amanda's life and informed her that her granddaughter was now fully recovered and was attending school again.

*... She seems to have abandoned the whole idea of deserting us and following you. In fact, she hardly talks about you at all. Of course, I blame myself for that, having said a few things about you that were not really true. I hope you forgive me, especially after you behaved so well. But believe me, it was the only way.*

*I would be quite happy if you would drop me a line from time to time, or even come to visit. But if you feel you would rather not, I quite understand.*

*Hoping you are keeping well and are successful in everything you do.*

*Yours very sincerely,*
*Lady Cornelia Davenport*

Malka Sternfeld could not help feeling worried when she saw the letter, hoping her daughter's experience had not left some mark, but her husband reassured her.

"Don't worry," he said. "I can see she is not affected at all by the letter. In fact, I would say that, if anything, the whole affair has strengthened her in her *yiddishkeit*."

"Yes, you're right, Leibel," his wife agreed. "And I think Michoel would have wanted her to do exactly as she did."

Three years had passed since Miriam's return from Wakebridge, uneventful but happy years, in the environment that she loved. Now, having finished school, she had come to Gateshead Seminary and, although she missed her family once again, it was quite different. Here she felt satisfied and fulfilled, studying subjects she enjoyed, surrounded by girls just like her. What was more, she was near Aunt Elke, with whom she still felt the closest bond and whom she visited a few times a week, sharing many a Shabbos meal with her and Uncle Yehuda.

If she ever thought about her time with the Davenports, it was as if she was remembering an interesting book she had been engrossed in. It was therefore an incredible surprise when she received a letter, forwarded to her by her mother, from Mandy. She did not read it straight away, afraid that it might distract her thoughts during the Chumash test they were having that morning, but immediately after dinner, when they had an hour's break, she sat down in a quiet corner and took it out.

*Dear Miriam,*

*I don't know why I'm writing to you after you said all those things about me, but I've decided to forgive you. Perhaps you were even right to say I was a horribly spoiled and selfish girl! I suppose I was, in a way. But I'm a bit older now, so maybe I've improved!*

*As you can see from the letter heading, I am now at boarding school... Roedean School in Brighton. It's quite exclusive. In fact, Princess Anne was here a few years ago! It's quite nice and, of course, it's by the sea so the air is terrific!*

*Now I must tell you the most exciting part of all. There is a girl here who's a distant cousin of mine! Her grandmother and my grandfather are first cousins. Her name is Samantha*

*Warrington-Browne but we all call her Sammy. She's great fun and we get on like a house on fire! So you see, even though you didn't really want to be my cousin, I have got one after all!*

*Hope you're well and enjoying life!*

*Love Amanda (Mandy) F.*

*P.S. You were right about not letting me be Jewish. I don't think I'd have kept it up, after all.*

Miriam could not help a smile of amusement as she read the letter. Mandy might indeed have improved, but she was still the same Mandy!

She sat very still, gazing distractedly into the distance. For the first time in three years, she allowed herself to think in detail about the time she had spent in Wakebridge. She had been so young and immature at the time, she reflected, and it was clearly only with immense *siyata d'Shmaya* that she had emerged from the experience unscathed. After all, the Davenports were her father's family and the knowledge of it could have influenced her. As it was, having for the first time in her life an insight into the lives of non-Jews had shown her—with absolute clarity—how fortunate she was to be one of Hashem's chosen people.

Mandy's letter, so typical of that "other world," just helped to deepen her sense of gratitude!

However, her main feeling was one of relief. Only now did she realize that a slight fear had still been hanging over her that she might one day be called to "them" again. Now, though, she could truly say that it was a closed chapter. At last she was completely free of her "distant cousin"!

# Glossary

*All the words listed in this glossary are Hebrew unless otherwise noted.*

Arbah kosos — four cups of wine drunk at the Pesach seder

Aveirah — sin

B'li ayin hora — lit., without an evil eye

B'nos — social groups for young Jewish girls

Bal tashchis — Biblical prohibition against wasting

Bar mitzvah — the occasion on which a thirteen-year-old boy assumes the responsibility of fulfilling the commandments of the Torah and is held responsible for his own actions

Bashert (Yidd.) — predestined

Beis medrash — study hall

Bitachon — trust; refers to trust in G-d

Biur chometz — the final act of ridding one's home of leavened bread, performed on the morning before Pesach

Bochur—young unmarried boy who learns in yeshiva

Borei p'ri hagofen—blessing said before drinking wine or grape juice

Boruch Hashem—thank G-d

Brochoh—blessing

Broigez (Yidd.)—angry

Bubbe (Yidd.)—grandmother

Challah, challos—braided loaves of bread made for Shabbos and holiday meals

Chapp arein (Yidd.)—take advantage

Charotoh—regret

Chas v'sholom—G-d forbid

Chasunah—wedding

Chavrusoh—study partner

Chazzan—cantor

Cheder—religious school for young children

Chessed—act of kindness

Chillul Hashem—desecration of G-d's name

Chillul Shabbos—desecration of Shabbos

Cholent (Yidd.)—a type of stew traditionally served on Shabbos, usually consisting of meat, beans and potatoes

Chometz—leavened food, of which even a minute amount is forbidden on Pesach

Chosson—groom

Chumash—Bible

Daf yomi shiur—a cycle for studying the Talmud in which a page of Talmud is studied each day

Daven, davening (Yidd.)—pray, praying

Der heim (Yidd.)—lit., the house; the old country

Divrei torah—words of Torah

Ehrliche yid (Yidd.)—an honest Jew

Eibeshter (Yidd.)—G-d

Eliyahu hanavi—Elijah the prophet

Emmesdig (Yidd.) — truthful

Emunah — belief in G-d; faith

Eretz Yisroel — the Land of Israel

Erev — the eve of

Ess gezunterheit (Yidd.) — lit., eat to your health; eat heartily

Farher (Yidd.) — exam

Frum (Yidd.) — religiously observant

Frummies (Yidd.) — those who are religiously observant

Gam zu l'tovah — this is also for the best

Geloibt is der eibershter (Yidd.) — Praise G-d

Gemara — the Talmud; the amplified discussion of the Mishnah

Goyim — non-Jews

Goyishe — characteristic of non-Jews

Gutten tug (Yidd.) — good day

Hashkafa — Jewish outlook

Halacha — Jewish law

Hatzlochoh rabboh — much success

Hatzlochoh — success

Havdalah — blessing recited at the conclusion of Shabbos

Hechsher — kosher certification

Heimishe (Yidd.) — traditional, observant

Kabbolas Shabbos — prayer recited at the onset of Shabbos

Kashrus — Jewish dietary laws

Kasher, kashering — to make kosher

Kavanah — concentration

Kibud av va'em — honoring one's father and mother

Kiddush — the prayer said over wine on Shabbos and holidays, proclaiming the sanctity of the day

Kol chamirah — prayer recited before Pesach to nullify all leavened bread remaining in one's possession

Kollel — a seminary of advanced Torah study

Kos shel eliyahu — a special cup of wine that is part of the seder on Pesach, intended for the prophet Elijah

Kugel (Yidd.) — a traditional pudding-like dish, usually made of potatoes or noodles, served on Shabbos and holidays

L'chayim — lit., to life; usually said over a toast

L'shem shomayim — for the sake of Heaven

Latkes (Yidd.) — pancakes

Limudei chol — secular subjects

Limudei kodesh — holy subjects

Maariv — evening prayer

Madrichah — female counselor

Maggid shiur — rabbi who teaches a class in Torah study

Mah nishtana — the four questions asked at the Pesach seder

Mashgiach — spiritual mentor in yeshiva

Masmid — one who learns Torah with diligence

Matzos — unleavened bread, which Jews are required to eat on the seder nights of Pesach

Mazel tov — good luck, congratulations

Mechalel, Mechalelei Shabbos — those who desecrate Shabbos

Mechilah — forgiveness

Mechutonim — the parents of one's son-in-law or daughter-in-law

Melava malka — meal eaten at the end of Shabbos to escort the Shabbos Queen

Melochoh — work prohibited on Shabbos

Mezuzah — scriptural sections placed on the doorposts of Jewish homes

Midah, midos — character traits

Minyan — quorum for public prayer service consisting of a minimum of ten men

Mishtara — police

Mitzvah, mitzvos (pl.) — lit., commandments; good deeds

Mizmor l'sodah — psalm of thanksgiving

Moichel — forgive

Mussaf — the additional prayer recited on Shabbos and Yom Tov

Mussar—rebuke

Nachas—pleasure

Nebech (Yidd.)—a pity

Negel vasser (Yidd.)—lit., water for the nails; the ritual washing
of the hands first thing in the morning

Nisayon—test

Oilom—lit., world; the crowd

Olov hasholom—of blessed memory

Parnossoh—a livelihood

Parshah—portion of the Torah

Pesach—Passover

Peyos— sidelocks; Halachah requires that the corners of the
heads of Jewish males, above the ears, remain unshaven

Pirkei Avos—Ethics of the Fathers

Porutz—wealthy landowner

Rebbitzen—rabbi's wife

Ribono Shel Olam—Master of the World

Rosh yeshiva—head of the yeshiva

Seder, sedorim (pl.)—the traditional meals eaten on the first two
nights of Pesach, conducted according to a specific ritual
order, which is outlined in the Haggadah

Sefer, seforim (pl.)—holy book(s)

Shabbos—the Sabbath

Shabbos hamalka—the Sabbath Queen

Shacharis—morning prayer

Shamash—caretaker of synagogue

Shayfeleh (Yidd.)—lit., little lamb; a term of endearment

Sheitel (Yidd.)—wig

Shiur, shiurim (pl.)—Torah lesson(s)

Sholom aleichem—lit., peace be upon you; hello

Shomer shabbos—follows the laws of Shabbos

Shul (Yidd.)—synagogue

Shvigger (Yidd.)—mother-in-law

Siddur—prayer book
Simchas—happy occasions
Siyata d'Shmaya—help from Heaven
Sofer—one who writes Torah scrolls and other holy writings
Tallis—prayer shawl
Talmid chochom—a scholar learned in Torah
Tefillin—phylacteries; boxes containing certain Torah passages,
    worn on the head and arm of Jewish males during morning
    prayers
Tefillos—prayers
Tehillim—Psalms, the book of Psalms
Teshuvah—repentance
Torah—the Bible
Treif—non-kosher
Tzedokos—charities
Yeshiva, yeshivos (pl.)—religious school(s)
Yetzer hara—evil inclination
Yid, Yidden (Yidd.)—Jew(s)
Yiddishkeit (Yidd.)—Judaism
Yiras Shomayim—fear of Heaven
Yomim Noroim—High Holy Days
Zechus—merit
Zeeseleh (Yidd.)—sweetie
Zeide (Yidd.)—grandfather
Zemiros—traditional Jewish songs, usuall ysung at the Shabbos
    and Yom Tov meals